Who You Wit'?

Also by Paula Chase

SO NOT THE DRAMA

DON'T GET IT TWISTED

THAT'S WHAT'S UP!

Who You Wit'?

A Del Rio Bay Novel

Paula Chase

Dafina
Books

KENSINGTON PUBLISHING CORP.
http://www.kensingtonbooks.com

DAFINA BOOKS are published by

Kensington Publishing Corp.
850 Third Avenue
New York, NY 10022

All Kensington titles, imprints and distributed lines are available at special quantity discounts for bulk purchases for sales promotion, premiums, fundraising, educational or institutional use.

Special book excerpts or customized printings can also be created to fit specific needs. For details, write or phone the office of the Kensington Special Sales Manager: Attn. Special Sales Department. Kensington Publishing Corp., 850 Third Avenue, New York, NY 10022. Phone: 1-800-221-2647.

Dafina and the Dafina logo Reg. U.S. Pat. & TM Off.

ISBN-13: 978-0-7582-2584-9
ISBN-10: 0-7582-2584-9

First Kensington Trade Paperback Printing: November 2008
10 9 8 7 6 5 4 3 2

Printed in the United States of America

For my fam

The Fifteen-Minute Make-out

"I hate how much I love you boy."
—Rihanna ft. Ne-Yo, "Hate That I Love You"

It feels too good.

It feels too good.

It feels too good.

Lizzie chanted to herself to break the spell of the warm frenzy building between her and Todd as he nibbled at her ear and stroked her side. Her breath hitched. Every time she attempted to move an inch or say something to slow the rush, he'd do something magical with his fingers or lips.

She tried again, managing to move her head an inch.

Victory. ·

She parted her lips to say something (anything), and Todd's lips moved to hers. She instinctively kissed him back, rolling the icy cool taste of Orbit spearmint around her tongue, savoring it. It was hard to chew gum now without thinking of Todd and flushing.

As a matter-of-fact, it was hard to do a lot of things without thinking of Todd.

The realization struck her dumb.

No matter how hard she tried, it was hard to connect that a practical, straight A, theatre geek like her not only had a serious boyfriend, but a popular, honest-to-goodness hot guy as well.

Six-foot one; blue eyes; unruly, light walnuty hair highlighted blond; and ready with a joke the second he opened his mouth, Todd had a hot surfer dude look going. Truth be told, even when he let the blond grow out, he was easy on the eyes. He was also a full member of Club Six-Pack. And his biceps and chest weren't bad, either. If Lizzie hadn't seen his body change with her own eyes, she would have never believed someone could go from skinny to sculpted in two years.

Yet it still took her by surprise when girls went out of their way to flirt with him or give her nasty looks when she and Todd walked down the hall together. To her, he was still the goofy, too skinny T who used to shadow JZ like a puppy when they were ten years old. Because of that, and their middle school friendship, she and Todd were a comfortable couple. She never felt self-conscious around him because whenever her nerves would attempt a takeover, like worrying that she had food stuck in her teeth and she had to get it off before he saw it, Todd would poke fun at it, reminding her that he didn't care about her being the perfect girl.

Everyone seemed to know Todd was hot, except Todd.

That made it easy to get caught up in his charm.

Except . . . Lizzie wasn't ready to be completely gaga.

She was changing, and some of the changes felt good. Really good, in fact.

But mostly, they were unsettling. Like now. Why couldn't she open her mouth to say, "Hey, let's take a break?"

How come her brain was directing her body to move, get up, put some space between her and Todd, and her body wouldn't obey?

Todd was becoming a priority in ways Lizzie had always secretly vowed no guy ever would.

Flubbing lines in theatre when he popped into her mind. Getting a B on her Chem test after their first real argument—she didn't recognize herself sometimes.

But things were about to take a turn if all went according to plan.

Todd's kisses rained down on her in quick pecks, like a yappy dog nipping at her heel. She met his lips with her own slow, but firm kisses encouraging him to gel with her, easing him back a little until their kissing was in sync. Her resolve melted. It always did around the twelve-minute make-out mark. Instead of panicking that things were going too far, Lizzie gave in, savoring Todd's warm breath on her neck, ears, then his lips on hers.

Step one of her plan would kick in in exactly five . . .

Todd's tongue darted in her mouth for a quick visit, then was gone. Four . . .

His hands pushed her shirt up just enough so Lizzie could feel their coolness on her warm belly.

Three . . .

He stroked her waist, careful not to go near her armpit (he'd learned the hard way that she'd burst into a fit of giggles, busting up the mood) but working closer to her bra.

Two . . .

Lizzie inhaled sharply as his hands made soft, smooth circles on her belly.

One . . .

Todd's fingers were on the front clasp of her bra just as Lizzie's cell phone blared "One" from *A Chorus Line,* filling the room, "One, singular sensation, ev'ry little step she takes."

Todd hesitated for a fleeting second.

Lizzie pushed herself upright. Her chest heaved as she ran her fingers through her tousled hair.

Todd's eyes, wide with surprise, skated from Lizzie to the phone in confusion.

Lizzie kneeled against the sofa, picked the phone up, and turned off the alarm she'd set right before she and Todd began making out. She was getting so good at doing it, fingers flying to set it before the kissing began, he never noticed. Smiling, she dipped her head and bunched her cascade of blond hair into a quick and dirty ponytail before standing up. She put her hand out to help Todd up from the floor.

His long body unfolded into a standing position where he tow-ered a full foot over Lizzie.

"Dude, I hate your phone." Todd shook his head, eyeing the phone with disdain. "It rings every time we . . ." He dropped down onto the sofa dramatically, pouting.

Lizzie pretended to check the missed call, even though there was none. "It's Mina. JZ should be here any minute to get us," she prac-tically sang, giddy that once more, her fifteen-minute make-out alarm had done its job.

Todd ran his fingers through his unruly locks, gathering himself. He looked shell-shocked and Lizzie, almost felt sorry for him.

Almost.

She felt (a little) bad for having to trick him, but she couldn't trust herself anymore to untangle herself from the increasingly hot and heavy make-outs. At some point, they were going to stop work-ing. Either Todd was going to throw her phone out the window—he was eyeing it now like he wanted to—or simply not let her jump up like someone had lit her pants on fire to check it.

She knew the day was coming. That's why it was time for the virginity pact.

Satisfied with herself, she plopped down beside a silent and pouty Todd.

"I'm starved. You?"

"Yeah, but not for pizza," Todd said, making googly eyes at her.

Lizzie planted a prim peck on his lips, allowing it to turn into a bit more before pulling away. Todd reached out to pull her back, but Lizzie was up in a flash, laughing as his hand swiped her tee shirt, catching only air.

He scowled, chiding her playfully. "Tease."

"Sucker." She sprinted clumsily as he chased her up the stairs.

The door bell rang as they reached the landing.

She hadn't planned it, but the cavalry had arrived right on time anyway.

Cldngirl

"Sumthing is gon' get done."
—Chris Brown, "Poppin'"

Mina looked at her cell phone, then stared out the sliding glass door of the sunroom for the hundredth time.

She and Brian were supposed to meet the clique at Rio's Ria at seven. She'd been waiting for him to swing by and pick her up for twenty minutes. He hadn't answered her text or calls, and she was decidedly annoyed. With a quick holler, "Ma, Daddy, I'm gone," she began the ten-minute walk from her house to his, hurrying to beat sundown. She hated walking down Dogwood at night—too many trees and not enough street lights.

She reached his house right before the last slice of sunshine fell permanently beyond the thick tree line of the cul-de-sac. Before she could knock, Brian's mom, a light golden-complexioned woman as tall as her son, a model in her teen years, opened the door.

"Hey, Mina. Come on in." Mrs. James yelled up the spiral stairway. "Brian, Mina's here. Timmy, come on before we miss this flight."

Brian's father thundered down the stairs, carrying a travel case ridiculously small and feminine for his tall stature. A former NBA baller himself, he was the older, darker chocolate version of Brian. He saw Mina eyeing the bag and laughed. "See, now you're hollering for me, and I was just trying to get *your* bag," he said.

Mina and Mrs. James laughed, sharing an unspoken joke as he handed the bag off as if it were a ticking bomb.

"Hi, Mr. James. Hope you guys have a good trip," Mina said.

Mr. James rolled his eyes. "I can think of a million other things I'd rather do. Weddings," he said like the word tasted bad in his mouth.

Brian came down the stairs two at a time, got last minute instructions from his parents, kissed his mom on the cheek, and saw them out the door. When they were gone, he turned to Mina, his eyes twinkling. "You hot 'cause I took so long?"

His lips brushed hers in a quick, affectionate peck.

Mina rolled her eyes. "I thought you had left me behind."

"My father didn't want to go. So he was dragging, and that gave my mother the chance to give me a few extra To-Do's." He shook his head, mildly disgusted. "Alright, hold up. I need to check on the pool. We're pumping it out." He sighed, scowling. "I don't know why my father decided to do it before he left instead of when he came back."

Mina laughed. "He probably thought it would give him a reason to stay home."

Brian agreed as he made his way to the back of the house. He walked outside through a set of French doors into the growing darkness and disappeared around the side of the large house.

Mina followed him as far as the kitchen, then sat at the counter where Brian's laptop was open to the Internet. She started to shut it down for him when a message popped on the screen.

Gldngirl: so whus up B, do u want an early graduation gift or what? ☺

Mina's breath caught in her throat.

Her emotions churned into a tornado, going from an EF0 to an EF5 in seconds.

Who was Golden Girl?

And exactly what kind of graduation gift did she have in mind? As if Mina had to ask.

Her hands shook. She glanced in the direction Brian had gone, didn't see him, and scrolled up to see the earlier portions of the IM discussion. Her fingers trembled so badly as she tapped the laptop's mouse pad, that only every other tap registered.

Her heart was in her mouth as she head checked outside to see where Brian was. Finally, she realized if she kept her finger on the button and rolled her finger over the magic mouse area, the cursor would zip to the top of the screen.

Duh!

She read the entire IM conversation, the spit drying in her mouth as she leapt into the middle of the conversation, the fly on the wall.

Gldngirl: what up B?

BJBBoy: ay girl nuttin

Gldngirl: u haven't been around da way in a while. 2 good for ur old set?

BJBBoy: Busy. Graduation, ballin, gettin ready 4 school

Mina's jaw clenched. Hello, busy with a girlfriend, too. How come he didn't mention that?!

Gldngirl: oh word, I heard u got into Duke. Go boy!

BJBBoy: yup. Full scholarship

Gldngirl: daddy's connections still hot like fiya

BJBBoy: go head w/dat u know ur boyz skillz fiya on their own!!! Believe dat

Gldngirl: LOL I hear dat. U know I know. Speaking of skillz . . . b4 u roll to Duke u gon' bless a chick w/those other mad skills u got?

Mina's heart did a karate kick. Her eyes scanned the screen so fast
trying to read Brian's reply, she had to read each sentence three times
to process the words.

> BJBBoy: there u go tryin get a dude in trouble. I ain't messin
> w/u and dat crazy azz Dre
> Gldngirl: Me and Dre so over. Damn B it's been a minute since
> we talked. Me and Dre been over 4ever
> BJBBoy: word?
> Gldngirl: if ur azz came back to DC more than evry blue moon u
> might know dat. Ur boys ain't tell u?
> BJBBoy: naw. I be in DC next weekend
> Gldngirl: real talk u tryin roll thru? get u a early grad gift. Don't
> sleep on MY skillz
> BJBBoy: LOL don't play. U gonna fug around and get ur ass
> tapped
> Gldngirl: um-huh thas the whole point!!!
> BJBBoy: BRB
> Gldngirl: aight
> Gldngirl: B where u at? U leave me hanging?
> Gldngirl: so whus up B, do u want an early graduation gift or
> what? ☺

Mina looked up from the screen. Outside, Brian wrestled with a
long white vacuum tube in the darkness. Anger blurred her vision.
She blinked hard for twenty seconds before it cleared. Fear coursed
quickly through her veins. She felt like a fish at the end of a hook,
struggling for air.

An early graduation gift?

Going to DC next weekend?

Brian was going to DC next weekend to hook up with this girl.
The whole conversation swirled in Mina's head. She imagined

Brian's face as he typed back—smiling, maybe licking his lips in anticipation of doing some ass tapping?

Her stomach clenched, and before she realized it, she was walking out to the patio, her short legs carrying her across the kitchen in seconds.

"Who is Golden Girl?" she blurted, sounding every bit as pouty as she felt. She folded her arms tight against her chest as if to hold back some of the emotion leaking out of every orifice. It took every ounce of willpower in her body not to throw herself on the patio, kicking and screaming, demanding to know why he was flirting with some girl who obviously already knew all about his "skills" off the hardwood.

Brian scowled. He wrestled with the tangled tube, cursing when the long white, Slinky-like contraption slipped from his hands and splashed water all over his sneakers. "What?" he asked, distracted.

Mina took a deep breath, told herself to calm down, but her voice rose another octave as she pronounced every word distinctly. "Who is Golden Girl?" She closed the distance between them and stood right next to him beside the pool. "Golden Girl, the person you were IMing before I got here. The one you're going to see next weekend so she can try out your skills for old time's sake."

By the time she got to the last sentence, her voice was muddled by tears.

Brian calmly fed the vacuum into the pool. He squatted to set it right before answering her. "She's just a chick I used to . . ."

"I know what y'all used to do, Brian. *That's* pretty obvious from the IM."

Tears dripped down Mina's face and neck. She kept her arms folded.

Brian's face was hard to read in the dark. The light from the patio only reached the edge of the pool, not touching the pool's far side. But his voice came out of the darkness, irritated.

"Mina, don't start tripping. Yeah, she's my ex," Brian said. He stood up, stared down at the pump once more as if expecting it to worm out of the pool and wrestle with him again, then finally faced Mina. "Why are you reading my IMs?"

"Oh, my God, Brian, don't do that," Mina exploded. "Do not go all 'why you all up in my business' on me. I was turning the PC off for you when the IM came in. Yeah, I read the whole thing. So?"

His sigh was thinly masked by the sudden churning of the pump. He let the grinding fill the air for a few minutes before walking away, back toward the house.

"Me and her was just flirting, that's all," he said over his shoulder.

Mina stood on the patio alone, stunned, as if Brian had smacked her instead of answering her question. Her legs moved automatically when he appeared back in the doorway, asking her, "You coming?"

When she got to the kitchen, he was shutting the PC down. Mina wondered if he'd bothered to say bye to Golden Girl or if he'd just IM her later, apologizing 'cause his psycho girlfriend busted his groove.

"That's it? That's all you're gonna say?" Mina asked. Her tears were dry, burned off by the anger that was once again spreading from her toes to her head. "I'm supposed to be cool with you going to see her next weekend?"

"So that's what I said to her?" He cocked his right eyebrow. "That I was coming to DC to see her?"

"You may as well have said it, Brian." Mina wanted to stay angry, but the fear returned, making her feel cold. She walked toward the warmth of the family room, and Brian caught her by the elbow.

"Did I tell her in the IM that I was coming to see her?"

He held her elbow gently, his gaze intent, not letting go. It forced her to look back.

"No," she answered meekly.

"You knew I was going to DC next weekend. My aunt asked me to help her paint her house. And JZ and Todd are going with me.

Remember?" Brian said. He sat atop one of the stools at the counter and pulled Mina toward him. "So what part of the IM are you so hot about?"

Mina blinked, and the tears rolled again. If this was what it was going to be like when he went off to college, she might as well check herself into the nearest mental facility. She was already a basket case.

She forced the IM from her mind. All she wanted was for Brian to hold her until August fifteenth, the dreaded day he'd hit the road to Durham.

The words to answer him wouldn't come.

Instead, she wept quietly and let herself be pulled into his embrace.

He kissed her ear, then whispered, "You were ready head to DC and drop them bows on her, weren't you, toughie?"

Mina chuckled through the tears, sniffling as she nodded.

She lifted her face to Brian's, and they kissed . . . and kissed, and this time when it went beyond the kissing, she didn't stop.

Virginity Pact

"Time may change me, But I can't trace time."
—David Bowie, "Changes"

Lizzie knew something was wrong when Mina and Brian stepped through the door.

No, not wrong. Different, she thought, watching Mina and Brian weave through the crowded tables of the Ria. Brian stopped to give pounds or handshakes to people, and Mina waited patiently behind him each time until they moved on.

Normally, Mina would be running her mouth, chatting it up with everyone they passed, or she'd say quick hellos and make a bee-line for the clique. As they got closer, Lizzie could see Mina's eyes were rimmed in red.

They had probably had a fight. Then again, Lizzie couldn't say that for sure.

With the countdown to Brian's departure imminent, Mina had been moody lately. One minute, happy and soaring, babbling non-stop about prom; the next, sad and sullen, thinking about life without Brian. She was testy with everyone. It wasn't far-fetched to think Mina had burst into tears spontaneously thinking about him leaving.

Lizzie was still trying to get used to her best friend's seesawing emotions.

Once the couple reached the table, JZ greeted them with a reprimand. "It's about time. We starving, waiting on y'all." He and Brian exchanged a pound before Brian made the rounds to Todd and Michael. JZ scowled at Mina. "What's wrong with you?"

Mina rolled her eyes at him. "Now, since when you wait on anybody to order food?" She took the open seat next to Kelly. "Sorry, Lizzie, Cinny, Michael, Kelly, and Todd, that we took so long. Brian had to clean out the pool first."

Lizzie watched as Mina's sullen demeanor slowly slipped away.

Minutes later, she was her old self, deep in several conversations, talking across the table to Michael about her prom dress, asking Lizzie about her upcoming driver's license test, and fending off a sleeper hold from JZ, who found a reason to pick at Mina like a big brother unable to resist tripping up his younger one.

The two of them exchanged playful barbs, going at it with their usual lusty verve.

JZ flexed his muscle and patted his arm, bragging about his sculpted frame.

Mina rolled her eyes, cutting him with a swift, "Man, nobody want feel those guns, except Cinny."

Jacinta's mouth dropped open. "How did I get in this?"

There was a raucous round of snickering. Jacinta and JZ's mutual flirting was a thing of urban legend among the clique—something they knew was taking place, yet played down or outright ignored.

"Let's see what those guns do for you if Raheem bust up in here and see you and Cinny all cozy," Mina said. Her eyes gleamed playfully.

"Ay, no disrespect to your man, Cinny, but you know I can handle mine if he start tripping," JZ said.

"Mina, why you starting stuff?" Jacinta's rolled her eyes. "Y'all know me and JZ . . ."

The entire table chorused, "Just friends," breaking them all up again, even Jacinta.

Lizzie rode the energy of her friends, feeding off their banter and dissing. She loved the nights they all hung out.

Nights that she and Todd hooked up with Mina and Brian to watch movies or play games at one of their homes were great, too, except inevitably they turned into make-out sessions—either Mina and Brian off in one corner, or if they were home alone, them in the family room, she and Todd in the living room, or sometimes, Mina and Brian left and went to his house. As much as Lizzie enjoyed it, preventing the make-outs from going twenty minutes or beyond was exhausting. It was the group outings she truly loved.

By the time the pizzas arrived, the Ria was on full blast, and the clique's banter mixed in with the general chaos of the restaurant. Soon, the musical chairs began, everyone hopping from their own table to their classmates', catching up on life, talking about the up-coming prom and summer plans. By ten-thirty, Lizzie had forgotten about Mina's red-rimmed eyes. And if Mina had been mad at Brian earlier, she wasn't by then. Whenever the two of them were at the table together, they were touching, holding hands, and smiling at one another.

Watching them, Lizzie knew this was the weekend she'd better bring up the pact, before it was too late.

But she didn't think about it again until the next morning as she and the girls lounged in Mina's room.

Kelly and Lizzie lay stretched out on Mina's bed. Mina sat atop her desk, cross-legged, staring at the posters on her wall, and Jacinta was stretched out on the floor reading a magazine. Having exhausted the topic of last night, they lazily debated if they wanted breakfast as music buzzed quietly in the background. No one was motivated to move beyond the bedroom, except Jacinta, who had gone to the bathroom a record four times since they'd woken up a half hour before.

With a lull in the debate, Lizzie popped up abruptly, the bed bouncing her like a trampoline. The girls eyed her sudden movement with idle curiosity.

Lizzie held up two fingers. "Okay, two words, guys . . . virginity pact." She beamed, smiling into her friends' confused faces as if she'd just invented the cure for cancer.

Mina's eyebrows jumped as if startled before settling back down. She picked up a blue and gold stress ball and stretched and pulled at its rubbery, dangling tentacles. She glanced at Lizzie before gazing over her head at the wall, the tentacles expanding as her fingers worked it overtime.

Jacinta looked up from the floor, her face caught between amusement and boredom, dropped the magazine she was flipping through, and pushed herself to a standing position. "I don't know what you're talking about. But obviously, I'm out." Before ducking out of the room she said, "Talk amongst yourselves about this new wild idea Lizzie has."

Kelly and Mina teetered. No one had to ask Jacinta what she meant. She and Raheem were going on nearly four years together, if you didn't count the time off during breakups, two and counting since the December of their freshman year. It was no secret their relationship was well past any sort of pact of abstinence.

"I'll bite," Kelly said. Her usual caramel complexion had a tawny glow from a recent trip to Hawaii with her mom, step-dad, and younger brother. With her thick chestnut hair, newly highlighted with dirty blond streaks, pulled back, she looked like she'd just stepped off a *Seventeen* mag photo shoot. She sat up, too, pushing her back against the wall, pressing Liz for more details. "I mean, I know what a virginity pact is but . . ."

"Okay, before you guys shoot me down, listen," Lizzie interrupted. She hugged Mina's body pillow to her, crushing it as she squeezed. Her eyes went a brilliant green, something that happened whenever she was excited. "Now that Mina and I have officially been able to date . . ."

"You want to take half the fun out of it by pledging to not have sex?" Cinny deadpanned, popping back into the room.

"I thought you were in the bathroom." Lizzie scowled, not hiding her annoyance with Jacinta's flippant attitude toward her idea.

"False alarm." Jacinta took a seat in the chair next to the desk. "But my bad . . . go ahead, Liz. This sounds like a fascinating idea," she said in a voice that sounded as thrilled as someone doing a play-by-play of paint drying.

Mina swatted at her to hush.

"No harm, Mina, but this is Brian's senior year. Y'all have what . . ." Jacinta furrowed her brows in concentration as she calculated. "Four months before he goes off to school? I can't see you wanting to make this pact right when he's ready to have even more chicks to choose from . . . college girls at that."

Lizzie cut her eyes at Jacinta. She wasn't going to let Jacinta win this one with her "I'm the relationship expert" bravado. This time last year, the girls were on collective lockdown, thanks to a secret road trip to O.C. to watch Mina and the Select Varsity team compete at Nationals. Not that she was blaming Jacinta for it. Lizzie had gone along willingly enough. But the trip, one part thrill, two parts disaster, had made Lizzie realize that she wasn't ready to go from zero to sixty with her relationship with Todd—no matter how good it felt to spend time with him.

"Cinny, are you saying that Mina's going to have to have sex with Brian just because he's ready to leave?" Lizzie rolled her eyes. The pillow caved in more as she dug into it. "That's crazy . . . and if anything, the fact that he's leaving is all the more reason she may as well not." She made sympathetic eyes at Mina. "Don't take this wrong, Mina, but . . . look, you're already down about him leaving. I think if you guys get any closer, it will be even harder in August." She took the challenge back to Jacinta. "Besides, they've held off all *this* long. What's the big deal?"

"Shoot, you just made my point for me. They've been together a year and a half." Jacinta's eyebrow rose to a skeptical steeple. "I can't believe Brian's been so patient. But I know he's expecting some sort of early graduation present on prom night."

She nudged Mina, smiling.

Mina's brown sugar face remained expressionless. Lizzie took her lack of smile or laughter at Jacinta's sarcastic hint as a small victory. She broke out in a toothy grin. But the poor rubber ball's tentacles were stretched to their limits as Mina stretched and pulled, stretched and pulled them methodically. Lizzie knew something was bothering her. She silently chastised herself. In her excitement about the pact, she'd broken an unspoken friend rule. She and Mina were the alpha friends of the quartet—she should have talked this over with Mina before presenting it to the whole group.

Having been best friends since fourth grade, by all rights, they could discuss serious friend stuff outside of the group without it being sneaky. They should have been presenting this as, "Hey, look what me and Mina are going to do."

But friend protocol was Mina's department, not Lizzie's. The pact had been on her mind so much lately, she'd been excited about finally sharing it.

Before she had a chance to analyze it further, Mina's voice, heavy with distraction, prompted her on. "Go ahead, Liz. Tell us about the pact."

Relieved, Lizzie threw a pillow at Jacinta's head to signal her annoyance had passed and that they were cool again. This wasn't the first time they'd been on the extreme ends of this topic. Truth be told, Lizzie always felt there was a silent tug-of-war between them for Mina's "vote" whenever they disagreed—a light air of friction that surfaced anytime she and Jacinta didn't see eye-to-eye.

Lizzie wondered if Jacinta felt it, too. Her eyes fell on Jacinta, sitting in the chair next to Mina's desk, her elbow on Mina's lap, her other hand cuffing the pillow Lizzie had just thrown at her. She didn't seem annoyed, bothered, or upset in the least.

The tension was very real to Lizzie. Whenever she and Jacinta were at odds, a tiny pebble lodged itself in her chest, a hard, cold feeling that spread as she worried whose side Mina would pick.

This isn't a competition, she told herself. But as soon as she thought it, she immediately went into overdrive, working to get Mina on her side.

Cinny wasn't going to win this one.

Lizzie cleared her throat.

"Look, I'm serious. We all have boyfriends now . . ."

"Not me," Kelly said. She groaned at Lizzie's open sympathy. "Okay, don't give me that look. Am I that pathetic?"

"No," Mina spoke up. "And if I have anything to do with it, you won't be single long anyway."

"And you know, once she sets her Cupid's bow and arrow on you, it's as good as done," Lizzie said, making the girls laugh and getting a tiny smile out of Mina.

Everyone was aware that the second Mina found out that Greg Canon, a quiet, but friendly chocolate cutie from her Spanish class needed tutoring, she'd known just the tutor to send him to. She'd slipped Kelly's number to Greg, a junior and the only black dude on the lacrosse team, and practically demanded that he call Kelly to arrange a tutoring session. Kelly had tutored him for two weeks before heading to Hawaii. Their sessions started up again Monday to ensure he passed the upcoming Spanish final. Lizzie knew Mina had been working behind the scenes to make sure the tutoring turned into a date soon.

"Well, you can still take the pact for when you do get a boyfriend," Lizzie said, giving Kelly one more sorry look. "If we take the pact together, it makes it easier to stick to it. You know?"

Her neck slow craned as she looked from Mina to Kelly for confirmation.

Kelly nodded, but Mina remained oddly detached.

Lizzie paid it no mind. When she had Mina to herself, she'd go all best friend on her and get them on the same page. For now, Lizzie focused the pact on herself.

"I'm just not ready to take it there with Todd," she admitted.

"I wasn't with Angel, either," Kelly said.

"Mi?" Lizzie said. Her eyes asked her best friend what her mouth didn't—"how about you?" But Mina was silent. Lizzie couldn't read her face. She pressed more than she had intended.

"I think it would take the pressure off with Brian." She smiled weakly. "No more ninety-nine percent nights."

They'd all had them—nights where make-out sessions went that-close to something more before they pulled back.

Lizzie chuckled and continued, "I think a pact is easier. But you could always try the Lizzie O' Reilly method for abstinence."

"I gotta hear this. What is it?" Jacinta asked, near laughing already.

They exchanged a childish second, sticking their tongues out at one another before Lizzie went on and sheepishly admitted to the girls about her alarm system.

Jacinta's eyes widened. "Lizzie, un-ah. And Todd hasn't called you on why your phone always goes off?"

"Nope. But when it goes off, I pull back and either start a new conversation or ask him to drop me home or whatever." Lizzie's shoulders popped. "It works for me."

Jacinta shook her head in wonder. "Seriously, y'all bobblehead 'burb girls got a plan for everything. Timed make-out sessions? I think I've heard it all."

"Why fifteen minutes?" Kelly asked.

Lizzie's shoulders shook as she laughed to herself. "Because usually, by fifteen minutes, he's completely in the zone and moving to unbuttoning, and it's when I'm really, really close to letting him." She shrugged. "The alarm literally wakes me up from how good making out feels."

"Okay, I'm not sure I want to stop that badly," Mina said with an apologetic smile.

Lizzie smiled back, but it was plastic. She wanted Mina to agree that there were ways to not do it, not shoot down her suggestions.

"See, that's what I don't get." Jacinta frowned. "If you want to do it . . . just do it."

"But I don't," Lizzie said. She fixed her eyes on Mina. "I mean, I really, really like Todd."

"You left some reallys out, didn't you?" Mina teased.

They giggled. "Okay, really, really, really, really like Todd." Lizzie sat up straight. "I admit I like him a lot. But that's my point. I like him so much he's distracting. Remember my B on my Chem test?"

Jacinta laughed, not unkindly. "First of all, in *our* world, there's nothing wrong with getting a B, Miss Liz."

"I know that's right," Mina said. She unfolded her legs and leaned back on her hands, warming up to the conversation.

"Second," Jacinta continued, "if you're doing all that, setting alarms and whatnot, just tell the boy you not down and save him the trouble of trying so hard." She snorted. "You *are* going to tell him you're officially refusing to do the nasty, right?"

"First of all, I wouldn't call it that," Lizzie said. She flipped her hair primly. "Second, it's totally my decision to do this. I'm not trying to be funny, but what does Todd have to do with something I'm choosing to do?"

"Hmm . . . let me think . . ." Jacinta looked to the ceiling. She rolled her eyes. "Because he's your boyfriend, Lizzie. How you goin' take a pact not to have sex and not let the boy know?" She raised her eyebrow. "You plan on the alarm thing working every time? Just how dumb is Todd?"

"He is not dumb, Cinny," Lizzie snapped, glaring.

"Liz, you know Jacinta was just trying to be funny," Mina said. She kneed Jacinta in the elbow.

"You know I love T, Lizzie," Jacinta said, taking the hint. "But real talk, you're treating him like he's stupid by going through all this. Just tell the boy . . . or are you afraid he gonna break up with you once you do?"

"Todd's too sweet. He'd never do that," Mina said, seeing the shadow of doubt-realization cross Lizzie's face. She sighed loudly.

"Come on, y'all. We don't have to fight about it. I mean, we all have our different views."

"True," Jacinta said. She turned and looked Mina in the eye. "But you know the deal, Mina. The clock is ticking. Ticktock. Ticktock."

"Did I miss something while I was gone? Is Brian pressuring you?" Kelly asked.

"The pressure is his fine body rubbing on hers," Jacinta cracked, dodging a Mina swipe at her head. "Todd's body is fiya, too. I don't know how you do it, Lizzie. Do you know how many girls are always talking about how cute he is?"

The thought had occurred to Lizzie. But she wasn't about to admit it. It was one of the reasons that fell in the Pro column of why she was taking the pact in the first place. She wasn't going to let the reality of competition push her, and she said so. "Am I supposed to have sex with him just because other girls would?" she asked sulkily.

"No," Jacinta said. "You're supposed to have sex with him if you want, period. If you don't, that's cool, too. Right?" She fixed Lizzie with a meaningful stare until Lizzie nodded, then brought her point home by saying, "So Mina, do you want to do it?"

Lizzie stared into Mina's face, trying to read it, the familiar pebble in her chest expanding with every breath.

"Okay, I'mma take that as a yes," Jacinta said, satisfied, mistaking Mina's long pause as solid confirmation that she wanted to have sex with Brian.

"No." Lizzie scowled. "Mina, you have to answer. Do you want to do it?"

"Yes," Mina said, then blurted, "and no."

Jacinta shoved the bony point of her elbow into the meat of Mina's thigh. "Princess is always walking the fence." She headed to the door.

"Where are you going now?" Mina asked.

"Bathroom," Jacinta said, disappearing.

Kelly frowned. "What, did she drink a Big Gulp without us know-ing? She's gone to the bathroom a million times this morning."

"Mina, since you're on the fence, now's the right time to make the pact," Lizzie said. Her words tumbled out over one another in an effort to get it all in before Jacinta returned. "I'm not saying it's wrong if you have sex. I'm just saying we don't have to. We can start off the pact just agreeing to not have sex for a year. Twelve months. Just one year." Her head ping-ponged between Kelly and Mina. "What do you guys think?"

"Well, I know it doesn't mean much now since I don't have a boy-friend," Kelly said with a slight apologetic shrug. "But I'm in, Liz."

Lizzie's grin touched her ears. She scrambled off the bed and was by the desk in one long stride. "Mi? Come on." She bumped Mina's foot with her hip. "I know Brian's a hottie, but he's waited this long . . . and it'll be easier to keep the pact once he's at school."

Mina's chuckle was humorless. "And what do I do for the next four months?"

"We'll make you a pair of boy shorts out of metal," Kelly quipped. She and Lizzie cracked up.

"Don't worry, Mi. We'll be there for each other," Lizzie said with a reassuring smile.

"And the shorts. We'll get you those shorts," Kelly said.

Mina chuckled softly along to Kelly and Lizzie's fit of giggling. Lizzie locked arms with Mina, tugging her off the desk.

"Now that that's settled, I'm starved," Lizzie said.

"Me, too. I'd kill for a waffle," Kelly said. She hopped off the bed, trailing behind Lizzie and Mina as they headed downstairs.

They knocked on the bathroom door on their way down, laugh-ing at Jacinta's impatient, "I'm coming."

With thoughts of waffle and syrup suddenly on their minds, for the time being, talk of the pact was on hold.

"First Times Suck"

"You got me doing things I never do."
—Day 26, "Got Me Going"

Mina hated to admit it, but hours later, as Mrs. Lopez's Benz SUV pulled off, Kelly in the driver's seat, her grandmother riding shotgun, Lizzie in the back, she felt lighter. The four of them had spent the rest of the afternoon picking out potential hairstyles that Mina could rock for prom night. Next weekend, Jacinta would help Mina try a few out until they decided which one was "the look."

Somehow, Mina had managed to sidestep committing to the pact, something she figured Lizzie would pick up on sooner rather than later. She'd gone along, forcing herself to act normal all day, but she felt queasy the entire time. If it hadn't been for Jacinta running to the bathroom every few minutes, Mina may have been in there herself.

But as Kelly drove off, some of the weight slipped off her shoulders.

Even though the whole pact idea had come out of left field, Lizzie had been so into it, Mina couldn't even get annoyed that she'd never uttered a word about it until now.

The pact itself was bad enough, but Kelly going along so easily had complicated things. If Mina had been up to it, she would have debated the issue a little—point out that Lizzie was being hasty, working too hard to control her feelings for Todd. She was sure

Kelly, who was always methodical, would have seen her point. They didn't have to take a pact, merely take one step at a time.

Then Kelly had gone and thrown her hat in the ring. It made Mina feel . . .

Deceitful.

Sneaky.

And worse, slutty.

Goose bumps prickled her arm, and she wrapped them around herself, gazing after the Benz, watching it stop for a full ten . . . fifteen . . . twenty seconds at the stop sign. The long stop had to be the work of Kelly's grandmother, frontseat driving.

Slutty. She couldn't believe she felt slutty. Brian was her boyfriend, not some random dude she'd hooked up with after a wink and head nod from across the room. Still, hearing Lizzie all excited about how great it would be to be in the pact together, how they all needed to do it, made her feel as if she'd torn her clothes off and served herself on a platter to Brian.

Her stomach shuddered like Jell-O, and a tiny flake of guilt itched at the back of her throat. She cleared it unconsciously.

"Alright, so you walking me home or what?" Jacinta said with her usual touch of gruff affection.

"Yup." Mina forced herself to smile. A cool breeze blew her new, short 'do, and a stray hair tickled her cheek. She pushed at the hair absently, tucking it behind her ear.

The look was a radical change for her. The back was layered and short, stopping at her hairline. The sides were also layered, but the hair was progressively longer as it came around to her face, covering her ears and angling to her cheek. If she combed all of the long layers, it was enough to pull into a half ponytail for cheerleading. Brian called it her Pomeranian look. A description Mina could have done without, even if it was accurate.

Her mom, who had been chatting with Kelly's grandmother,

came and stood beside her. "Decided what you're doing with your hair for prom yet?"

"I'm gonna hook her up with a few choices next weekend Miss M," Jacinta said. She twiddled with Mina's hair, pulling and pushing it around gently. "She gonna be looking fly."

Mina and her mother chuckled.

"Okay, let me go get my bag," Jacinta said. She walked briskly, disappearing into the house.

"Does that mean another girl's weekend here?" Mina's mom asked. Her eyes rolled in exasperation, but there was a pleased lilt in her voice.

Mina nodded.

Her dad would often declare an entire week girl free, because the girls spent so much time at the Mooneys'. But Mina knew both he and her mom (mostly) enjoyed the chatter that broke up the usual quiet of their three-top family.

"I better warn your father," her mom said. She started inside, stopped, and turned back to Mina. "You okay?"

For a second, Mina felt the same close, uncomfortable suffocation she'd felt when all the girls had been hanging out in her room earlier. She froze as her mother's brown eyes gazed her up and down curiously.

For one excruciatingly long second, Mina knew without a doubt that her mother could smell on her that she'd had sex. Her throat tightened as the air locked in her larynx. "Yeah," she squeaked. She swallowed hard, forcing moisture down her gullet, reminding herself that if her mother smelled anything, it was the sickeningly sweet aroma of eau de Britany, J-Lo or Paris Hilton. Earlier, the girls had smeared one another with the scented pages of a magazine as a form of torture until they couldn't take any more of the celeb fragrances. She tried again, this time hitting normal. "Yeah. I'm fine. Why?"

Mariah Mooney's head cocked as it shook slowly. "Nothing. You all must be cooking up something. Mae Bell and I actually had a conversation on the opposite side of the car at the same time as you girls." She laughed. "That's gotta be a first."

"Just tired." Mina managed a phony yawn that turned into a real one midway through. "We were up late last night chatting with Michael." Her eyes rolled. "He refuses to even let me see a picture of my prom dress."

Mariah snorted. "You trusted him to hook you up. Let the boy do his work."

"Dag, Ma, pick favorites much? I knew you'd take his side," Mina grumbled.

"Don't I always," Mariah joked.

It wasn't far from the truth.

After weeks of overly loud discussions with her mother about what type of dress she'd wear to Brian's prom, Michael had stepped in and settled the whole thing by agreeing to help design and make a dress for Mina.

Mina's vision was Beyoncé on the red carpet at the Oscars— long, slinky, and cut low enough to accentuate the obvious junk in her trunk, while her mom's was pastels, frills (tulle?! Not!), and every body part covered, except Mina's arms—more first communion than first prom.

Michael, God bless him, had several things going for him.

He was a master with a sketch pencil and a demon with a sewing machine and needle.

He knew Mina like he knew the back of his hand—hanging out with someone since age four does that.

And most importantly, he could do very little wrong in the eyes of Mariah Mooney. As long as the dress he designed did not have any peekaboo elements or a high wardrobe malfunction capacity, likely Mariah would approve.

In February, when he'd come back with a sketch of a dress that was revealing without being "grown" and flirty without being sexy, both the young and older Mooney fell in love with it immediately. It was no joke that Michael was her mom's pet.

"Picking him over your own daughter. So wrong," Mina said dryly.

"Love ya, Boo-Boo," Mariah laughed. She opened the door to the house, bumping shoulders with Jacinta as she exited.

"Bye, Mrs. Mooney. Thanks for having me over," Jacinta said.

"You're welcome, sweetie," Mariah said. She closed the door behind her.

"Ready?" Jacinta asked.

Mina nodded. Her mind raced as she thought about her behavior today. Had she been acting different? Did she look different? Was she different?

Jacinta hoisted a blue bag with yellow polka dots onto her shoulder. She and Mina walked in sync, their footsteps thudding lightly against the blacktop, silently at first, until Jacinta began to lecture Mina playfully.

"Why are you starting all this nonsense about me and JZ last night? All I need is for some rumor to get back to Raheem that JZ trying to holler, and then I've got *that* drama to deal with." Jacinta chuckled, barely aware that she was now walking a step ahead of Mina and that Mina hadn't answered her. Her voice carried, growing more animated as she chattered on. "The messed up part is it's me Raheem gets all pissy with, not JZ. I mean, he still plays pickup with JZ sometimes. And he don't say boo to JZ about me. But oh naw, let me be late calling him or answering his call, and I gotta hear . . ." Her voice deepened, mocking Raheem's, "Oh, so where you been . . . with ol' boy?" She sucked her teeth. "I'm like, Raheem, yeah I was with JZ *and* a billion other people. I can't help that I like chilling with Jay, though. That's my boy. Shoot, can I help that he fine as hell, too? Still, you're not help—"

"Me and Brian did it. We had sex," Mina blurted, stopping Jacinta in her tracks.

Her bag slipped from her shoulder and hung heavily in the crook of her arm.

Her eyebrows furrowed, then she snorted. "You know what . . . I knew it."

Mina's eyebrows knitted. "You did? How?"

"Was it yesterday?" Jacinta peered at her. "Y'all took too long to roll by the Ria." She hefted her bag back onto her shoulder. "First, I thought something was wrong. Me and Lizzie kept blowing up your cell, and you never answered. When you finally did, you were just like 'yeah, we're on our way.'"

Mina laughed low in her throat, confused. "And that meant we had sex?"

"No," Jacinta chuckled. "But any other time, you'd give us a game time analysis of everything that was holding you up. Brian had to do this or that. You lost your shoe, or your mother added a new rule, whatever. You would have told us every detail about why you were late."

She and Mina laughed at the truth in the observation.

The good vibrations of the laughter rolled around in Mina's head like a pinball, touching her frayed nerves. Telling Jacinta felt really good. Good like what happened between she and Brian wasn't so alien, after all. Good like maybe she wasn't a slut. Good like, thank God someone else knows, and the world is still spinning on its axis, good.

Jacinta's laugh went up a notch. "Good grief, and Lizzie talking about virginity pacts and whatnot." She shook her head in amusement. "No wonder you were so quiet." Her voice turned tender. "So . . . y'all did it, huh?"

The gentle question irritated and soothed Mina. It sounded like the voice someone would use on a person on the brink of a break- down. But she sort of felt like a person on the edge of a breakdown. And she laughed suddenly, as if to prove it.

By the time she spoke up, they were on Jacinta's front step. Jacinta placed her bag on the landing, then took a seat on the step. Mina sat beside her, the concrete chilling her butt through the cotton flood pants. She hunkered down and endured the chill rising up her backside.

"It feels like I have an X on my forehead or something," Mina said. The suffocating feeling pushed its way back up, burdening her once again. She hugged her knees, lying her head on her lap to pass some of the body heat from her upper body to her lower. "Do you think anybody else thought that's why me and Brian were late? I'm not really ready to broadcast it."

Jacinta's face crumbled in concentration as she pondered, then she shook her head. "I mean, Lizzie was worried 'cause you weren't answering your phone." She chuckled. "JZ was just worried that we were gonna wait on y'all to order the food. Michael joked that you were probably changing outfits."

Mina snorted. "Yeah, he did say something like that when we walked in."

"Honestly, we all believed y'all when you said the pool pump acted stupid. And later, when you told us the two of you had got into an argument, that explained why your eyes were all red."

"Both were true, actually," Mina said, brightening.

Normally, this was the exact sort of thing she'd share with Lizzie ASAP, but now, with Liz pushing the whole twelve-month abstinence pact, it felt as if she'd just been uninvited into some sort of special club in which Lizzie was not only a member but also president. Or at least, she'd be uninvited once Lizzie found out. And she'll have to find out, right? Mina thought, mind whirling between ways to keep it from Lizzie and how to break the news to her.

Her head pounded.

"Do you regret doing it?" Jacinta said.

"Brian asked me the same thing." She frowned. "I don't regret it. Well . . . I mean, I'm not happy I did it, but I'm not sad, either." She blew out a long breath and sucked her teeth. "That's stupid, isn't it?"

"Not really," Jacinta said.

Mina winced. "You're just saying that 'cause I'm all to pieces right now."

"You 're always all to pieces, Princess," Jacinta teased. "Over cheer competitions, track meets, what to wear." She shrugged. "I'm used to it."

"Real talk, I want to throw up," Mina said, then laughed. "Not exactly a glowing endorsement for not regretting it. But . . ." The IMs from Golden Girl blazed in her head. She hugged her knees tighter as the cold moved from her butt to her thighs. She lowered her voice, talking less to Jacinta than to herself. "We were so . . . close for those few minutes. I don't regret that. But . . ."

Her voice hitched as the feeling—wanting Brian to hold her in his bear hug forever—overwhelmed her again. Nausea hit in a swift-rolling wave. She swallowed until the urge to cry or throw up passed. Still gripping her legs, she laid her hot face into her cool lap, turning her head toward Jacinta as she talked. "It didn't feel like I thought it would."

Jacinta only nodded.

Mina lifted her head, sniffling. "It's definitely overrated." She straightened upright at the weird smile on Jacinta's face. "What?"

Jacinta shrugged. "Nothing."

"No, it's something. You've got that smirk you get when you're trying and about to fail at not saying what's on your mind." Mina snickered. Jacinta didn't hold back on her thoughts very often. But when she tried, the look was always the same.

"I just think if we talk about this again in a few days, weeks, or whatever, you're gonna be saying something different," Jacinta said.

Mina frowned, but before she could say anything, Jacinta continued, "First times suck. I'll just say that. But second or fourth times?" She shrugged, a knowing smile playing at the corner of her mouth.

Mina started to object. But a sliver of doubt plucked her heart.

Declaring there would be no second time was about as sincere as someone shouting, "it wasn't me," when they were caught red-handed. Already, thoughts of lying beside Brian warmed her in the chilly breeze. Who was she fooling to say it would never happen again?

She squinted up at Jacinta. "So I'm guessing it's too late to make that pact with Lizzie and Kelly?"

Jacinta chuckled, knocking shoulders with her. "I'm thinking, yeah."

Competition

The next morning, Lizzie waited for Mina amidst the usual muted morning cacophony echoing throughout the corridor—a mix of excitement to be back among one another for the school year's last few weeks and disgust at having to put up with classes simply to get a social fix.

Traffic built around Lizzie in pockets, then buzzed by, making room for the next shift. Poised patiently against Mina's locker in a yellow vintage Gotta Have My Pops! tee shirt, she blended in with the bright dandelion-colored locker bay. Every few seconds, her back vibrated as lockers jangled open and clattered shut with students going about their morning.

Angling her shoulder so Mina's neighbor could maneuver, Lizzie glanced down the crowded hallway, hoping to catch Mina rushing through. She wanted to put in a quick plug for the pact and get Mina's final answer.

Plug for the pact. It sounded like a commercial pleading for a cause.

Don't forget to wear your plug for the pact. Show your support today.

In a way, it *was* a cause. And Lizzie was definitely campaigning for Mina's support. An idea took hold, making her chuckle to herself.

She should get ribbons made up. Red for AIDS, pink for breast cancer . . . and white for virgins. White made the most sense, of course, because it stood for purity. So she, Mina, and Kelly could wear tiny white ribbons. No one would have to know what they meant. It would be another one of their inside jokes.

Or we could tell people, and soon, all the virgins will want one, Lizzie thought, snickering quietly. She dodged to the side, barely missing getting clipped by a locker closing, and backed into Todd.

"Don't tell me you're laughing at another guy's jokes. You'll break my heart." He laid his arm around her shoulder, hugging Lizzie to him. She was squeezed gently against his stomach. "So what's so funny?"

"Nothing. Just having an imaginary conversation with myself," Lizzie said.

Todd leaned down and planted a kiss on Lizzie's lips. Her face warmed at the affection. She still wasn't quite used to public affection. But Todd, either unaware or (most likely) unaffected by the attention a few passing girls paid to them, straightened up, his arm still firmly around Lizzie's shoulder, and kept talking. "I have conversations with myself all the time. As a matter-of-fact, I had a good convo last night when my girlfriend blew me off to study. I said, Todd." Todd's face was a cartoon as he conversed with himself. "And I said, What's up, dude? And I'm like, dude, she blew you off for homework. You're losing your touch. I was all, Du-u-u-ude, it's no big. And then . . ."

Laughing, Lizzie put her hand up to stop him. "Okay, okay. Let me guess . . . dating etiquette says I should apologize for leaving you hanging last night?"

Todd touched one finger to his nose and pointed another at Lizzie, smiling.

"Sorry. I'm worried about my AP Lit final." Lizzie shrugged in apology. "I really had to study."

What she didn't share was how badly she'd wanted to ditch studying to talk to him. She'd been tempted, very tempted. Todd had no idea just how much he filled her thoughts. At least, she didn't think he knew, and she wanted to keep it that way. It was bad enough she was already one of those girls who grinned like an idiot whenever she was around him.

Todd's eyes rolled in exasperation. "Lizzie, you're a straight A Alice. Seriously, dude, *you* should be teaching the Lit class." He began walking, nudging Lizzie along with him. She glanced back, checking for signs of Mina. Seeing none, she let herself be guided off.

I'll catch her later, Lizzie thought, enjoying being in the crook of Todd's arms. She felt the soft, downy hair on his arm against her neck, tickling, and stifled a giggle.

Every other person they passed said hello to Todd, dapping him up with pounds and hand shakes, exchanging quick inside jokes or weak one-liners. He acknowledged them all without missing a beat with Lizzie. "I'm just saying, the Bay Dra–da season is over, and I thought maybe . . ." He wiggled his eyebrows. "You might make a little more Toddie time."

They stopped in front of her AP Lit class, side by side, her still tucked under his wing.

Lizzie looked up into Todd's blue eyes, bright with mischievous humor. Her face burned under his intensely amused attention. But her chest filled with a warm happiness at the thought of spending more time with him before he left for Cali to visit his brother for a few weeks and before summer theatre kicked into high gear.

Respecting Lizzie's aversion to being called out by a teacher for hallway PDA, Todd ducked in for another quick, yet teasingly lingering kiss.

The soft memory of his kiss tingled Lizzie's lips, and she merely nodded in agreement as a long, leggy brunette with thick, curly hair stopped in front of them. Lizzie recognized her as a junior on the volleyball team. The girl's legs, tawny, tan, and athletic, went on for days in an ultra miniskirt. She was nearly Todd's height. They towered above Lizzie.

She gave Lizzie a quick, perfunctory hello before launching into a lengthy and animated discussion with Todd. Her polite ig took Lizzie by surprise, but only for a second. There were a few things that came with being Todd's girlfriend that she still wrestled with:

1) The Hallway PDA, though admittedly she'd grown to like that more than she'd ever admit.
2) Being half of a "popular" couple.
3) Being ignored by girls who assaulted Todd with their silly, pointless banter as if they were on some hidden camera date show and gaining points for being the girl who laughed the hardest and loudest at Todd's barrage of corny jokes.

Lizzie wasn't sure which grated on her more—the being a popular couple thing or getting the ig from girls like Miss Teen Volleyball.

As much as she hated it, she was almost used to the ig. It happened all the time. After getting the ig from some girl, Lizzie always had to inform Todd that the girls were totally flirting with him. She never brought it up in a jealous way, just as an observation. Todd always joked it off.

"I never believe my own hype, Liz-O," he'd say with that infectiously devilish grin.

It was that "Aw, who me, popular?" way about Todd that Lizzie loved. Even though secretly, it angered her how blatantly the girls ignored her to flirt with her boyfriend.

Hello, and right in my face, she thought, eyeing Volleyball Girl's hair toss and wide-eyed head shake at one of Todd's cracks.

Lizzie grimaced. She refused to be that openly infatuated with anyone, even Todd. Although, more than once, in the middle of one of their fifteen-minute make-out marathons, Todd's arms wrapped around her, her body pressed against his hard chest, she'd definitely thought how envious those girls would be if they could see that.

Take that, Volleyball Girl! Lizzie thought, secretly disliking the brunette chatting up her boyfriend.

She almost wished he'd let the full walnut brown-colored hair grow back and stop working out until his abs showed good ol' rib, like it used to. Maybe it would cut down on chicks like Volleyball Girl here stopping to . . . to what, exactly?

She listened in to the conversation for the first time.

Todd talked easily, as if this weren't their first encounter. He brushed hair out of his face, a nervous habit of his, and joked with the girl about how her long legs would equal a sick vertical leap if she played basketball. And, of course, Volleyball Girl laughed.

Lizzie rolled her eyes, marveling at how Todd made witty banter with anyone.

Conscious that Todd still had his arm around her and that she probably looked like a pod person, standing there gape-mouthed, Lizzie cleared her throat. Catching the hint, Todd brushed his hair out of his face and wrapped up the conversation. "Cool. Look, Cassie, I'll talk to you later."

"See you, Todd," Cassie said, wiggling her fingers slowly in the world's flirtiest wave. She turned and swayed her way down the hall.

Sure that Todd was watching Cassie's long model-volleyball legs in that ultra miniskirt, Lizzie slyly ping-ponged from Cassie to him. But Todd was looking her in the face.

"Alright, so you gonna blow me off later, too?" Todd asked, his face an exaggerated wince. "Maybe you have some Russian to study or something?"

"You know I don't take Russian," Lizzie said, happy that Todd hadn't watched Cassie's smooth, leggy exit. Her grin practically wrapped around her head.

"Well, French then? Spanish? Physics?" Todd threw up his hands in surrender. "What else is gonna come before your dude?"

Lizzie took his hand in hers. "Chillax, dude."

She laughed up into Todd's smiling face.

"Seriously. Wanna meet at the Ria?" Lizzie asked.

"Well, my stahs, Miss Lizzie, ah yew asking lil' ol' me on a date?" Todd said in a poor Scarlett O'Hara southern accent.

The first bell rang. "Right after school," Lizzie said, firming up the plans.

"Cool." Todd pulled Lizzie to him and gave her a full kiss on the lips. "I'll wait for you by the flagpole."

Lizzie watched him saunter down the hall. He was obviously in no hurry to beat the second bell. A few people fell into step beside him. Before she turned to head into her classroom, Lizzie heard Todd's voice—she couldn't make out what he said, but she waited a few seconds and sure enough, the expected eruption of laughter from his audience followed.

S*#% Happens . . .
All the Time

"These sleeping dogs won't lie."
—All-American Rejects, "Dirty Little Secret"

If Mina had any lingering day after regrets or jitters, Jacinta couldn't tell. The ride to school was same as always: Jacinta walked to Mina's house. Brian drove up in his Explorer and blew the horn once. Jacinta hopped in the back, mumbled a "how y'all doing?" to the guys; Michael, still waking up, gave his usual nod while JZ hollered, "hey, girl," louder than necessary at six-thirty AM as Mina waited impatiently for him to relinquish his hold on the front seat. The two exchanged a few obligatory barbs, "Move, big head," followed by, "Why can't you sit in the back?" even as JZ obliged. Then Mina stepped in, bent over the middle console, and planted her sweetie kiss on Brian's lips.

End scene.

It was the same morning every school day—had been for fifteen months.

For all of Mina's confusion and uncertainty yesterday, today was just today, same as last Monday and every Monday before it.

Jacinta toyed with that thought as the clique joked around her, amazed at how the world kept going even when something huge was happening to people. Watching Mina nag at JZ and tease Michael, all while keeping her arm just near enough to Brian's on the console that they touched, Jacinta had to remind herself that just twelve hours ago, Mina had been a total wreck.

A bitter envy stung Jacinta at the way Mina went wherever her emotions carried her. She thought she was used to Mina's very public highs and lows. Whether she was being embarrassed in front of half the student body on a beach or rambling in the hallway excitedly, Mina wore how she felt on her sleeve and dared anyone to give her grief for it—which Jacinta did.

At first, Jacinta teased Mina's brimming emotions because it irked her. She wasn't used to being around girls so open with their feelings, and sometimes, being around Mina was like having a single fly swarm your head. You could swat and swat, but the fly kept flitting about.

Jacinta poked fun at Mina simply because it was easier than admitting that she wished she could be so free with her emotions, at least every now and then. But crying in public or gushing about how much she loved Raheem just wasn't her.

She wished it was because then, maybe at some point the other day, she could have found a way to bring up her own minicrisis.

Mini was putting it mildly. But she was sticking to that adjective to hold off the panic lurking at the corners of her mind.

The clique's clucking grew louder as Michael joined in, his early morning freeze thawing at the same exact spot as always—as the SUV glided slowly out of The Woods and onto the main strip, where it would take ten minutes to get to DRB High. Always ten minutes. Twenty if Brian stopped at the Blarney Bean, an early morning hangout that served the hottest (and in Jacinta's opinion, nastiest) coffee ever.

Her disdain for the Blarney was the minority opinion. The shop was routinely packed with students and commuters alike in the morning. The only equivalent was Rio's Ria in the afternoon, after the high and middle schools let out. If Jacinta didn't know better, she'd swear both places laced their food with crack to keep the streams of people spilling out of their doors. She loved the Ria. But slurping up Blarney iced or hot coffee was one 'burb habit Jacinta passed on.

She silently willed Brian to bypass the coffeehouse this morning and cheered inside when the truck crawled along in the dense traffic instead of joining the left turn lane. No espresso today, she thought relieved. Just the thought of the strong coffee's thick scent tugged at her empty stomach, making it cramp. The involuntary contraction stopped her swirling thoughts. She held her breath for a beat, waiting and getting what she wanted—another lurching clench.

Yes!

Jacinta relaxed in the leather seats and waited for the cramps to grow from a whisper to a squall in her belly and for the first time in days, allowed her mind to go to the other reason she was glad her period was coming.

It was late. Three days late, to be exact.

She shuddered at the four-letter word.

JZ nudged her. "Want me put the window up?"

Jacinta shook her head. It was an unseasonably warm morning, and the cool spring air floating into the truck actually calmed her. Still, she absently hugged her arms closer to her body, as if warding off the chill coursing down her spine from the thought of L-A-T-E.

JZ gave her one last confused frown before answering Brian about their weekly pickup game. Mina loudly reminded Michael that he would be missing the game or risk her wrath because he'd promised to deliver Mina's prom dress that day. Jacinta laughed along with everyone else at the empty threat. Michael was every bit of five inches taller than Mina's petite five feet. She was hardly someone to fear, unless you just didn't feel like hearing her mouth. No one knew that better than Michael, and he went along good-naturedly.

Yesterday had been the first time Jacinta had ever seen perpetually upbeat Mina so freaked out. Check that. Mina could overreact with the best of them. But it was always coupled with a bright side or a plan. Mina had been planless, yesterday, torn about the pact and the fact that there was no way she could take it.

No matter how many times Jacinta pointed out that everything couldn't be broken down into steps, her friends believed in preparing like some people believed in God. In Jacinta's opinion, as much as she had grown to love her 'burb girlfriends, their obsession with planning was exactly why they were always so lost when something unexpected hit them.

Not like her.

Shit happens . . . all the time. That was Jacinta's philosophy.

It was why when Raheem smacked her at the cheer competition (the girls still talked about that like it had happened yesterday instead of last year), then Jacinta had smacked him back to remind him that he was fool crazy for raising his hand at her.

It was why she and Raheem broke up, then got back together and argued on occasion (many occasions).

It was why, since Raheem had made it official that he was committing to Georgetown, he'd suddenly been "we, we'ing" her to death.

Every time they talked, it was "we this," and "we that," about their future.

And, it was why her period was late. Shit happens . . . all the time, even apparently, when you did what you could to prevent it.

Jacinta zoned in on the passing scenery, large houses, small houses, lush green trees blooming with pretty flowers, nothing like the sparse landscaping in her old neighborhood, and realized she actually knew who lived in at least half a dozen of the homes they passed. And not just knew them, but had hung out with them, made memories all along the corridor that led from the high school to the neighborhoods surrounding Cimarra Beach.

To the left was Todd's house, a big brick house with a stone driveway, and Jared Cornwell's was the bright yellow rancher. Jacinta and the girls had once chased Jared halfway to the school after he water ballooned them. In a second, the truck would pass the spot where JZ had smacked the bottom of Kelly's peppermint mochachino cup, making it fly out of her hand and all over the sidewalk. It was the first time Jacinta had ever seen Kelly get seriously angry—so mad that JZ had to walk back to the Blarney and buy her a new one.

Jacinta couldn't say when it happened, but The Woods and DRB High school had finally become her home. It had been an unsettling realization at first, but now she had so many connections to the people and the places she saw everyday that it had been forever since she'd cursed how slow the week went, aching to be back in Pirates Cove on weekends. Now, it was the opposite. She'd go to The Cove to see her family and count the hours to head back and check in with the clique, especially JZ, who had become her escape. Around him, she didn't have to think about boyfriends and futures or (no disrespect to Mina and the girls) being so correct and proper, worrying about hurting someone's feelings with one of her blunt truths.

Jacinta never worried that any drama would pop off when she dropped in to see JZ, something she'd taken to doing (apparently not as on the low as she thought) after especially cloying weekends with Raheem. And lately, every weekend with Raheem was smothering.

Hanging out with JZ wasn't anything she hid from the clique, just not anything either of them announced or talked about. They were just friends. If the friendliness dipped into a fierce game of flirting . . . well, who could blame her? JZ was . . .

Jacinta inhaled sharply at another dull twisting of her insides, stronger this time. As the clenching subsided, her breath leaked out slowly in relief.

Yes, it's coming, she thought excitedly.

Even though she was used to shit happening, words couldn't describe how happy she was to ride the crimson wave this month.

Not one single word.

But seven hours and ten trips to the bathroom later, she did have a few words to describe how she was feeling: terrified, on edge, and sick. The dull warning of the cramp storm had stopped shortly after her first class. Distracted, Jacinta had spent the day asking to be excused to the restroom by every single teacher, plus a few stops in between classes, hoping, praying that the cramps would return and bring the flow of her cycle with it.

With the last bell still echoing in her ears and students spilling out all around her, Jacinta stood at the double doors of the school's entrance, staring out into the teacher's parking lot, a sea of cars and SUVs that went on for rows. The vehicles waited patiently for their turn to leave while students' cars revved up and sped out in the surrounding lots. Jacinta gazed out at the still lot, wishing for some of its stoic silence to quiet her mind.

Mina was in front of one of the concrete benches under the flagpole, talking to three girls, two cheerleaders and a girl Jacinta didn't recognize. The four of them stood clustered together, deep in conversation. Every few seconds, one of them would look up, smile, flirt, laugh, or shout good-bye to friends passing by before going back to the discussion.

No doubt solving a real crisis, like whether to choose polyester shorts over mesh for next year's cheer camp, Jacinta thought, unable to avoid the disgust crawling up her throat. She swallowed it like a bitter pill, refusing to feel sorry for herself. She closed her eyes for a second—to better hear her own body—last check to see if the cramps were lurking somewhere deep inside. But her stomach was silent, minus a low rumble to remind her that she'd skipped lunch.

She snorted softly, defeated, before pushing the doors open and walking into the swirl of students heading toward buses and their own cars. Her steps, slow and deliberate to ensure Mina's friends were gone before she reached the flagpole, clicked lightly against the walkway. Exhaust from the buses pulling off got tangled in the warm air and wafted her way. She wiped at her nose absently.

"Hey," Mina called when Jacinta was only steps away. "Brian had some after school . . . thing. Some graduation meeting. Wanna walk to the Ria and meet JZ, Liz, and Todd?"

"Okay, Mina. We'll talk to you later," one of the cheerleaders said.

"See y'all." Mina waved, turning her full attention to Jacinta. "I'm not all that hungry. But I'm down for heading to the Ria if you are. Brian said we could wait for him. He's only gonna be like a half hour. But we could have been home and back by that time."

"Mina, give me a second," Jacinta snapped softly. She sat on the concrete bench and dropped her tote bag beside her. It kiltered dangerously near the edge, threatening to spill her books.

"My bad." Mina's eyebrows raised slightly. She took a seat beside Jacinta. "Bad day or boy trouble?"

"Both," Jacinta said glumly.

Still holding on to the straps, she nudged gently at her tote with her butt, letting it fall down to the ground. She folded one leg under her and turned toward Mina. "It's a really bad day, and it's 'cause a boy got me in trouble."

Mina laughed loudly and was about to make a joke until she saw how serious Jacinta's face was.

"Wait. Trouble like what?" Mina's eyes narrowed.

Jacinta rolled her eyes at Mina's playing dumb. Her eyebrows spiked, and she stretched her neck in a comical prod, as if to say, "now, what do you think?"

"Trouble like detention? Or suspension?" Mina leaned in, whispering. "Or trouble like, somebody ready to be a momma up in here?"

Jacinta laughed at that. Hearing Mina come close to revealing her problem sucked some of the fear away. Not a lot, but some. She nodded. "Yeah, trouble like that . . . the third one."

Mina scooted closer, and she folded her legs under her, going into full-scale friend mode, so she and Jacinta were only inches apart. "Oh, my God. Are you freaking?" Her hand thumped on her chest dramatically. "Oh, my God, I'd be freak-ing."

"I'm alright," Jacinta lied.

"Alright?" Mina's voice rose. Her head bobbed to the left, then right as she checked out the near empty campus. Aside from a few teachers filtering out, she and Jacinta were practically alone out front now. "Does Raheem know?"

"He knows my period is late. But I really thought it would come on this morning." Jacinta shook her head in disbelief that it had betrayed her. "I told him to call me to check. He should be calling soon."

As if summoned, Jacinta's phone shouted, "Partner, let me upgrade ya," then proceeded to play a bar from the Beyoncé song before Jacinta flipped it open.

"Hey, Heem."

"Wassup, girl," Raheem said.

"Nothing." Jacinta leaned her elbows on her thighs and away from Mina's curious gaze. Immediately, all the control fled. She silently cursed the tight knot in her stomach, willing its tightness to be from her period and not the doom she felt crowding her. Telling Raheem was the easy part compared to . . . well, she didn't want to think about telling anyone else.

Easy or not, she braced herself for Raheem's rant. She'd probably have to hear all about how not ready he was to be a father. Like she was ready to be a mother? But he was heading to Georgetown University late this summer—she was pretty sure they didn't allow babies in the dorm.

Mina tapped her, mouthing something.

"Hold up for a second," Jacinta said to Raheem. She brought the phone away from her ear. "Huh?"

"Want to walk to the Ria or just stay here?" Mina asked.

The Ria was only a short five-minute walk across the school's soccer fields and the main street, but walking, doing anything would be better than nothing. Jacinta stood up, picked up her bag, and signaled that she wanted to walk.

They took their time, using the sidewalk around instead of cutting through the teacher's lot.

"So, what's up? Did it come on?" Raheem asked.

"Nope."

Jacinta's heart pounded in her ears as she waited for Raheem to flip out. Instead, his voice came back a hushed whisper. "Damn. For real?"

"For real," Jacinta said.

The short answers were helping her keep her cool. Keeping her from screeching into the phone, "What are we going to do? What? Huh? What are we going to do?!"

"So we gon' have a little baller, huh?" Raheem said, the smile in his voice unmistakable.

Jacinta took the phone off her ear and stared at it, scowling, like it had licked her.

"What?" Mina asked. "Dead spot?"

"Raheem, are you serious?" Jacinta asked, her voice hitting that note of incredulity that meant she wasn't just confused, she was pissed.

"Well, I guess it could be a little girl. But girls be hoopin' too," he said.

Jacinta stopped abruptly. Mina sputtered to a halt beside her. "Alright, where is the real Raheem? And who the hell are you?"

Raheem laughed. "What? You thought I was gon' trip?"

"Yes. I'm tripping. Why aren't you?"

Jacinta kept taking the phone off her ear and staring at it.

"'Cause there's worst things that could happen, I guess," Raheem said, a shrug in his voice.

"Yeah, like my father killing you and me."

"I know that's right," Raheem said. There was silence on both ends; then with another verbal shrug, he said, "But Jamal know I'm gon' take care of mine."

"Alright, look, we need to have this conversation in person," Jacinta said with real authority. She shook her head. "'Cause I don't know if you're joking or what. But . . ." She paused, as if pondering another option, then snorted. "Naw, we need to talk." Her eyebrows squinted in genuine confusion. "You heard me right? About my period?"

"Yeah. You said it's not coming on or . . . whatever, it was supposed to come on a few days ago, and it didn't," Raheem said matter-of-factly like Jacinta was the crazy one. "But alright, holler at me later. I can dip by today or tomorrow."

"Bye, Heem," Jacinta said. She flipped the phone shut, still shaking her head in a slow tick tock motion.

She and Mina stood on the sidewalk, waiting for the light to turn so they could cross over to the Ria. Traffic was light this time of day, the calm before the rush hour storm, and cars floated by lazily.

"What did he say?" Mina asked, raising her voice to be heard above the passing cars. "Was he mad?"

"Naw, he wasn't mad," Jacinta said. Her eyebrows tightly knit, she shook her head. "But I wish he had been."

Good Boys vs. Bad Boys

"We headed out something proper like."
—T-Pain ft. Akon, "Bartender"

Monday's reluctant return to the end of the stretch countdown turned to Tuesday's frantic gallop to get the week going. End of the year fever was in the air. Even late in the afternoon, with classes over, the hallways were louder as students, emboldened by the thought of freedom, ignored the inside voice etiquette. Teachers, fighting their own battle fatigue, gave lackluster warnings, knowing that neither they nor an administrator felt like dealing with an after-school detention with only fifteen days left. Even the hall walls, usually vivid with school spirit signs and informative flyers—Order your yearbook NOW—were silently blank, minus a few forgotten "Prom Tickets For Sale."

Prom was next week. Tickets had stopped being sold yesterday. The random signs were only another clue that each day, everything from the schools walls to its faculty were on a countdown to desertion.

Greg Canon was in on that countdown, and Kelly could tell. Their tutoring session dragged. Greg was getting even simple sentences wrong. Too polite to show her frustration, Kelly swallowed an explosive sigh building in the back of her throat and corrected Greg's mangled translation for the fourth time. Mina had been right, Greg was adorable but hopeless. Kelly had serious doubts he was going to get the C he needed on this exam to avoid failing Spanish. Most likely he'd be *volver otra vez* to Senorita Caridad's Spanish level four course.

For a second, she was tempted to speak aloud to see if Greg knew what the phrase meant just to break the monotony. But the thought that he wouldn't be familiar with the simple word for "returning" swelled her chest with another unuttered sigh. Her Sidekick tinkled lightly, and Kelly quickly fished it out of her purse. It was after school, but cell phone use in the library was frowned upon. Her breath caught as she read the text from Angel.

Whaddup ma?

Angel had stopped texting her months ago, once it was clear she wouldn't answer. The chill she felt goose bumping down her arms, once delicious anticipation, now was a curious dread. What did he want? And why was he so casual like they were still dating or, heck, had even talked recently?

She flipped the Sidekick shut when Greg's voice, stuttering over yet another sentence, reached her ears. This time, she did sigh—a small, fluttery breath of air—but smiled apologetically to cover it up. She absently placed the Sidekick on the table as she said, "No. It says, 'Martinez was unable to understand Nunoz's frustration.' She snorted at the irony of the sentence. "You said, 'Martinez did not know Nunoz's frustration.'"

Greg flashed a smile, and Kelly found herself smiling back, her irritation at bay.

He sucked at Spanish, but boy, was he a cutie! His low cut hair framed a round pie face, which was baby soft clean, except a small patch of hair above his lip that would only be considered a 'stache if it had lots more follicle company. Narrow, almond-shaped eyes and a constant, upturned impish grin gave the impression that he was perpetually happy.

"Mí no bueno en esto," Greg said, his grin sheepish.

Kelly let out a belly laugh, then smacked her hand over her mouth, her eyes searching for the librarian, Mrs. Bostwick. She wasn't sure if Greg had purposely spoken the sentence grammatically incorrectly or not. But it was close enough. She nodded. "You're right . . . you're not very good at this."

"Usted procura. You try," Kelly said, meaning it. The Sidekick tinkled again, but Kelly ignored it. "Not to be mean or anything . . . but why are you still taking Spanish if you're struggling with it so much?"

Greg's eyebrows shrugged. He sat back in his chair, lacing his hands behind his head. "I know it's crazy. But if I want to get into a good lax school, I need certain courses and grades."

Kelly didn't know much about lacrosse, much less what made a college qualify as a good lax school. But she nodded sympathetically. Now, with only two weeks left in their sophomore year, a lot of her peers, her included, really had college on the brain. It was as if a bell had rung, and everyone realized they only had two more years to goof off. Some people took it to heart and were goofing off more. But some of the more motivated achievers were already planning to take the SATs over the summer to gauge whether they'd need a course to help them pass it. Getting good grades had always come easy to Kelly. It was no secret she was a loner and the classic quiet girl while at elite McStew Prep. She hadn't gotten a social life until transferring to DRB High last year and meeting Mina. Still, even with a serious uptick in social activity, Kelly's grades continued to stay on track.

"Couldn't you just take Advanced English?" Kelly asked. She had her doubts about Greg passing level four, and thoughts of him going to level five made her cringe for him. By level five, the entire class was taught in Spanish, no breaks, no English. He'd be lost from day one.

Greg nodded. "I think so. But you know it looks better when you have a foreign language."

"Do you know what schools you're going to apply to already?"

Greg sat up straighter, his eyes shining. "Hopkins, UNC, and probably Syracuse. Hopkins was the NCAA lacrosse champions last year. . . . That's definitely my first choice."

"Maybe you should look to see exactly what their requirements are," Kelly prodded. "If you don't need Spanish . . ."

Greg laughed. "I should run now while I have the chance?"

Kelly nodded, chuckling along.

"I feel like I know the stuff, but I just can't translate it when Senorita Caridad goes so fast."

"Actually, you're not doing too well reading it off the paper, either," Kelly said apologetically.

Greg chuckled. "Okay, okay, I suck."

"Admitting it is half the battle," Kelly joked.

The two of them muffled their laughter. Kelly's Sidekick rang out again, and Greg picked it up without flipping it open.

"These things are cool. You like it?"

"Yeah. I mean, the phone part sort of sucks, but I mainly use it for texting anyway," Kelly said.

Greg nodded. "Yeah, I've heard other people say that." He handed it over to her. "It keeps ringing. Must be your man."

Kelly's eyes fluttered in a half roll, half pop as she protested, "Nope. I don't have one."

"No?" His eyebrow crinkled in concentration for a second. He chuckled almost to himself. "Then maybe I'm not crazy. Is Mina trying to hook us up?"

Kelly laughed openly, and sure enough, Mrs. Bostwick appeared behind Greg, frowning. Kelly tucked her chestnut hair behind her ear and covered her mouth respectfully. She waited for Mrs. Bostwick to walk away before she giggled softly.

"She's so busted," Kelly whispered.

Greg's smile widened. "I knew it. I actually already had a tutor, but she kept saying you were the best and that I had to meet you if I wanted to pass."

"The best?" Kelly shrugged. "No. But I've spoken fluent Spanish since I was three."

"Word?" Greg nodded, impressed. "Are you Hispanic?"

"I'm Latina, yes," Kelly said.

"I didn't know that," Greg said. "I just thought you were mad good at speaking Spanish. No wonder you sound so . . . authentic when you speak."

"Authentic?" Kelly cocked her head to the side in mock question.

Greg leaned in, apologizing. "No, I mean . . . I didn't mean—"

Kelly smiled. "I know what you mean."

"Mina was right, then. You are the best. Sorry I'm a lost cause."

"No, you'll pass. We'll just have to . . ." Kelly frowned, searching for the right solution. She finally decided upon, ". . . Work harder."

"So, should we tell Mina the jig is up or"—Greg leaned in, lowered his voice, and said in near perfect Spanish—"should we go get a slice of pizza together?"

"I'd love to," Kelly whispered back in Spanish. She smiled. "That's the best I've heard you speak since we started."

Greg beamed. "I practiced that one." He gathered his books. "How about Friday?"

Things were moving so fast Kelly could only nod. Before Greg could sprint away, she reminded him, "And don't forget we have another session on Thursday."

He winked at her. "Thanks. See you, Kelly."

Kelly took her time gathering her books. The Sidekick tinkled again insistently. There were five more messages from Angel. She cruised through them, her eyes wide as saucers.

Whus up ma? hit me back

Kelly come on, I need a favor

Wanna kick it Friday?

Cm on girl I wan ask u smthng

Be my date for Sam-Well's prom

By the time Kelly joined the clique in the student parking lot at Brian's Explorer, they were ready to break camp and head their separate ways. The truck idled noiselessly as Mina hung out the window, gabbing with Lizzie. Mina's face lit up when Kelly joined them.

"How's the 'tutoring' going?" Her air quotes dangled in the air as she waited on the answer.

"Well, Greg's on to you," Kelly said. Her face beamed with obvious pleasure. "He had a light bulb moment today and realized you've been trying to hook us up."

Michael's window came down. "And it only took him, what? A month to figure that out?"

Mina shushed him. "Was he happy or . . . sad or what about that, Kel?"

"I'm going for happy," Lizzie said. She smiled when Kelly's face lit up more.

Kelly nodded.

"Yay! Happy?!" Mina grabbed Kelly's hand and swung her arm side to side to a soundless rhythm.

"Very cool," Brian said sarcastically. He tugged at Mina's shirt. "Can we go? Dude's a little hungry."

"Word," JZ hollered from inside.

Mina waved them off. "I want all the dee—" she started when Brian stepped on the gas, jerking the car forward and a foot away from Kelly and Lizzie. "Brian," she pouted. "I almost hit my head. Come on, one more minute."

JZ, Michael, and Jacinta laughed in the back, fueling Brian's antics. "No. You been one more minuting me for the last fifteen minutes."

Kelly and Lizzie jogged over to the truck.

"At least let me say bye. That's so rude to just pull off," Mina lectured.

Brian gestured to the open window. "A minute . . . starting now."

"So did he ask you out, Kelly?" Mina asked. She sat back down in the seat and buckled herself in as she talked. "Did I work my magic right?"

"Fifty seconds," Brian sang out.

"Brian, stop. I can't even hear her."

"He—" Kelly started.

Brian pulled the truck forward an inch. "Forty . . . thirty-nine . . . thirty-eight . . ."

JZ joined in. "Thirty-seven . . . thirty-six."

"Oh, my God, y'all are so common," Mina yelled over their countdown. "Kelly, call me later, or text me or something." She turned to Brian, a sly glint in her eye. "And I'm gonna remember this countdown next time *you* want something from *me*, Mr. James."

"Son, she threw the lockdown on you," JZ said gleefully.

"Man, she showing off for y'all. She know she can't resist me." Brian tickled Mina's side, getting a smile from her.

"Kell, for real, call me," Mina managed to get in as the truck pulled off for the final time.

"Mina and Brian are so cute," Kelly said, watching the Explorer glide slowly through the parking lot.

"So are puppies," Lizzie said with a playful eye roll.

Kelly put her arm around Lizzie's shoulder. "Aww, you miss hanging out with her, don't you?"

Lizzie nodded. "Yeah. But I was only joking. Brian's cool."

"You'll have the old Mina back all to yourself next year," Kelly said.

"No, I'll have the depressed and missing Brian Mina to myself next year," Lizzie said, unable to keep the hint of bitterness at bay. Hearing herself, she switched subjects. "I was going to hang out and help some of the cast pack up props and stuff. But Mr. Collins had an emergency and called it off. Wanna chill?"

"As long as you don't mind riding with me. I've got to drop my brother off to a swim meet," Kelly said. She made a face. "Grand doesn't mind letting me drive solo to run errands."

In answer, Lizzie's footsteps fell in sync beside her as they headed off the school's campus and to Kelly's house.

"So, *did* Greg ask you out?" Lizzie asked.

"Yes. We're going to the Ria on Friday." Excitement bubbled in Kelly's voice, making her sound like a little girl. "He's really nice. Kind of shy, but still willing to force conversation when things get too quiet. It's cute. I just wish he'd have a Spanish light bulb moment."

A stream of passing cars covered her and Lizzie's laughter.

"Tough tutee, huh?" Lizzie asked.

Kelly shrugged. "I've had tougher. But he's definitely in my top ten of tough people to teach."

"Try saying that fast ten times," Lizzie laughed. "Toptenoftough-peopletoteach, toptenof toughpeopletoteach, toptenoftuppupilto-teach . . ."

Kelly joined in until they'd sufficiently mangled the sentence into another language. They passed through the gated entrance to Kelly's neighborhood, their voices the loudest thing in the quiet tony enclave of mansionettes.

Kelly's shoulders shook through the last spasms of laughter before her face grew serious. "Angel texted me while I was tutoring Greg today. He wants me to go to prom with him."

Lizzie stopped in her tracks. "What?" Her green eyes searched Kelly's hazel ones for a hint of teasing.

Lizzie had her own thoughts about Angel (she didn't like him), but she also didn't like Raheem much. It was their personalities that turned her off. Angel was too slick and smooth; Raheem, too gruff and sometimey with pleasantries. But she knew that it was too weird a coincidence that she disliked both the best friends from one of Del Rio Bay's most notorious low income neighborhoods. She didn't need an equation to show what that added up to—snobbery.

Lizzie resisted the urge to roll her eyes for fear Kelly would think she was judging this new bit of news. Instead, she stood patiently, waiting.

Finally, after a few seconds, Kelly resumed walking and talking. "I haven't answered him or anything. He kept texting me the last half hour of me and Greg's session. I read them just before I met you guys in the lot."

"What are you going to say?" Lizzie asked, forcing calm nonchalance into her voice. She fought the urge to scream, "Oh, my God, run! Run, Kelly, run!"

"Lizzie, I'm not going to prom with him," Kelly said. She tittered nervously, prompting Lizzie to stop walking.

She quickly gathered her thoughts. She and Kelly had grown an easy, comfortable bond, nothing like the fragile tug-of-war connection she had with Jacinta. It wasn't so long ago that Lizzie had thought Kelly was weird. Her first impression of Kelly was that she was some sort of freakishly quiet bookworm. But Kelly had proven to be one of the most honest, straightforward people Lizzie knew. And it was that honesty that prodded her forward.

"Kelly, are you thinking of going? I mean . . . you know, did it cross your mind?" Lizzie asked. Before Kelly could answer, Lizzie pushed forward. "I'm just saying, if it did, it's cool to just say so. I won't judge you . . . well, I mean, I'll try not to come off judgmental." She sighed, shaking her head. "It seems like . . . I don't know . . . like we're all only half sharing with each other now because of our boyfriends. Nobody wants to hear the truth." Lizzie squinted, focusing on her next words, letting them pour carefully. "Like, I'm not jealous of Brian or anything. But it seems like maybe Mina isn't really telling me everything . . . I don't know. Maybe that's just how it is, you know? You can't confide in eight million people. And he is her boyfriend and . . ."

Kelly's soft voice broke into Lizzie's stream of words. "Liz?"

"I . . . sorry," Lizzie smiled, embarrassed.

Kelly laughed. She took a few steps and waited until they were walking in sync again before she said simply, "Yes."

"Yes, what?" Lizzie said. "I think I blacked out in the middle of my ramble. What did I ask you?"

They laughed long and hard, unable to pick up on the conversation again until they were in the car, Kevin, Kelly's twelve-year-old brother, tucked in the back, head nodding to the impossibly loud music. Kelly switched all of the music to the back speakers so she and Lizzie could hear themselves.

She nodded her head to her purse. "Get my Sidekick out, please."

Lizzie fished it out and thrust it toward her.

"No," Kelly said, taking her eyes off the road for a second. "Text Angel back for me."

"Me?" Lizzie said, her eyes wide. "What do you want me to say?"

Kelly smoothly changed lanes. She peeked in her mirror and checked on Kevin. His head nodded vigorously to the music. Caught up in the tunes, his eyes were half closed. "Ask him what's going on with the invite to prom," she said finally.

Lizzie read it aloud as she typed:

Y me? We haven't talked in months.

Kelly nodded. "Yeah. That sounds like me."

"Guess we're officially friends then. We can pose as one another when we're messaging." Lizzie grinned. "So you're really thinking about going?"

Kelly's brows furrowed. "I'm just curious why he's asking me." She snorted. "I know he's not hurting for a date." Her head shook slightly, and her voice lowered as if she was talking more to herself.

"Do you know how bad I wished Angel was just a regular guy?" She rolled her eyes. "A good boy."

Lizzie nodded her head, though she wasn't entirely sure. Kelly was a pretty girl. Smart, too. She didn't get Kelly's attraction to Angel at all. No matter how cute he was, his attitude ruined it for Lizzie. She couldn't see past it. But she kept that to herself.

"He really is a nice guy," Kelly said, as if reading her mind. She looked at Lizzie long enough to relay an apologetic eyebrow shrug, then chuckled nervously. "But too much drama for me."

"Greg seems like your type," Lizzie said.

"He's a total sweetie. I think he's even shyer than me when it comes to dating . . . I like that," Kelly said, laughing.

The Sidekick tinkled, and both girls looked down at it as if it had spoken.

"What did he say?" Kelly asked, her voice tense.

Lizzie read it, "Haven't talked in months 'cause of you, baby girl. I been right here, waiting for you to stop tripping. So what's up?" Lizzie looked over at Kelly's thoughtful face. She fought the urge to lecture or beg Kelly to stop going down this road again. No wonder Angel was such a good drug dealer—he certainly did a good enough job pushing himself on Kelly. It was like she couldn't help herself. When Kelly didn't say anything, Lizzie prompted. "What should I say?"

Kelly eased the car into the deceleration lane and turned into the North Rio Swim Center. She pulled up to the front of the building, turned the radio down, and looked up at Kevin in her mirror. "Gerard's dad is bringing you home, right?"

Kevin made a face at her. "Yes, mom."

"I'm just making sure, Kev," Kelly scolded.

He laughed, his hazel eyes crinkling in the corners. "Yeah, I have a ride. Thanks. See you at home."

He dashed out without a second glance.

Kelly waited for him to go inside before pulling away from the curb.

"So . . . what do I say now?" Lizzie asked.

Kelly tucked at her hair until it was completely smoothed behind her ears. She gnawed at her bottom lip as she spoke. "Tell him that I lost sleep wishing he wasn't who he is. And that I really believed him when he said he'd stopped selling drugs. And that I still think about him even though I totally don't want to. And that I wish I could un-meet him because he's on my brain so much it makes me feel crazy." She looked at Lizzie, her pretty face frowning. "Tell him that," she said softly.

Lizzie smiled, chuckling as she pretended to type. "Okay, what came after losing sleep?"

Kelly cracked up, shaking her head. "Just tell him I'm busy that night."

Lizzie eyed Kelly's head, shaking slowly back and forth as if she was holding a conversation with herself. She wasn't sure if Kelly was shaking her head over Angel's ballsiness or her own inability to resist him. Seemed like all of them were addicted to their boyfriends in some way or another. Her stomach fluttered, hating the feeling of powerlessness. She typed back quickly, then pulled her phone out and sent her own message to Mina. Speaking of powerless.

Tomorrow

"I know I got to be right now,
'cause I can't get much wronger."
—Kanye West, "Stronger"

"**S**ee . . . now, what am I supposed to say to that?" Mina asked. She flipped her phone open so Michael could see the text from Lizzie:

So, Mi u never said . . . r u in or out, girlie?

Michael looked up from his sketch long enough to read the message, then went back to drawing. He and Mina sat on the floor of his basement room, their backs against the sofa. Music filled the room, covering their conversation.

Mina flipped the phone closed and looked to Michael for an answer.

"So, let me get this straight," Michael said. He looked up from his sketch pad to the ceiling, a look of exaggerated concentration on his face, and tapped his chin with a pencil. His eyebrows worked in his dark chocolate face, rising and falling before settling into a steeple. "You and Brian did it?"

Mina nodded, ignoring the lectury vibe shimmering in Michael's voice. Lectures from Michael, she was used to. They kind of went with getting advice from him, a necessary evil. She didn't like them, but she was used to them.

"And Lizzie doesn't know?" Michael's eyebrow went up another

notch. "You're the one with all the best friend rules. What's the expiration date on sharing something that huge?"

Mina snorted, rolling her eyes. "Like an hour. I'm way passed that
expiration, Mike, seriously."

"But you told *Cinny?*" Michael's voice rose to a telling, now-
you-know-that's-wrong pitch.

"Gah! I know. I know I shouldn't have told her first but . . ."
Mina dropped dramatically, her back across Michael's outstretched
legs, crushing his sketch pad. "Why didn't Liz tell me about the pact
sooner? I swear, if I'd known . . ."

"You wouldn't have done it?" Michael's grin made it clear he
didn't believe that, and Mina didn't dispute it.

She crossed her arms over her eyes as she answered. "I'm saying,
if I'd known she was thinking about something like that . . . then either I would have gone ahead and taken the stupid pact or not. It
would have been either I was in or out. But it's all bad timing now."
Her foot shook with an involuntary tic. "It's like, if I tell her now I
can't take it, she'll be all 'why not' and . . ."

Michael shrugged. "And you can just tell her why." He tugged at
his sketch pad until it popped from under Mina, then laid it on top
of Mina's arm and sketched. "Just tell her that somehow Brian fell on
top of you, and his . . ."

"Michael," Mina screamed, sitting upright, upsetting Michael's
human desk. She fixed him with a disapproving stare, resisting the urge to
laugh. "For real, it's not funny. I don't want Lizzie to think I don't have
her back on this whole abstinence thing . . . even though I sort of don't."

Michael pulled Mina back down, placed her arm back over her
eyes, and resumed his sketching. "Just joking, Diva. Real talk, just
truth up. That's what you'd tell anybody else." He lifted the pad and
Mina's arm and peeked down at her. He waited until she opened her
eyes. "Wouldn't you? Shoot, didn't you tell JZ to truth up when him
and Lizzie got into that beef over him cheating off her Algebra test?"

Mina only nodded.

"What? No special exceptions for your case?" He patted her arm as if he were an old grandma. "Aww, my girl growing up."

Mina rolled her eyes. "Growing up sucks."

"Just tell her, Mi. She won't be mad that you can't take the pact—" Michael paused, making Mina take her arms away to look up at him.

"Why'd you stop?"

He laughed. "Okay, she might be a little mad."

Mina bolted upright. "What? Do you know something I don't?" She frowned. "You and Liz be keeping stuff from me now that y'all always at some theatre thing together."

Michael's eyes rolled to the ceiling. "Okay, somebody who just lost her virginity and told someone other than her best friend should not be talking about who sharing what secrets."

Mina smacked at him. "Stop being right, daggone it!"

"Can't. It's a bad habit," Michael joked. He started as his cell phone vibrated beside him. He picked it up, looked at the number, then stood up, letting Mina's head slide to the floor. "Hey, what's up?" he said into the phone, walking off to a corner in the far side of the room.

"Dag, leave me hanging much?" Mina yelled to him. She sat up, flipped her phone back open, and read Lizzie's message again.

"Truth up," she murmured.

She began typing a response, then stopped. She couldn't text something like this. But calling Lizzie and telling her over the phone wasn't much better. If telling your closest friend you were no longer a virgin didn't merit a face-to-face, she wasn't sure what did.

Her fingers flew across the QWERTY keyboard of her phone.

Don't be mad . . . but I'm out for this one.

She scanned the message quickly, then hit "send."

Telling Lizzie something was better than nothing at all, at this point, she reasoned, then silently lectured herself, *Tomorrow . . . we'll talk tomorrow.*

Pinky Rings and Promises

"I promise not to hurt you, I promise not to lie."
—Tiffany Evans ft. Ciara, "Promise Ring"

The pool's water glistened, a perfectly still glass of blue until JZ threw a beach ball, raft, and floating chaise chair into the middle. A shockwave of ripples bounced the items around. They bobbed furiously like they had invisible ghost riders.

"Good job, Jay," Mina muttered. "Remind me never to get you to help me do anything."

"What?" JZ asked, his voice muffled as he rummaged in the tiny shed at the corner of the large pool. He came back out with a tiny basketball hoop. "We can switch jobs if you don't like how I'm doing it."

He dropped the hoop in and rushed toward her, threatening to scoop her up and dump her in. Mina fended him off with a flick of the long-handled net she was using to clean the pool, wetting him.

"Alright, kids. Play nice," Jacinta warned, a safe distance from the flying water. She lay back in a brown-striped chaise, soaking in the afternoon sun.

"I'm just saying. He was supposed to be stacking the stuff, not throwing it in." Mina squinched her nose at JZ's eye roll. She set the net on the concrete, then plunked down next to it and dipped her feet in the pool, wincing at the freezing cold water. "Okay. It's officially too cold to swim, y'all."

"It's not too hot for the hot tub, though," JZ countered.

Brian came through the French doors at the back of the house. "Who said anything about swimming? Y'all the hired, unpaid help."

"That's messed up about you, B," Jacinta said. "For real. Your exact words were, 'y'all want come over and get in the pool?'"

Mina laughed, nodding along.

"Un-ah, you misheard me." Brian ducked the beach ball Jacinta threw his way. "I said, 'can y'all come over and *clean* out the pool?'"

JZ threw a few more pool toys into the water, then pulled a chair up next to Jacinta's. He stretched his long legs out and put his arms behind his head, relaxing. "I'm finished."

"Truthfully, it already looks clean to me," Jacinta said, eyeing the pool's pure blue clear to the bottom.

"Yeah, it's pretty much ready for some action," Brian agreed. He gestured to the cushions, toys, and floats. "But pulling out all this mess goes faster with a crew." He sat down next to Mina, letting his long legs dangle in the water. "Y'all can thank Mina. She's the one inviting people over on Friday and whatnot."

"Shoot, I didn't think that meant I was gonna have to work," Mina grumbled. She kicked lazily at a float heading her way. She bumped shoulders with Brian. "You have a problem with me trying to spend as much time with you as possible before you go off to college and forget all about me?"

She cut her eyes cut toward him.

"Now, there you go. Ain't nobody forgetting anybody." He nudged her back.

Jacinta kicked at JZ's foot. "Mama Zimms have any good snacks at y'all house?"

"Always. She gotta keep her baby boy happy." JZ grinned. "We be right back, y'all."

"Where y'all rolling to?" Brian asked.

"Yeah? Together and all couplelike," Mina said. She stretched her eyes at Jacinta, who waved her off.

"Over to my crib," JZ said. "Look, we're hitting the Jacuzzi when we get back."

"You're getting in, Cinny?" Mina asked, surprised. She figured Jacinta didn't feel like getting her hair wet in the middle of the week. Normally, it wouldn't be a big deal, but Jacinta had let her hair grow out. No longer a short curly dyed blond 'do, it was now her natural shade of dark chestnut and cut in a cute pixie to her ears. It was longer than Mina had ever seen it and actually made Jacinta look younger and less mature than the brassy blond look had.

"Sounds like I don't have a choice," Jacinta said, hunching her shoulders. "So, yeah, I guess."

She trailed behind JZ, and they disappeared around the corner of Brian's house.

"Anyway, as I was saying . . . that's what they all say," Mina said, lowering her voice, bringing the conversation strictly between them. "We'll see when you're a bigtime Duke freshman."

"Want to make a bet?" Brian challenged.

Mina squinted at him. "A bet? That you won't forget about me?"

Brian nodded.

She put out her pinky, and Brian hooked his around it. They shook, then released fingers.

"Bet."

"Bet," Mina repeated.

Brian folded his arms, smiling smugly. "See, you're gonna be so burnt."

"Not like I'm trying to lose the bet. But I can see you coming home with a new swag." Mina bopped her head to a silent tune, mocking a cool walk. "Thinking you're all that. I'm gonna be all, 'Brian, hey, it's Mina.' And you gon' be all, 'hey, high school girl.'"

Brian shook his head, grinning, biting back a laugh.

Mina laughed hard enough for both of them even as she hoped like crazy the scenario was as exaggerated and unlikely as she intended.

"So that's how it's gonna be?" Brian's eyebrows rose, skeptical.
Mina nodded.

"I guess you know, toughie. I mean 'cause you have had all of . . ."
He looked down at the pool, his hand stroking his chin as he pretended to think. "What? One, maybe two boyfriends?"

Mina smacked at him. "So? I know how y'all do. Especially y'all
ballers."

Brian rolled his eyes. "The best part about you knowing everything is me proving you wrong all the time."

"Pssh," Mina cackled. "And how many times have you proven me
wrong?"

"Pssh," Brian mocked her, his chuckle a deep contrast to her giggle. "You mean how many times have *I* been right? Try every time.
Like when I told you Craig . . ."

Mina dunked her foot into the water hard, spraying water all over
Brian, cutting him off. "Let's not go there."

"Oh, yo, that was wack."

Brian wiped his face, hopped down into the water, and before
Mina could react, bear-hugged her, pulling her in. He cradled her
like a baby.

She screamed at the cold water icing her butt, soaking her pink
and white plaid Bermuda shorts. "Oh, my God, boy."

Brian held her just above the water.

"Okay, now how many times have I been right?" he asked again.

"None." Mina squealed as he walked her to the middle of the
pool. The bottom of her shorts were soaked and cold.

Brian's grip tightened, and he dipped her to her lower back. "How
many?"

Mina struggled. "Don't get my hair wet, Brian . . . please."

"How many?" He ignored her, keeping her butt immersed.

"Okay, okay. You've been right . . . once." Brian dipped her to the
middle of her back. She screamed, "Twice. I meant twice."

"The correct answer is, 'all the time, Brian,'" he prompted like a teacher to a student.

He pretended to lose his grip. Mina kept herself afloat by squeezing her arms around his neck. "Okay, all the time, Brian. Just don't get my hair wet."

He walked her back to the ledge, setting her down gently.

"And now I'm right again." He plucked something out of his shirt pocket and held it in front of her face. "See. Would I give you this if I planned on forgetting you?"

Mina squinted at the small piece of silver in his hand, heart-shaped with a small stone in the middle. Her hands were shaking too bad to pluck it from his fingers. But Brian made no move to hand it to her, just kept it floating in front of her face. A million questions raced through Mina's head. Her heart lodged itself square in the middle of her throat, cutting off her ability to make spit.

"Oh, what? Toughie at a loss for words?" Brian teased. "I figured by now, you would be used to me being right."

Mina remained silent.

"Earth to Mina, hello," he continued. He palmed the ring and pulled himself out of the pool to sit beside her. "What? You don't want it?"

Mina finally let the breath she was holding out. "No. I mean . . . what is it?"

"It's a new car." Brian's eyes rolled. "It's a pinky ring, toughie."

He lifted her left hand and slipped it on her pinky.

Mina's hand floated robotically to her face. "I mean, I know that." She tore her gaze from the ring long enough to look at Brian as she asked, "I mean . . . what does you giving it to me mean?"

His brown eyes teased. "How come it has to mean anything?"

Mina's face burned. "Don't play, Brian. I'm serious." She spoke in a hushed tone. "I mean . . . to me, it means . . ." She looked down at it again, so teeny, so adorable. Very her. She fought the tears welling.

That's all she needed was to scare him off with melodrama, now that he was making . . . what, a commitment to her? She glanced off across the pool, afraid to look him in the eye, steadying her voice. "I know what I think it means. But I'm saying, what does it mean to you?"

"That you my girl. My shorty." Brian tugged at her finger playfully. "And that I'm right, *again*. Because I wouldn't do all this if I planned to just go to school and forget all about you. Right?"

Mina's eyes fluttered furiously, battling the unshed tears. She swiped at her eyes to hold them off.

"Hold up. Let me go get my phone and take a picture. It's a Kodak moment when you're speechless." Brian stood up and started walking away.

Mina tugged at his basketball shorts, still dripping from their soak in the pool, and he sat back down.

"It's really cute," she managed to say but cut herself off before she got too sappy.

"I know you like tiny stuff. Cell phones, miniskirts . . ." He smiled. "Come to think of it, I like tiny skirts on you, too."

Mina smiled shyly. "I really like it."

"Good." Brian leaned in so their foreheads almost touched. His eyes stared right into hers. "So we can squash all this 'Brian gonna forget about me' stuff. Right?"

As she nodded, he pressed his lips firmly against hers, sending shivers up and down Mina's spine. Her body broke out in goose bumps even as her face and lips warmed. She kissed him back eagerly, angling her head just right so she could feel the full pressure of his lips on hers.

Suddenly, Lizzie's voice echoed off the pool. "Now, I just told Kelly it wasn't really hot enough to swim. But I see that it's definitely hot enough here for it."

Mina pulled away reluctantly, irritated that their moment was disrupted.

"What's up, y'all?" Brian said. He stood up. "Alright, I'm going to change."

Kelly and Lizzie chorused hello, then giggled as they bum-rushed Mina, poolside. Kelly sat to her left, Lizzie to her right.

"Seriously, I think I need to take a dip to cool off from that kiss, so I know you do," Kelly teased.

Mina wiggled her fingers in their faces. "You guys likey?"

Lizzie grabbed her fingers to still them. "Mi, this is adorable. When did you get it?"

"Just now," Mina said.

"Brian gave it to you?" Kelly asked in a scream-whisper. "Let me see."

Mina nodded as she shoved her hand in Kelly's face.

Lizzie's eyes popped. "He did? So it's like a . . . promise ring?"

Mina cheesed, her head bobbing up and down.

"Oohhh. It's like the pre-pre engagement to the engagement," Kelly said.

"Kell, you've totally been hanging around me too much," Mina said.

But she secretly liked that description of the ring's purpose just fine.

They all laughed, but Lizzie cut hers short. "Wow. So is this why you're flaking on the pact?" She nudged Mina playfully. "Guess it means you promise to give him your goodies, too."

Mina peered at Lizzie to see if she was joking, being sarcastic, or what and saw that Lizzie's green eyes were clouded with worry. She draped her arm around Lizzie's shoulder, wiggling her newly ringed finger playfully. "I don't think it means all that, Liz. And um, I didn't even have the ring when I texted you yesterday about the pact." She squeezed Lizzie's shoulder. "Are you mad that I'm not in it with you?"

"Disappointed, yeah," Lizzie admitted. "I guess I'll just have to settle for having Kelly on board."

"Dang, thanks a lot, Lizzie." Kelly pouted.

"That totally didn't come out the way I meant it, Kel." Lizzie pulled away from Mina's hold so she could see Mina's face better. "Just remember to give me the play-by-play when it finally happens, 'kay?"

Mina's smile froze. She nodded woodenly.

I should just tell her now, she thought. *Just do it . . . tell Lizzie now.*

"It's sweet," Kelly said, admiring the ring.

"Who, me?" JZ asked as he snuck up behind them.

"Boy," Mina yelled, startled. She smacked at him.

"How come y'all still don't have on swimsuits?" he asked, frowning.

"Heyyy . . ." Mina said. She pointed at the keys in Kelly's hand. "Kelly, did you drive?"

"Yes." Kelly beamed. "Grand finally let me drive solo . . . I mean, for something fun."

She and Lizzie laughed.

"And I picked up Lizzie," Kelly said proudly.

"Sweet. That's all but me and Liz driving now." Mina put her hand out for a high five, and Kelly dapped it up. "I start taking Driver's Ed next month."

"Remind me to stay off the streets all month," JZ said, ducking Mina's flailing arm. "Okay. Seriously, where are y'all's swimsuits?"

"Jay, we have them on under our clothes," Mina said. She flashed the strap of her two-piece. "Happy?"

"Very. I'm going to turn on some tunes." JZ walked away.

"No getting my hair wet, JZ. For real," Jacinta called after him.

He waved dismissively without looking back.

"For real," Mina chorused. She tugged lightly at Lizzie's long hair, already pulled back in a high ponytail. "Very regretting getting my hair cut right now."

"I knew you would," Lizzie said in a boastful, told-you-so tone.

"Thanks, Liz," Mina groaned.

The girls stood up and peeled off clothes. They headed to the large Jacuzzi, a separate section at the back of the pool.

"It's cute, Mi. I still love it on you." Kelly ran her fingers through her own highlighted chestnut tresses as she pulled it into a ponytail with a squishy fat bun on top. "I was thinking of getting mine cut."

"Kelly, Mina's hair style would look really nice on you," Jacinta said.

"I can't see myself with short hair," Lizzie said. "Too much work. Plus, if I can't French braid it every now and then, I feel lost."

Jacinta snickered. "Dramatic much?"

"Always," Lizzie sniffed playfully as she eased her way into the roiling water of the Jacuzzi.

"Is everybody still coming over here on Friday?" Mina asked, looking from Lizzie to Kelly to Jacinta. They all stepped lightly into the hot tub, slowly letting their bodies get used to the hot water, instinctively raising their voices over the loud bubbling.

"I'm coming and bringing Raheem," Jacinta said. "We might get here late, though."

"Well, me and Greg are grabbing a slice at Rio's Ria." Kelly smiled triumphantly. "That's what I was trying to tell you yesterday."

"Ooh, Kelly, bring him here instead," Mina said. Her eyes gleamed.

Kelly's light brown eyes flickered uncertainly. "But we already sort of made the date. I don't want him thinking . . . I don't know, that I had better plans and just asked him along."

"Way overthinking that." Jacinta snorted.

"Can't you guys just come afterward?" Lizzie offered.

"I'll think about it." Kelly said. She rolled her neck, letting the heated water ease her muscles.

"Where's Todd?" Mina asked Lizzie.

Lizzie's head relaxed on the rim of the Jacuzzi. She closed her eyes as she answered, "Family ob. But he's coming Friday."

Hip-hop suddenly blared from a nearby speaker in the tiki bar only a few feet away from the spa, followed by JZ's loud rap mimic as he walked over. Brian was right behind him. JZ slid down between Jacinta and Lizzie, Brian between Kelly and Mina.

"Brian, Kelly's driving solo," Mina announced. "Know what that means?"

"I can finally stop being Jeeves, the chauffeur?" he cracked.

"Well, I wasn't gonna put it like that, but yeah, I guess." Mina highfived Kelly. "One more solo driver to the mix."

"Son, everything set for pickup tomorrow, right?" JZ asked. His head nodded to the music. Jacinta and Lizzie swatted at him as his fingers wandered aimlessly with a mind of their own, tickling Jacinta's neck and tugging at Lizzie's ponytail.

"Yeah. I think just about everybody's coming," Brian said. He slid his arm around Mina, and she snuggled closer.

"Who's coming over tomorrow?" Jacinta asked, nosy.

"Varsity team," JZ and Brian sang in answer.

Jacinta lowered herself until the water was up to her chin. She yelled to be heard over the jets. "Umph, is that fine ass Stefan gonna be there?"

Lizzie's head popped up. "Boyfriend much? What about Raheem?"

"Shoot, I can still look. Cause Stefan is like, woah," Jacinta said, sending the girls into laughter.

JZ flicked water at her. "No girls allowed, shawty."

Jacinta flicked water back, setting off a battle royale of water sloshing and ruining any mood of mediation and unwinding.

"Hello, my hair," Mina yelled, standing up to avoid the moisture. "I'm gonna look like a Pekingese-Chow tomorrow if I get wet."

Brian cracked up. "What is a Pekingese-Chow?"

He tugged playfully at her thighs. Mina sat on the hot tub's rim, refusing to get back in. "I don't know. But I'm sure it would look a hot mess."

"Jacinta," a voice boomed from across the yard. "What you doing in there, girl?"

Everybody froze, drawn to the voice.

Raheem stood at the shallow end of the pool. He sauntered over and gave a head nod to Brian and JZ. They nodded back, the O.C. beef behind them in the grand tradition of guys getting over things faster than girls.

"Hey, Mina . . . Lizzie . . . Kelly," Raheem said before frowning at Jacinta. "I thought getting into Jacuzzis was bad for the baby?"

Single Teen Mom

"What is meant to be, will be."
—Lauryn Hill, "Everything Is Everything"

Jacinta was so hot with Raheem she could barely see straight. She stepped out of the hot tub, and the cool air broke her entire body out in goose bumps, making her teeth chatter. Snatching her towel off a nearby bar stool, she rubbed at her skin as if the water was hard to remove, the whole time glaring at Raheem. He stood, his back to her, by the hot tub, bumping his gums with Brian and JZ, asking about the weekly pickup game, making noise like he might stop through.

The guys were playing it off good, like Raheem hadn't just spilled some major beans. Jacinta glanced at Lizzie and Kelly, too embarrassed to make contact and read their eyes. Even from where she stood and with only the tops of the girls' heads visible, she could see they were dumbfounded. Mina head checked Jacinta's way, but Jacinta busied herself putting on her miniskirt and top. She grabbed her tote and hollered over to Raheem, "I'm ready." Without waiting, she took her time heading to the side fence. As burnt as she felt, she wasn't about to get all spastic and race out crying.

"See y'all tomorrow," she called out extra loud without looking back.

The clique mumbled back good-bye.

"Hold up, girl," Raheem hollered. He dapped up Brian and JZ before jogging to catch up.

Jacinta kept walking until she was safely in Raheem's car. He got in, grinning, and leaned over for a kiss. Jacinta's hand flew up before his lips reached hers.

Raheem pulled her hand down, leaning closer. "You don't have a kiss for you boy?"

"Let's just go." Jacinta pulled back further.

For a second, they eyed one another. Raheem's smile slowly turned down. His eyebrows furrowed, and he shook his head.

"What? What are you hot about?" He started the car and backed it down Brian's long, flat driveway. "I came over like you asked."

"Nearly two hours late," Jacinta spat. "I figured you weren't coming. I wouldn't have bothered to get in the Jacuzzi if I thought you were coming."

Calm down. Calm down, she told herself and was almost there when Raheem said, "I ain't know there was a time limit on showing up. I had to get my hair braided." He glanced over, his eyes narrowing. "Oh, so you had me penned in for three, and your boy JZ for four?"

Jacinta clamped her mouth shut against the rant rising in her throat, nearly biting her tongue.

Raheem snorted. "I must be right."

"Or so wrong . . ." And stupid, Jacinta thought, ". . . that I'm not gonna bother to answer."

"Then what difference it make what time I showed up?" He pressed. "You told me to come over. I did."

He lifted a hand off the steering wheel in a "what?"

Jacinta waited. She wasn't going to let this turn into them fussing over small stuff. Or in Raheem's case, nonexistent stuff.

Raheem rolled the car smoothly down Dogwood, stopped at the Stop sign, made a right, and headed to Jacinta's house. When he'd gone past Michael's cul-de-sac, then Mina's, Jacinta felt ready to talk.

"Raheem, what did I tell you was my only rule since I moved over here to The Woods?"

"What rule?" He scowled.

A slow, silent sigh seeped through Jacinta's clenched teeth before she replied. "I told you that I never spread my business with the clique." Her eyes locked on him, waiting. When he finally glanced over warily, she finished, "How you gonna bust up over Brian's and put my business out there like that?"

She closed her eyes for a second to hold back the tears of frustration. When she opened them again, Raheem was pulling into her drive. He turned the car off and cocked his head, looking at her.

"My bad. I thought you told your girls everything."

Jacinta didn't detect any sarcasm in his words. But she knew Raheem wasn't that dense. Even if he thought she'd told the girls, that had nothing to do with Brian and JZ. He'd told on purpose. She was sure of it. But proving it would only take the conversation into crazy circles.

"Well, I hadn't told anybody."

"Not even Mina?" Raheem asked, obviously not believing her.

"Not even Mina," Jacinta lied.

He chuckled under his breath. "My bad." He rubbed her arm with the back of his hand. "So, we gonna talk about the baby or what?"

Jacinta scowled. "I just said my period was late. Why are you talking like—"

"You're pregnant?" He said it like maybe Jacinta wasn't very bright. "I thought that's what missing your period meant. Or does it mean something new now?"

Jacinta shrugged. "It could. I mean . . . look, I'm not all into having no baby."

"If you pregnant, you're pregnant." Raheem shrugged. "What did the test say?"

Jacinta's eyes rolled. "I didn't take one."

"Then take one." Raheem's eyes questioned, but when Jacinta didn't respond, he asked aloud, "What you waiting for?"

For it to come on, Jacinta screamed in her head. She didn't want to take a test. She'd been having cramps off and on for a week. Maybe something was blocking it off. It had to be coming. It felt like it wanted to.

Raheem stared at her, waiting for an answer.

The usual gruffness in his voice disappeared. "Alright, that's on you. But I'm saying, if you are, then I'm gonna take care of mine. Ya heard?"

"If I am—" Jacinta shook her head. "I'm only sixteen. I don't want a baby."

Raheem's lips puckered in disapproval. "Well, I'm not down with no abortions. The baby half mine, too."

"Okay. Well, are you gonna take *your* half to Georgetown?" Jacinta's eyebrows arched in defiance.

"You know my mother would help out," he said as if that were a grand plan.

"I don't want a baby," Jacinta repeated.

"Well, it ain't about you."

The matter-of-factness in Raheem's voice grated on Jacinta. She shifted in her seat, aware that her bottom was wetting the car's seats. She'd hear about that later. Raheem loved that car like it was a . . . baby.

A soft shudder rippled through her.

Raheem was gruff. He hated complications and was one of the most impatient people she knew. But he was one thing more than any of those. He was loyal. When he loved something, he *loved* it, period, end of story.

The car.

Her.

Even Angel in a "that's my boy, my homey" kind of way.

He also had two nieces and a nephew that he spoiled bad, ages five, three, and two. They were so hardheaded Jacinta couldn't stand being around them. They didn't listen to Raheem's mother or his sister (their mother), but they listened to Uncle Heem without fail. And he loved their little bad butts back for that.

No doubt, he'd love his own child, their child.

Jacinta winced. The phrase made her stomach drop. She opened the car door slowly, as if it weighed a ton. "Alright. I let you know what's up after I take the . . ." She muttered the last word. ". . . .test."

With one leg out of the car, Raheem's words stopped her.

"It's gonna be cool. Don't worry, alright?"

She nearly broke her neck whipping around to look at him. "Are you serious? My father is gonna trip, for sure." Her eyes locked with Raheem's. She tried once more to make him understand. "It's not gonna be alright."

"Your father know how things go, Cinny." A tiny smile crossed Raheem's face. "I'm not saying he ain't gonna trip. But it's probably not gonna be as bad as you thinking it will." His face grew thoughtful. "When Shay got pregnant with Deonte, my moms went off." He shook his head at the memory. "My father wanted to straight kill Tank. Things was mad tense for a few weeks. But . . ." He shrugged. "It got better. And you know my moms spoil Deonte to death. Shoot, she spoil all of Shay's kids."

"Well, I don't wanna be like Shay." Jacinta spoke the thought aloud before she could stop herself.

Raheem's lids lowered. It looked like his eyes were closed. But they weren't. He did that when he was mad—let his eyes fall so you couldn't read them. The brewing argument between them was inevitable now, so Jacinta spoke her mind.

"My father sent me to live with Aunt Jacqi over here so I wouldn't end up a statistic."

"Oh, so Shay a statistic?" His voice was low, working to stay calm.

"I didn't mean it like that." Jacinta kept her voice level. "But Shay was seventeen when she had Deonte, and—"

"And she got a job and takes care of her kids. How is that being a statistic?"

Jacinta took a silent gulp of air, swallowing her real answer—three kids, two before she was twenty, by two different dudes. Hello, statistic.

She let her breath out slow, quiet, then answered. "I'm just saying I don't want kids, and—"

"Nobody saying we gonna have three," Raheem interrupted.

Jacinta let her anger subside before replying. "So, you're at school, and I'm . . . what? Working? Living with your mom with Shay and her kids? Doing what?"

Raheem frowned as if Jacinta was being ludicrous. "By the time you graduate, I be ready to hit the NBA."

Jacinta's eyes popped. The last few months, he'd gotten more serious, talking about how he'd stay at Georgetown for two years, then enter the NBA draft. But Jacinta had never let herself believe it could happen. Even if it did, two years—her last two of high school—felt like a long time to play single teen mom.

It sounded like a bad reality TV show.

Single teen mom or not, there was also the matter of Raheem planning out her two years with this "we" and "us" talk. He was ready to go to school. She'd never said it to him, but the "we" that they were would be . . . well, out of sight and out of mind. She would never admit it out loud, but she was looking forward to having a break from Raheem. The thought of a baby tying them even closer made her head ache.

"You and the baby be set for life," he said. "You won't even have to work after you graduate."

Jacinta let a few seconds pass, let the silence in the car wash over her before she shrugged. "I see you got the whole plan on lock so . . ." She swung her legs out, pushed herself out the front seat, and closed the car door.

"Ay," Raheem called out the open window.

Jacinta leaned in. "What?"

"Most chicks would be glad their man gonna handle his business."

Then go knock them up, she thought, forcing a thin smile on her face.

"And I'm not even gonna make you sign a prenup." Raheem winked and burst out laughing.

"Lucky me," Jacinta said. "I holler at you later."

She walked off and into the house, not bothering to watch Raheem pull away.

Outing Secrets

"I was blown away. What could I say?"
—Daughtry, "It's Not Over"

The hot air of the blow-dryer sucked greedily at the moisture on Lizzie's skin, scorching her. She dipped her head to her waist, giving her tight face a break, and let the arid heat do its job on her damp locks.

The scent of chlorine that had clung to her nostrils was finally gone, and the wetness that had chilled her bones from sitting in the Jacuzzi on a warm, but not quite hot enough day had worn off. The only thing still lingering from their midweek romp in the hot tub was the aftershock of the bombshell that Jacinta was (might be?) pregnant.

Lizzie cut off the dryer. She fluffed her hair, feeling dampness in the roots but not caring. It was dry enough. The whine of the dryer echoed in her ear a few minutes more. In the airy silence, the thing bothering her leapt out of her mind as if someone had booted it to the forefront.

When Raheem had outted Jacinta's . . . condition, everyone had been floored. You could have popped an olive in Kelly's mouth, she was so shocked. And Lizzie was positive she'd seen JZ take a literal scoot away from Cinny, like he might catch something. Then again, maybe that was him distancing himself so Raheem wouldn't think anything was up between them. Though, it was the word baby that had made JZ slide over, Lizzie was certain. Everyone had been stunned.

Well, not everybody, she thought as she brushed her hair. She used soft, long strokes, coaxing the reality out of herself. Everyone had shown some sort of surprise or discomfort, except Mina.

First, Lizzie thought she'd imagined it. But she and Mina had been sitting right across from each other. Lizzie had a clear, wide-open view of Mina's reaction. And when Raheem dropped the bomb, Mina had looked concerned. Her eyes hadn't popped like, "What?!" They'd narrowed in an "Oh, crap."

Lizzie wanted to be wrong. She'd stared across at Mina, trying to get that BFF ESP going, but Mina's eyes had flitted away from her gaze and back at Jacinta, worried.

Worried.

You can't worry about something you just found out. Could you? Lizzie wondered.

She parted her hair, forcing herself to take her time. She wanted to rush to her laptop and log on. She knew Mina would be on, and she'd promised Todd she'd ping him, tonight. But she needed to calm down first. Rid herself of the prickly jealousy that kept lodging itself in her mind.

How could Mina choose this—pregnancy drama—over the peace of mind the pact could give her?

Her fingers slid through her hair, some of the blow-dryer's warmth still present, and easily divided it into three segments. The braid formed almost instantly as her fingers danced, soothing her. By the second braid, Lizzie didn't feel quite so jealous. Even if she hadn't imagined the knowing she saw on Mina's face, it was swazy. Clique secrets were becoming the norm, it seemed. She and JZ had shared one last year, and she and Mina always had a secret or two stored in their friend vault. Usually, when the time was right, the secrets always came out and became general clique knowledge.

Sometimes, it was just easier to tell it to one person first, Lizzie justified.

She smirked. It sounded reasonable enough. Yet it still made her sad. The line between secrets and lies was blurring. She didn't have to talk to Mina to confirm it. She just knew. Felt it like she sometimes knew with absolute certainty that she'd nailed or failed an audition.

She wrapped the end of each braid with a rubber band, patted her hair, then smiled quizzically at her image in the mirror before heading to her bedroom. She rushed through the formality of getting the laptop booted up and herself signed on. Within minutes, Todd IMed her.

BasketballT: What up l-boogie?

Grinning, Lizzie pushed the laptop to the head of her bed and stretched out toward it.

Liz-e-O: nothing how wuz da family ob?
BasketballT: fam+out of town cuzzins+skating= l-l-lame!
Liz-e-O: LOL ur crazy
BasketballT: like a fox. did u guys hang out?

Lizzie's eyes rolled. "Boy did we," she muttered as she typed.

Liz-e-O: Yup ttly missed sme juice
BasketballT: dish l-boog
Liz-e-O: ok did u jst ask me 2 dish?!
BasketballT: so sick of b/n w/fam im actn like a ol' beyotch LOL
Liz-e-O: u said it not me
BasketballT: so what up? Iz dat more manly?
Liz-e-O: a little. Cinny is preg
BasketballT: WTF?! Serious?
Liz-e-O: tttly
BasketballT: dayum wat did JZ say?

Lizzie chuckled.

Liz-e-O: nothing. surprised I guess

BasketballT: tht sux

Liz-e-O: 4 who? Cinny or JZ

BasketballT: LOL both. Dude, jay likes her

Liz-e-O: he tol u tht?

BasketballT: no so dnt go tellin ur girls. jus sayin I thnk he does

Liz-e-O: me 2

Just then, the sound of wind blowing announced Mina was on. Lizzie's heart skipped excitedly. She waited a few seconds, willing Mina to IM her first. She forced herself to keep talking to Todd, rather than ping Mina first.

BasketballT: mayb crazy ques—is Cinny kirkin out abt being preg?

Liz-e-O: she wuz defntly po'ed Raheem outted her but same ol Cinny, cool as a cuc

BasketballT: man, Raheem makin babies n I can't evn mke it 2 2nd base

Liz-e-O: o ha ha w/e T

BasketballT: j/k . . . kind of

Usually Todd's humor was cute, adorable even. But he'd hit too close with that crack. She gladly switched conversations when a message from Mina finally blew through.

BubbliMi: hey Liz. Crzy dy huh?

Liz-e-O: mos' def. hey did u alrdy knw Cin ws preg?

BubbliMi: Mon she tol me her pd wuz late. She's still not 100% sure she is

Lize-e-O: I'd b freakin!

BubbliMi: u n me both!! :-0

A buzz of pleasure widened Lizzie's smile. She'd half expected
Mina to be nonchalant about the whole thing. She was glad to hear
a very Mina reaction. The ringing of messages from Todd forced her
to click back over to him.

BasketballT: r u iggin me?
Liz-e-O: no
BasketballT: o u didn't ansr me

Lizzie scrolled back up to see what she'd missed. She squirmed as
she read his previous messages.

BasketballT: now I guess we'll never do it?
BasketballT: gtta rmbr 2 thnk Raheem 4 this. Thx bro ☹

Lizzie decided to play dumb.

Liz-e-O: so wuts da ques
BasketballT: LOL gotta luv a grl who plys hrd 2 get
Liz-e-O: gotta luv a guy who lvs da chase ;-)
BasketballT: LOL hw lng u gnna run? A dude's legs r gttn tired
Liz-e-O: well . . . me n Kelly took an abst pact

There she'd told him. Now maybe everyone would get off her
case. When Todd didn't answer immediately, she went back to Mina.

Liz-e-O: ur pinky ring is so cool
BubbliMi: OMG Liz he tttly cght me off grd
Liz-e-O: I bet. Hey, so it's cool and all . . . but how come u don't
wanna do da pact?
BubbliMi: cn I b honest?

Lizzie's stomach clenched, but her message back was casual.

Liz-e-O: of crse Mi! we're girls fo' life rmbr ☺
BubbliMi: taking it feels like I'm choosin b/w u n Brian
Liz-e-O: not tryna mk u choose . . . jus wtchg out 4 my grl
BubbliMi: I knw <3
Liz-e-O: no big. me n Kel will go it alone

Lizzie blanched at the lie. It did matter. But she wanted Mina to want to take the pact because she wanted to, not just to please Lizzie. She laughed at the lie.

They'd been doing stuff like this—having each other's back, agreeing with stuff that they didn't necessarily want to go along with—for an ice age. Heck, yeah, she wanted Mina to go along just because.

Just because that's what girls do.

Just because it would be taking Lizzie's side on the issue.

Just because, period.

Mina not taking the pact definitely stung, especially since Lizzie was sure it was something Mina would have willingly done a year or two ago. She fiddled with one of her braids, then reluctantly minimized the box and picked back up with Todd.

BasketballT: ok pls tell me abst stands for absence frm schl or smthg. Pls!
Liz-e-O: LOL nope means abstinence . . . u knw frm sex
BasketballT: ummm does ur bf gt a say in ths?

Lizzie shot straight up. She crossed her legs and balanced the laptop on her lap.

Liz-e-O: dnt take it wrng bt no
BasketballT: thas not cool Liz

Lizzie's cell phone vibrated, buzzing its way across her desk. She pushed the laptop aside, hopped off the bed, and picked up the phone, saving it from nose-diving off the edge. Todd's number flashed from the screen. She took a deep breath and answered. Todd jumped right in. "Look, I knew you weren't down with us doing it right now . . ." He sighed loudly before continuing. "But never? Dude, isn't that extreme?"

"It's just for a year," Lizzie said. She winced at the pleading in her voice. She wasn't asking for Todd's permission. Even the anger in his voice, a rare tone, wouldn't budge her. She'd made this decision and didn't regret it.

"I don't get it. So you talked about this with Kelly, but not me?"

Lizzie frowned. "It's not that we discussed it." She fumbled to explain. "I just . . . we . . . I'm not . . ."

"It's not like I was all, 'Lizzie do it or we're hist.'" Todd mimicked a nag. "Dude, it just sucks. 'Cause we're always straight up with each other. And now you're like making decisions about our relationship without me."

"I am being straight up," Lizzie said, exasperated. She eyed the laptop, but Mina had logged off. "Shoot," she muttered.

"What?" Todd snapped.

"I. . . nothing."

"So I guess you and Kelly already took this oath? Signed it in blood or whatever?" Todd asked, openly sarcastic.

"Pact," Lizzie corrected him automatically. "No blood, just an agreement. And I had hoped Mina would do it, too, but . . ."

Todd's chuckle was bitter. "Good luck with all that."

"Why do you say that?" Lizzie scowled.

"Because Mina and Brian already did it."

"Do you want a pickle?"

"Shut up, just shut up, shut up."
—Black-Eyed Peas, "Shut Up"

The next morning, the silence in Brian's truck was so thick it even seemed to smother the light strain of chatter streaming from the radio. The abnormal quiet got to Michael. He was usually the only zombie in the morning. As the truck rolled down the sleepy street, he looked from Jacinta over to JZ and peeked up at the rearview mirror to catch Brian's expression. He was sitting behind Mina's seat and couldn't see her at all.

Whatever it was, and it had to be something, everybody was in on it but him.

He waited a few minutes more for someone to say something.

He knew if he got Mina alone, she'd dish in a minute. But it was too weird that no one was talking. He couldn't take it anymore.

"Alright, what did I miss yesterday?"

His question was met with Mina peeking over at Brian, JZ's knee jumping, and Jacinta staring past him, looking out his window.

"It must . . ." he started, but Jacinta cut him off.

"Go ahead, somebody tell Michael." She pursed her lips. "The whole world knows now anyway."

"Not the whole world, Cinny," Mina said softly. "Just us."

"Knows what?" Michael asked. He leaned up so he could see over to JZ, then looked at Jacinta beside him. His face searched theirs for answers.

JZ's knee jumped double-time, as if it was keeping time to a silent tune.

"My period is late. Okay?" Jacinta exhaled like she'd been holding it since she'd gotten in the truck. "My. Period. Is. Late."

Eyebrow arched, Michael glanced over at JZ again, who suddenly had found something really interesting outside his own window. His neck was going to snap if he stretched it any further toward the window.

"Let's have this conversation once, so we don't have to do it again," Jacinta said. She rounded her shoulders and sat up straight. "It's late. I haven't taken any test. It doesn't even mean I'm pregnant. It's just late. I'm pissed that Raheem outed me like that. Can we talk about something else?"

"Please," JZ muttered.

"Do you want a pickle?" Michael asked.

Jacinta scowled. "What?"

"A pickle."

"No." Jacinta's eyes rolled.

"Oh. Well, you're not pregnant then."

Jacinta looked at him as if he'd lost his mind.

"When you pregnant, you're supposed to have cravings and stuff. So you must not be." Michael raised his hands as if to say, "see, that simple."

There was a brief moment of collective confusion until they all realized he was joking. Michael shook Jacinta's knee and smiled.

Mina tittered, then Brian and JZ chuckled—one of those begrudging, "man, that was stupid" kind of laughs.

Finally, Jacinta snorted and chuckled along, too. "Boy, you crazy."

"Let me just say I haven't heard the word period used so many times this early since seventh grade when I had language arts first class of the day," Michael said, still clowning.

"I wish you would stop using it *now*," JZ said. "Let's just ban it for the rest of the day."

"Yeah, well, Mack D-a-d-d-y, you better hope all those girls you be creeping with use the word often, as in they got theirs," Mina chided.

More laughter smoothed out the tension.

"Naw, for real, can we stop talking about it?" JZ pulled his cap down over his eyes and slumped in the seat.

"Dra-ma," Mina sang. She balled up a piece of notebook paper and threw it back at JZ.

He batted it away, then reached across Jacinta to tap the back of Mina's head.

"Stop, bighead," Mina whined.

JZ continued to pluck with Mina the rest of the ride. They played their usual game of friend tug-of-war, attempting to get Michael and Jacinta to side with them as they verbally sparred, dissing one another. By the time they got to school, everyone happily left the awkward topic of Jacinta's cycle behind.

Later that day, Mina, Michael, and Lizzie sat in Mina's room waiting for the big unveil. Lizzie sat on the bed, silently throwing darts with her eyes at Mina. All day, she'd tried to process what Todd had told her on the phone. She wanted to believe that he was mistaken or maybe just taking a snitty jab at her, because of the pact. Their conversation hadn't ended that well, and Todd had avoided her the entire day at school. But Lizzie knew he'd been telling the truth. Her chest was tight with anger and hurt.

But Mina was too eager, dying of curiosity about the prom dress hidden under the garment bag hanging on her closet door to notice.

"Come on, Mike. Stop playing," Mina scolded, hiding a smile.

But Michael was enjoying every moment of teasing out the big reveal.

Mina plopped on the bed beside Lizzie and gave Lizzie a "he's tripping" eye roll.

Lizzie's eyebrows popped slightly, but her face remained expressionless.

Michael stroked the white garment bag concealing the dress, purring at it under his breath. The last anyone had seen of the dress, it was a swatch of vibrant, sapphire satin draped over a mannequin in a jumbled mass. Once Michael was assured his measurements were on, he'd refused to let Mina see the dress even when she'd harrumphed that Jennifer Hudson probably got a look at her dress before Oscar night.

"Well, if she did, she saw it in the dark," Michael had shot back. "'Cause that thing was wack. I got this, diva. Just trust me."

Lizzie knew that if Michael came even close to his sketch, the dress was going to be gorgeous.

Mina's knee did an involuntary dance in anticipation as she begged this time, "Come on, Mike. Please."

Michael pulled down the zipper of the garment bag in a dramatic sweep, and both Lizzie and Mina gasped.

Michael grinned, his handsome, dark chocolate face complimenting the soft electric blue of the short satin dress. His hands pulled lightly at the skirt of the dress, making the pleats shimmer softly.

Mina gawked. She stood in front of the dress, taking in every detail. The pleats fell perfectly from a wide band covered in beads. Michael and his bead work. It was like he refused to take the easy way out of a design, and Mina told him so. "Mike, how long did it take you to sew on all those beads? Are you crazy?"

Despite the light scolding, her voice was hushed in reverence.

Michael shrugged. "Long enough that I'm gonna be pissed if your boy Brian pull any off messing around."

Mina smiled sheepishly and rushed on. "It's gorgeous. Isn't it, Liz?"

Liz nodded, speechless. She was usually the recipient of Michael's off-the-chain designs for the school's productions. But he'd gone out of his way for Mina, and it showed. The dress *was* gorgeous.

"It's like . . . that dress is so Mina," Lizzie said finally, her eyes admiring the dress from its V-neck and spaghetti straps to the pleated skirt.

Mina nodded.

"Well, I figured that the empire waist would help hide some of that apple bottom." Michael chuckled as he nodded toward Mina's rear. "So I know Mama Mooney will like that. But you got your top out with the V without having to worry about your girls hanging out."

The three of them laughed.

"Not that my girls are all that big," Mina said.

"I love it," Lizzie declared.

Mina beamed.

Lizzie smiled back, the smile never reaching her eyes. A flicker of confusion crossed Mina's face before she said, "Mike, can you take us over to the mall so I can finally get the accessories and shoes?"

"What? On my magic carpet?" Michael said.

Mina picked up her tiny purse from the desk. "Brian and JZ are balling over at JZ's. He'll probably let you use his truck."

"Well, if he lets me, yeah, I'll take y'all," Michael said.

He and Lizzie trailed behind Mina and headed down to JZ's.

Busted

"So I want to take this time out
and apologize for things I have done."
—Akon, "Sorry, Blame It on Me"

The heavily wooded cul-de-sac where JZ's and Brian's houses stood by themselves was packed with cars and SUVs. Mina, Michael, and Lizzie followed the sidewalk around the side of JZ's house until it led them to the NBA regulation-sized court. The game was in full swing. Six more guys sat, watching from the bleachers, waiting for their turn to be subbed in.

"What up, Mike-Man?" JZ hollered before heading back down the court.

"What up, Jay?" Michael exchanged dap with a few players sitting on the sideline.

"Hey, T," Mina called to Todd.

He waved hastily and hustled down the court.

Mina waited for Brian to look up, then waved him over shyly. He pointed to one of the eager guys on the sideline, who ran in, taking his spot.

Sweat glistened in his black curly hair, pouring down his face. He mopped it off with his tee shirt before peeling the shirt off and throwing it to the side. A little tingle of appreciation ran through Mina as she eyed Brian's well-toned pecs and biceps.

Who's a lucky girl? Me! she thought as he walked up to him.

Brian exchanged a pound with Michael and nodded at Lizzie,

who gave him a small, frozen smile. He sat on the bottom bleacher so he and Mina were almost face-to-face. She stepped closer and stood in between his legs.

"What's up, toughie?" Brian asked, tapping the back of her thigh lightly.

"Can Mike use your truck to take me and Liz to the mall?"

Brian smelled like a gym, even outside, but Mina had the urge to kiss him. His hand caressed her leg softly as he considered her question.

"Mike, you cool driving my truck, man?"

"Yeah. But I'm not mad if you want take the diva yourself," Michael said, cutting his eyes playfully at Mina.

Brian snorted. "That's all you, man." He leaned back, reached for a DRB Blue Devils duffle, and rummaged around for his keys. "Just don't be getting no tickets or nothing."

"It's swazy. I'm used to driving my grandmother around." Michael rolled his eyes. He caught the keys Brian chucked at him. "You know how slow I gotta go with her in the car."

"Thanks," Mina said.

Brian winked at her, and she grinned. She started to walk away. Brian tugged at the back of her tee shirt, and she let herself be pulled back toward him.

Brian frowned. "So what, I gets nothing for being the good boyfriend who letting some other dude drive you around . . . in my truck?"

Mina played along. "My bad. What did you want?"

He pulled her close enough to whisper in her ear. She grinned as he said, huskily, "I'll tell you later."

The trip to the mall was uneventful enough. Lizzie and Mina teased Michael, who drove an elderly thirty-five miles an hour the entire way. Michael reminded Lizzie that soon she'd know exactly what it was like to become an overnight chauffeur with her parents badgering her to "slow down." He promised to return the teasing when the time arrived.

Things were feeling almost like old times. Mina found the perfect earrings, a pair of crystal tear drops, and held them next to the crystal strappy heel sandals Michael had approved.

"This is going to be hot," she said, grinning broadly.

"Hey, Mi, did you and Brian have sex already?" Lizzie blurted. Her arms were folded tight against her chest, her face set in grim determination.

Michael's eyebrows steepled. He played it cool and kept his eyes on the shoes Mina held frozen in midair.

Mina's face cracked like a day-old mud mask. Her voice rose to a liar's squeak. "No. Why?"

Lizzie's eyes clouded, becoming a dark green.

That's when Mina realized, too late, that Lizzie already knew. But she was in the middle of the lie and couldn't pull out.

Lizzie's face turned a dark pink as she shrugged and mumbled something to the effect of "just wondering."

Usually the voice of keeping it real, Michael kept mum.

Leaving Lizzie standing by the rack of shoes, Mina quickstepped to the register and paid for the glittery sandals. Her hands shook as she gripped the bag.

The three of them walked the mall in silence, their footsteps hurried.

Mina attempted to say something, but her chest tightened, clutching the words, trapping them. She was working just to breathe, much less have a conversation.

In her head, she practiced.

"Okay, this is messed up, but . . . yeah, we did it."

"Liz, I didn't know how to tell you. The pact was so important to you, and . . ."

"I'm a total liar. But I had my reasons."

None of the icebreakers sounded good enough. So she kept silent, all the while willing her brain to connect with her tongue to say something—even something lame, just to get her mouth working.

Beside her, Lizzie's breathing was ragged. Mina didn't have to look to know a storm was building.

Say something, say something, she screamed to herself.

They reached Brian's Explorer. Mina rode shotgun, Lizzie in the back. As Mina strapped herself in, she turned toward the back and started, "Lizzie . . ."

Lizzie stared her in the eye. Her words were icy hot. "When did you become such a liar?"

Michael cursed under his breath. His hand froze on the ignition. The keys jingled lightly as they swayed.

Mina swallowed.

I can't be mad. I deserved that, she told herself. *I did lie. I can't be mad.* She exhaled slowly, but instead of apologizing, she said, "Who told you about it?"

Lizzie exploded. "So it is true?" Tears of anger streamed down her reddening face, and she swiped at them. "All day long, I kept hoping it wasn't true. Even though I knew you were acting shady."

Mina felt like she'd been punched in the stomach. Now, every excuse she'd made for not telling Lizzie sooner felt flimsy. Her eyes pleaded with Lizzie, but it wasn't enough to penetrate the darts Lizzie shot at her.

"When did all this happen?" Lizzie asked, sniffing. She held her head higher. Her voice steadied, and the tears stopped leaking. "If you tell me weeks or months ago . . . I swear, Mina, our friendship is over."

"No. No, it was just last Friday," Mina said. She nearly sighed with relief that it hadn't gone that long. It was a minor victory but one all the same. She unstrapped her seat belt and knelt in the seat so she was facing Lizzie head on. "I wanted to tell you. But then you brought up the pact, and it just felt . . . I felt . . ." Mina paused. She wanted to get it right. "I felt weird enough after it happened. Like not sure it was cool to do. And you were so excited about the pact I thought you were gonna be pissed at me that I'd done it."

Lizzie's face softened. For a second, she seemed to consider the merits of Mina's excuse before her eyes blazed again. "It's not cool that we're keeping secrets from each other."

"May I drive, ladies?" Michael asked over their bickering.

When they didn't answer, he pulled out.

"I didn't do it to be sneaky, I swear," Mina said. She hesitated, then asked again. "Who told you?"

"Todd," Lizzie said. Her voice hardened. "And I guess that's another reason he's so pissed at me. Every flipping body is *doing it*."

She spat the last two words.

Mina took her seat, buckled up again, turning her body as far as she could to keep eye contact with Lizzie. "Todd's mad at you because of me and Brian?"

Lizzie rolled her eyes. "It's stupid. He's mad that I didn't discuss the pact with him before taking it."

Michael scowled. He looked in the rearview mirror as he spoke. "Wait? You took a pact to not have sex, but you didn't tell him you were taking it?"

Mina felt her eyebrow inching to an arch and forced it back down. She agreed that was all kinds of wrong. But she was still in the hot seat, so she kept her comments, and her raised eyebrow, to herself.

Lizzie sighed noisily. "Okay, okay. I get it. I should have told him first. But if I had, and he said he wasn't down with it, then what?" She folded her arms, challenging Michael and Mina.

Michael chuckled. "My bad. I'm not even in this."

"I guess I don't need to ask whose side you're on, Mina," Lizzie said.

Mina frowned. "What does that mean? Just because me and Brian had sex doesn't mean I'm like the poster child for it."

Tears shimmered in her eyes. She turned to face the front, afraid Lizzie would see how hurt she was.

"I didn't mean it like that," Lizzie huffed.

"How *did* you mean it then?" Mina rolled her eyes, and a few tears spilled. She turned to the back and snapped, "That's exactly why I didn't tell you right away."

"Whatever, Mi," Lizzie snapped back. "But I bet you told Cinny."

Mina's silence was answer enough. It hung in the air the rest of the ride home.

Game Over!

*"Not worth the aftermath, after that . . .
try to get you back."*
—Maroon 5, "Makes Me Wonder"

When they arrived to JZ's to drop off Brian's truck, the game was over. Brian, Todd, and a few stragglers, including Stefan, the cutie, lounged on the bleachers talking smack about who had brought their A game.

Michael dropped the keys in Brian's hand. "Next week, I'm balling. One of y'all can take these crazy dudes to the mall or whatever." He jabbed his thumb over at Mina and Lizzie, standing tight-faced and tight-lipped off to the side of the court.

JZ walked over, stood between them, and put his arm around them. "What's wrong with my girls?"

Mina shrugged his arm off. "Brian, can I talk to you for a minute?"

There was a chorus of oohs as the guys teased Brian about being in trouble.

"Uh-oh," JZ said. "And this is why the kid rides solo."

"Naw, you ride solo cause you keep getting caught dipping with two shorties at a time," Stefan said.

JZ brushed his shoulder off. "I know, right."

Brian doled out pounds and handshakes amid the laughter as he grabbed his bag. He sauntered over to Mina, his eyes peering through the darkening evening as if trying to gauge what was on her mind.

Todd stood up, stretching his long, lean body before grabbing his bag. He put his hand out for another round of pounds. "I see y'all later, dude." He and JZ exchanged a grip and pound to the back. "Deuces, Jay." As he passed Mina, whose arms were tightly folded against her chest, Todd said a low-key hey, then said the same to Lizzie.

For a second, Mina's anger faltered. She instinctively went to protect Lizzie. "Todd, what's . . ." But Brian pulled her by the hand, leading her away.

"Come on. What you want talk about?"

As she and Brian headed out, Mina heard JZ say, "Ouch. What the hell is going on with everybody? You need a ride home, Liz-O?"

Mina took one last look back and saw Lizzie nod her head before she and Brian disappeared around the corner toward his house.

Mina had never seen Todd act like that. Never. And she'd known Todd for six years. Her mind swirled, ping-ponging between thoughts of Todd and Lizzie and she and Brian. She resisted the light pull Brian had on her hand, forcing him to stop walking. They stood at the top of JZ's driveway.

"What's up?" Brian asked. He cracked open a Gatorade and drank.

Mina folded her arms again, almost by instinct, as she reprimanded him. "Why did you tell Todd about us?"

Brian's eyebrows scrunched. "About us? What about us?" He wiped his mouth with the back of his hand.

Mina pursed her lips and raised her eyebrows as if that were somehow the answer to the question. "That we had sex, Brian," she whispered loudly.

He scowled. "I didn't tell Todd."

"Then how'd he find out?"

Brian shrugged.

"Did you tell anybody?" Mina asked.

"Did you?" Brian snapped.

"Cinny. But . . ."

"Do you see me tripping over that?"

"No. But maybe you would if Cinny went off and told someone you weren't ready to tell." Mina's voice rose.

Brian shook his head. "Okay. I can tell you're ready to start popping some stuff that's either gonna be nonsense or some old bullshit only you and your girls would understand." His right eyebrow arched. "So just say what you're pissed about. I'm ready take a shower and chill."

Mina faltered. Brian's straightforward way always kept her slightly off balance. It took her a few seconds to figure out her own point, but she found her voice. "I'm just saying it's not cool that you're bragging about it. What? Did you and Todd have some kind of bet or something, and you won?"

"You watch too many of those corny ass TV shows, Mina." Brian snorted. "Nobody had a bet."

She looked him in the eye. "Then how did Todd find out?"

Brian sucked his teeth. "I told him. Alright?" His voice carried in the quiet cul-de-sac, making Mina wince. She wondered if JZ and the rest were still out back and if they could hear. Brian walked toward his house, taking long strides, forcing Mina to speedwalk to keep up. "And it wasn't all dramatic like you making it. Nobody was sitting around dogging y'all out." He cut his eyes at her as if he knew that's exactly what she was thinking. "Me, Todd, and JZ were kicking it. Todd was joking, saying how Lizzie wasn't really down with sexing and that he was putting down his best game trying to change her mind. JZ said something crazy about how you and her are best friends, so if one of y'all did it, the other one would, too. So they kept tripping, asking had we done it. After a while, Todd was seriously asking, wanting to know, and I told him. So that's how he knows."

"JZ knows, too?" Mina groaned.

"Is it really a big deal?" Brian asked, annoyed. "It's not like they're not your peoples and don't already know everything else about you."

Mina couldn't argue that. Still, she'd wanted to tell her friends in her own time and way. No doubt, if she voiced that, Brian would only say she was being dramatic.

They stood in front of Brian's driveway under a street light, silent. Stefan blew his horn as he drove past, and a few minutes later, JZ stopped his mom's Volvo convertible right next to them. He had the top down. Lizzie sat up front. It looked like she'd been crying. Michael sat in the back.

"You want a ride, Mi?" JZ asked.

Mina was about to say no.

"Yeah, she does," Brian said. He gave JZ a pound, then Michael and headed up the driveway. "See y'all tomorrow."

Mina's mouth fell open. She stared at the empty space that had been Brian seconds ago before climbing in the back with Michael.

Hours later, her homework done, Mina sat at her desk, phone on vibrate in case Brian called to apologize, PC on but Away message blazing, "I'm away B*tches," until someone she felt like talking to logged on.

Michael's satin blue masterpiece, hanging from the closet door, caught Mina's eyes every few seconds. She smiled at it, willing herself to think good thoughts about prom instead of the fact that both Lizzie and Brian were now mad at her.

Check that, Lizzie wasn't just mad—she was righteously pissed. But at least she had a good reason to be mad. Brian was just being pissy.

Eyeing the computer monitor, double-checking for Lizzie's entrance online, Mina shook Brian out of her head. She was not going to think about him right now. She had to make things right with Lizzie, let her know that she hadn't meant to let the secret linger. She would have definitely told her by . . . well, this Friday. She was sure of it.

Definitely by Friday, she told herself, eyeing the phone. She tapped the digits for Brian's phone number on the keypad.

Why hadn't he called or texted her?

She hated when he got pissy. If he'd just told her he'd told Todd, she would have had to come clean with Lizzie sooner, pact pressure or not. How in the world was he the one mad?

Just then, Todd's screen name bolded on her screen.

Lizzie was MIA tonight, but this was the next best thing. Maybe she could help fix things.

BubbliMi: Hey T. Wassup?
BasketballT: Nuttin.
BubbliMi: heard a vicious rumor today.
BasketballT: uh-oh. It wasn't me
BubbliMi: LOL see I knew it had to be all lies tht ur mad@ my girl Liz

Five minutes went by before Todd finally responded.

BasketballT: u tryna trap me into flaming her? Wht is she there w/u?
BubbliMi: T it's not like that. 4real! Y r u mad @ her?
BasketballT: it's b/w me n Lizzie

Mina's face warmed, but she pressed on.

BubbliMi: I know. Not tryna b up in ur mix. But she's straight bummed
BasketballT: me n' her both. She played me
BubbliMi: Todd, no harm but u know Lizzie is not like tht. Honestly, I thnk she's jus not rdy is all
BasketballT: and she couldn't jus tell me tht? She had 2 take a pact?

Mina felt the same way. But she didn't want to agree with Todd. She was saved when Cinny appeared online. Scrambling to ditch her away message, she was rewarded by a message immediately.

CinnyBon: I missed all the fun huh? ☺
BubbliMi: wht fun?
CinnyBon: don't play it off. I'm on da phone w/Jay now
BubbliMi: Ok it's official—JZ likes u. anytime he on the phone gossiping something gotta b up!
CinnyBon: ROFL he tol me 2 tell u stop tripping!

Mina laughed, embarrassed that Jacinta had shared what she said with JZ.

BubbliMi: Dayum Cinny. I didn't know u was gon' drop dime on me like that!

She switched back to Todd.

BubbliMi: u know how Lizzie is. Very organized. A pact is very her ☺
BasketballT: she "organized" me right outta the whole decision. WACK but w/e
BubbliMi: she really likes u T. jus talk 2 her. Plse!!
BasketballT: Oh like she talked to me abt the pact?
BubbliMi: 2 wrongs don't make a right
BasketballT: umm . . . did u just go ttly parental on me? LOL
BubbliMi: yes. LOL seriously tho, jus talk. Please. Maybe it's not 2 late 2 meet in the middle
BasketballT: wht's the middle of no sex and having sex?
BubbliMi: a BJ? J/K. Totally J/K!!!
BasketballT: LOL I like the way u think

BubbliMi: T, I was j/k!!! if u tell Lizzie I said that I will so deny it
☺
BasketballT: I promise I'm not printing this as we speak.
BubbliMi: better not be. I jus want u guys 2 b cool again
BasketballT: yeah, I know. Gtg c u
BubbliMi: c u

Mina shook her head, smiling. It was hard to put this Todd together with the sweaty, stony-faced person he'd been this afternoon. She realized Todd hadn't made any promises about making up with Lizzie, but he also didn't sound mad anymore. She'd settle for that.

A trail of messages from Jacinta littered her screen. Apparently, JZ had given Jacinta the entire scoop from earlier, and Jacinta wasn't above teasing Mina for getting herself bombed out by Lizzie.

CinnyBon: now look @ u breaking ur own rules—lying 2 ur girls and whatnot. Bad Princess, Bad.

Mina read it and Cinny's other messages, laughing. Jacinta had a weird way of making Mina feel like her problems were small and silly. And compared to the pregnancy scare hanging over Jacinta's head, the squabble with Lizzie and Brian's tude *were* silly.

Mina picked up the phone. She couldn't take both her boyfriend and her best friend being mad. Having neither of them call or online was like extreme isolation. Like they'd both gotten together and decided to cyber ice her.

Paranoid much, Mina thought, snorting nervously.

Still, the silence was deafening. She had to squash one of the beefs. Her heart pattered against her chest.

How come admitting you're wrong is so nerve-wracking, she thought as she dialed.

She took a deep breath and braced herself for a scolding.

Sprung

"Got me doing things I'll never do."
—T-Pain, "I'm Sprung"

The next evening, Brian's backyard was a virtual carnival of activity. People splashed in the pool, crammed into the Jacuzzi, ran ball on his basketball court, hung out at the Jacuzzi's tiki bar, and filled any and every seat or empty spot surrounding the pool.

What had been intended as a clique get-together had turned into a full-blown party with a slew of varsity athletes and various other senior glitterati once word-of-mouth of the event hit the halls of DRB High.

Mrs. James had flipped once the tenth caravan of jam-packed cars showed up. She lectured Brian about "misrepresenting" the gathering. The lecture, given discretely within the confines of the house away from the partiers, was sharp but short. Rather than clear the area, she settled for cutting off any more from entering. She and Brian's dad stationed themselves on the front porch, ensuring no one else snuck by.

Mina and Lizzie sat poolside, Mina's late-night apology soothing the tension that had blistered between them. Lizzie's hair, pulled in a side pony, made her look like a little girl. Her pink polka dot bikini top added to the effect. Typical of Lizzie, she wore shorts, hiding the bottoms. In contrast, Mina sat comfortably in only her green and yellow-striped two-piece, the tiny transparent sarong around her waist for fashion and not much more.

Mina kicked lazily at the bathtub warm water and JZ, who tugged at her feet. Michael lowered himself in and nabbed a floating chaise before it escaped. He flipped himself into it and anchored himself by the girls by holding on to the ledge.

"It's so good to see you two girls playing nice," Michael said with singsongy sarcasm.

Lizzie laid her legs over the arm of his chaise, pulling the chair to them. Her eyes scanned the area for Todd.

"He's over on the basketball court," Mina said with a smile.

"That's pathetic that I'm so obvious." Lizzie's feet kicked absently, making the chaise bump lightly against the pool's wall.

"I can't lie—it's funny to see you open like that, Liz-O." JZ smirked. "Mina? We all know she rummin' cause Brian got her sprung. But you're usually the smart one."

Mina cupped her hand into the pool, scooped up some water, and aimed toward JZ's face. "That's wrong, Jay. I'm not sprung."

He laughed as the water fell short. "Man, please."

Michael nodded. "You can't even deny that one, Mi."

"How mad is he?" Lizzie asked, ignoring Michael and JZ. She twisted a strand of hair around her finger. Her eyes brimmed with anxiety. "Tell me what he said again, last night."

Mina patiently relayed her and Todd's IM chat from the night before for the fifth time. She left nothing out, even the BJ comment, which made Lizzie wince.

"Liz, you know why he's mad, right?" Michael said.

"Yeah, 'cause you doomed the dude to an indefinite sentence of dating his hand," JZ cracked. He dipped underwater to avoid another handful of flying water. He resurfaced, grinning. "Liz, I'm joking. But on the real, Todd's a good guy. Shoot, he too sweet in my opinion." JZ shrugged. "But I bet you could have just told him you wasn't with sexin', and he would have been cool."

"For how long?" Lizzie asked, eyebrow raised in a challenge.

JZ shrugged again. "I can't answer all that. But he likes you, so who knows. Maybe as long as you needed him to."

Mina touched Lizzie's arm. "I can't believe I'm saying this, but I think JZ's right." She turned her head as JZ splashed at her as a thank you. "You know Todd. He's the most easygoing person we know."

"I know he is. But I hate that you guys are saying I needed his blessing to take the pact." Lizzie made eye contact with each of her friends before shaking her head in frustration. "It was *my* decision. Even if I went about it wrong, it was still my decision to make. Not me and Todd's, mine."

Her face reddened as people nearby stared. "I'm just saying," she went on, lowering her voice. "I know I need to apologize, and if he stops avoiding me, I will. But I'm not apologizing for taking the pact. Just for . . ." Her eyebrows knitted as she thought about it for a second before deciding on, "For not telling him first."

JZ's eyebrows arched. "Alright, Liz, you boss. But . . ." He looked off toward the basketball court, barely visible because of the number of people surrounding the pool.

"But what?" Mina and Lizzie asked together.

"Look, y'all know T's last girlfriend was a straight bitch," JZ said. "She played him, and he's not down for getting played again. Todd's cool, but he not gon' play nobody's punk." He shrugged. "Man, look, that's y'all business. Just do you, Lizzie O'Reilly." He stuck out his fist for a pound. Once Lizzie tapped his with hers, he swam off.

"Liz, is it worth you guys breaking up?" Mina asked softly.

She and Michael stared intently in Lizzie's face as her eyebrows furrowed, straightened, then creased again.

Lizzie snapped lightly, "I'm not going to have sex with him just so we won't break up, Mi."

"I didn't mean you should," Mina said patiently. "I guess I'm asking . . . are you sure that . . . if Todd can't get with the pact and wants to break up, will you be alright with that?"

"I guess I'd have to be," Lizzie said. She hugged her knees to her chest in a sullen pout.

Mina saw the uncertainty in Lizzie's eyes. She knew Lizzie meant it, but saying you were cool with a breakup and living through one were two different things. Goose bumps crawled up her arm in the warm night, and before she could squash it, one selfish thought entered her mind—*I'm running out of time to spend with Brian. Where am I going to find time to be there for you if you guys break up?*

She dunked her feet in the water, butterfly kicking them to distract herself from her own thoughts. Her hands fluttered to check her hair, safely secured in its Pomeranian ponytail, smoothing the sides absently.

As if summoned by her thoughts, Brian appeared by her side, towering over her. He touched the top of her head. "Hey. Come here for a second."

Mina stood up. "I'll be back, y'all."

"Sprung," Michael mouthed before tugging Lizzie onto the chaise with him and shoving off and into the middle of a volleyball game.

Mina followed Brian into the house. It was deathly silent inside compared to the cacophony beyond the French doors. Mina shook her head to make her ears pop. She hesitated when she realized Brian was heading upstairs.

"What about your parents?" she whispered, peering around for any signs of them.

"They're out front on guard duty." He ignored the quizzical look on Mina's face, took her hand, and urged her along the stairs.

They walked into his darkened room, which overlooked the backyard. A wide slice of light from the pool filtered in from a window, brightening a single spot in the room. Mina stood in the slice of light, looking out over the fun.

"So, you mad at me?" Brian asked over her shoulder. His chin brushed her spiky pony.

Mina's shoulders hitched even as relief flooded her body. She'd pretty much expended all her energy making up with Lizzie last night. It was too hard to be mad at him while Lizzie was mad at her. It was like flying without a net.

Brian stepped in closer behind her.

It took every ounce of Mina's willpower not to turn around and throw herself in his arms, but she kept her vigil over the party below them. Her waist grew warm when his hands rested there on her bare skin, just above her sarong. The feeling intensified when Brian's lips brushed her ears, giving her the warm chills.

"You got me in trouble," he said.

Mina craned her neck to look at him. "How? What did I do?"

Brian nodded toward the backyard. "You and your party."

"I didn't invite all these people, honestly." She mentally ticked off how many people were in attendance, stopping at forty because it was hard to count with so many people moving around. "You know stuff gets crazy whenever it gets out an upper is having something." Mina gnawed at her lip. "Should I tell your mom it was my fault? Is she really po'ed?"

Mina felt Brian shake his head no against her ponytail.

"What's your punishment? She's not letting you go to Duke?"

Brian laughed. "You wish."

"You know I do." An involuntary sigh of resignation escaped her lips.

His hands wrapped around her as he spoke. "I didn't mean to leave you hanging yesterday."

"Really?" Mina scowled in the darkness. "Because it sure looked like you meant to."

"I was mad at how you came at me."

"I'm sorry," Mina said. Her eyes wandered the yard until she spotted Lizzie and Michael in some oddball lounge race. "I did come at you wrong. But Lizzie was mad at me, and I was mad at myself. So I took it out on you."

Brian tweaked her side. "It's cool."

Mina took a step forward and sat on the window's ledge, facing Brian. "Everybody's saying you've got me sprung."

"Umm, 'cause you are," Brian said. He pulled her off the ledge and toward him. They kissed long and full, his hands kneading her waist. Just when he'd gotten Mina to the point where the rest of the world ceased to exist, he pulled back, smiling down at her. "What's wrong with being sprung?"

Guess who's coming for pizza?

I *could get used to this,* Kelly thought.

She and Greg were having a great time. She'd been a little freaked out about going on a solo date—it was her first one—and had told herself it would be just like a tutoring session. Thinking of it like that had calmed her down lots. But now, sitting across from Greg in the booth at Rio's Ria, she realized it was nothing like tutoring at all. And that was a good thing.

Greg was much more confident when he wasn't bumbling over translations. And instead of being frustrated by his weaknesses, Kelly could focus on how funny he was, how he seemed to know so many people, as evidenced by the number of people, especially girls, who stopped by to say hello, and how dang cute he was. His nearly hairless face made him look like a little boy. But when he'd shown Kelly a slash he'd gotten on his leg at a lacrosse game weeks before, the bulge of his calf muscle reminded her, a little boy he wasn't.

So this was what it was like to be with a nice guy.

A flash of shame bolted through Kelly's mind. Angel wasn't really a bad guy. He . . . oh, my God, don't think about Angel right now, Kelly chided herself.

She tucked a piece of hair behind her ear and smiled brighter, hoping Greg didn't realize she was daydreaming.

"I'm surprised it's not packed in here," Greg said, gazing over the thick, but not wall-to-wall crowd.

Kelly nodded, then it hit her. "I think I know why it's not as crowded."

Greg's eyebrow raised in question.

"Do you have anything to do after this?" Kelly's heart fluttered.

Greg shook his head as he sipped from his soda. "You?"

"Actually, yes." A deep fissure of pleasure zipped through Kelly's heart when Greg's face fell. So he cared that she had something to do. Score! Goal or whatever you say in lacrosse.

Greg glanced down at his cell phone. "Do you need to go now?"

Kelly's head swished back and forth. "No. But do you want to go with me later? Brian James is having a pool party tonight. So I was heading over there afterward."

Greg's face lit up. "Yeah? I know Brian. We had gym together last semester."

"Well, you know that's Mina's boyfriend, right?"

Greg nodded slowly, as if he were trying to reconcile his memories while answering.

"That's where I'm going." Kelly balled up her napkin and sat back. She continued shyly, "Mina told me to invite you. But I wasn't sure if you already had something else to do or whatever."

Greg grinned. "First, I thought you had double booked. I was like, 'snap, she nexting me.'"

He and Kelly laughed, and just as Kelly was about to say something witty in reply, her tongue froze. Either her mind was playing tricks on her, or Angel was walking in, heading her way.

She tried to tear her gaze away, but couldn't. His smile, stretching from his thin lips to his light brown eyes, was easy and confident. Kelly noticed that his brown hair was much longer on top, thick with waves, than when she'd last run into him at Jacinta's a few months back. Finally, Greg turned around to see what she was looking at. By that time, Jacinta and Raheem were also in. Kelly saw the worry on Jacinta's face. It looked like Jacinta was trying to get to the table first, but the Ria was too crowded for her to do any zipping by Angel, who seemed to have a radar on Kelly as he beelined for the table.

"You know them?" Greg asked.

"I . . ."

"Wassup, mami?" Angel said. He sat on Kelly's side of the booth, scooting her in as he made himself comfortable. He stuck his fist out for a pound from Greg. "What's up, man? I'm Angel."

Greg tapped Angel's fist lightly with his own. "Hey, man, I'm Greg." His eyes glided over to Kelly, confused, questioning. If he didn't know who Angel was, the terror in Kelly's face was probably giving him a clue.

"Hey, Kelly." Jacinta finally reached the table. "Sorry to barge in. But you weren't answering your phone, and I had to ask you something."

A few million unasked questions floated between the two girls as Raheem muttered an introduction to Greg, followed by more fist pounding.

"So, Kellita, what you been up to, girl?" Angel's platinum grille shone as he grinned. He winked suggestively at Kelly, and her stomach dropped. He nodded toward Greg. "Is he why you too busy for me?"

As if that was the proof or signal he needed, Greg stood up. "I'll be back, Kelly."

Angel snickered once Greg walked off. "Damn, he a ol' punk. How he gonna let some other dude bust up in here with him and his girl and then leave?"

He put his hand out for some dap, and Raheem smacked it lightly.

Kelly's chest heaved. She spoke evenly, anger and fear lacing her words. "Angel, what are you doing?"

"'Cause I texted you the other day, and you didn't get back to me. So." His shoulders hitched, finishing the thought—I'm here.

"Kelly, honestly, I did try and call you. Is your phone on?" Jacinta asked.

"I can't hear it in here," Kelly said. She pulled the phone out and saw Jacinta's five missed calls.

"So what, that's you now?" Angel thumbed over to Greg, who stood talking at a table of his lacrosse buddies.

Kelly shuddered as visions of a gang fight screamed across her mind.

"Angel, I don't want to go to prom with you." Kelly spoke like she was lecturing a child. "Why would you even ask?"

Raheem and Jacinta made themselves scarce.

Angel's light brown eyes darkened. "'Cause I think you tripping. I know you was pissed about that little traffic stop—"

"You mean drug bust?" Kelly snapped.

Angel chuckled. "Okay, bust? The cop didn't even know I had something on me."

"Because you made me stash it in my pocket." Kelly spoke through clenched teeth.

"Alright. But that was last year. It's not like we got arrested." His voice softened to what Kelly called his romantic thug lilt, and he asked in Spanish, "You telling me you still mad?"

For a second, Kelly's limbs went jelly, remembering how safe that voice used to make her feel, however brief she and Angel's time had been. "I'm not mad," Kelly admitted. "But you lied to me, saying you had stopped dealing drugs. Well, you did what you had to, and so did I."

Angel's head reared back. He looked Kelly up and down. "Look at little mami, all spicy." He chuckled. "See, that's why I can't stop thinking about you, girl. Look at you, got me all sprung, chasing you and shit."

Kelly fought back a grin.

It's not cool to be happy about that, she thought. Still, she couldn't help it. She tucked her hair and swallowed the smile before it spread.

"Angel, I'm serious. I don't want to go . . ."

"Come on, Kelly. I leave for school in August. Hang with me one more time," Angel said.

"School? What school?" Kelly asked curiously.

He winked. "Yeah, see, you thought I was gonna be a ol'buster just running the streets."

"I didn't say that," Kelly stammered. Of course that's what she'd thought.

"I'm going to Towson University." He nudged her. "So you more down with going now that you know I'm ready give up my life of crime?"

"If you had given it up last year, we wouldn't be in this mess," Kelly muttered.

Angel leaned in close, his lips touching her ear. "You don't need to answer me right now. Call me tomorrow."

"Prom is next week. What am I supposed to do about a dress?" Kelly asked, flustered, knowing full well she had a whole closet full of what her grandmother called cocktail dresses—more than perfect for any prom. But she didn't know what else to say.

Angel's grin was a mile long. "You know I got you. I'll take care of that." His eyes softened with innocence as he said, "You know, *if* you decide to go."

He stood up, winked, and strolled away from the booth. Kelly watched him go over to Greg, say something, then point at her. She wanted to fall through the floor.

Jacinta laid into Angel once they were back in the car before Raheem could pull back into traffic. "That was ignorant. Man, just let her be, Angel. She not trying to get with you."

From the back seat, Angel's light brown eyes blazed with a smug satisfaction. "Then she need say that." He licked his lips. "If she was all into the dude she was with, why she sit there and let him walk away?"

Jacinta rolled her eyes. "Because that's Kelly. She wasn't going to make a scene just because you trying to get your swagger back."

"What you talking about? I never lost it," Angel snapped. He railed against Jacinta. "This between me and Shorty anyway. So be 'bout your own business, girl. Go play mommy."

"Man, whatever." Jacinta sucked her teeth. But Angel's comment had accomplished his goal. She sat in the front seat, arms folded, glaring out the window.

Raheem nudged her playfully. "You take the test yet?"

"I haven't even bought one yet," Jacinta said. She felt Raheem's eyes on her, narrowed in confusion or maybe, disapproval. She pretended not to notice.

"She don't need no test to tell her what she already know," Angel teased, practically basking in Jacinta's discomfort.

"When you gonna take it, Jacinta?" Raheem asked.

The gentle tone of his inquiry surprised her. She glanced over at him through the darkness and saw that his eyes questioned softly. It flooded her with a mix of guilt and wariness. She had no intention of taking any test. She was going to wait her period out, that was that. But she wasn't going to get into it with Angel in the car. Seeming to understand that, Raheem moved on.

"Since I'mma have a room to myself at Georgetown, you and the baby can visit anytime you want." His teeth flashed in the darkness as he grinned. "I mean, I don't know about staying the night, though. I need to see if Coach is down with getting me a hotel room when y'all want to stay the weekend."

Angel laughed along. "Naw, they probably not down with no crying baby in the dorm."

Jacinta gritted her teeth. She absently scratched at a spot on her face, hot and tingling with frustration, and wondered how Raheem could see them so clearly with a baby, like it was getting a dog or having his nieces and nephew for the weekend. The whole picture made her stomach clench. She knew a girl who had gotten pregnant when they were twelve, Taquon. She'd walked around with her big belly hanging out, still trying to wear baby doll tee shirts and mini-skirts. Jacinta thought Taquon looked a hot mess, but no one else seemed to think it was a big deal. A few adults even said Taquon looked "cute, all tiny with that big belly."

And Taquon never seemed embarrassed. If anything, she had a certain hip-swaying walk like she was proud of it—well, until she was too big and could only waddle.

Taquon worked at the Auntie Anne's in the mall now. Last time Jacinta had seen her was last year when she'd gone to get a pretzel and they had caught up on old times. Taquon had shown Jacinta a picture of her four-year-old son, and they'd popped some yang about getting together one day. Something they knew wasn't going to happen. They weren't really friends to begin with, but once Taquon had gotten pregnant, her father made sure Jacinta knew he expected better.

Jacinta hadn't given Taquon a second thought until recently. Now she couldn't get Taquon off her mind.

Taquon wasn't the only young chick from Pirates Cove Jacinta knew who had gotten pregnant, but she had been the youngest. And Jacinta still remembered her father watching Taquon walk down the street in a bikini top and bootie shorts, stretch-marked stomach on display, shaking his head and wondering aloud where her parents had been while she'd been out having sex with a boyfriend who was fifteen but still only in seventh grade.

Up until that day, Jacinta had never heard her father speak a bad word about their community or anyone in it. He'd been, and still was, actively involved in community affairs, neighborhood watch, the whole nine yards. Everyone knew him, and he seemed to know them. But it took seeing a twelve-year-old with a stomach the size of beach ball for him to utter the first negative words about the place she'd grown up.

"Don't you ever call yourself strutting around like it's some badge of honor that everybody know you been laying with some dude," he'd said so angrily Jacinta thought he was mad with her. "People around here act like using a condom is a federal crime."

Raheem and Jacinta had just started going out the summer Taquon had her baby. Sex was the last thing on Jacinta's mind. And by the time it was on her mind, her father's narrow-eyed anger floated back into her head, and she'd made sure she and Raheem always used a condom.

Now she couldn't remember the last time they'd used a condom. They hadn't on a regular basis since she started taking birth control at thirteen.

Suddenly, Taquon's voice, stuck in an automatic happy customer service tone, saying, "Girl, we need to hook up and hang out one day," mixed with her father's steely, angry words, "Don't you ever call yourself strutting around like it's some badge of honor that everybody know you been laying with some dude," in her head. She closed her eyes, pushing both voices to the back of her mind, working unsuccessfully to mute them.

Her eyes fluttered open when Raheem said, "Am I still dropping you over to Brian's house?"

Jacinta nodded, then realized Raheem couldn't see that in the dark. "Yeah," she said simply.

"What, you don't want to hang with me and Heem tonight?" Angel pushed on the back of Jacinta's seat.

No, Jacinta thought. *I don't. I want to be somewhere I don't need to think about babies and boyfriends and futures.*

But out loud, she said, "Naw, I'm hanging with my girls tonight." As an afterthought, she added, "And stop pushing my seat."

Angel pushed at it again with his foot for good measure before laughing and lapsing into a conversation with Raheem about the rest of their night. Jacinta let them go on. She stared into the night, gladly tucking the idea of pregnancies and babies away the closer they got to The Woods.

"Dude, This Sucks"

"It was nice to know you, but I got to move on."
—Young Berg, "Sexy Lady"

Lizzie pushed up through the water. Coming from the muted, warm depths of the deep end to the loud, cool surface made her ears pop. Her head swiveled left to right, checking on the whereabouts of her competition.

"Did we win?" she yelled over the party's noise to Michael. Dog-paddling to the side of the chaise, she gripped the edge of the float and asked again. "Mike, did we win?"

"No. We won," Marissa declared.

There was a lighthearted, but slightly heated exchange between Michael and the skinny, horse-faced guy Marissa had been pushing in the chaise race. The game had grown more intense with each round of competitors working to knock Lizzie and Michael out of the champion spot.

Lizzie was certain they'd won again, but she let Michael challenge Marissa's claims that only Michael's chair had touched the wall, not his hand, which was the rule. While Michael debated the finer points of water chair racing, Lizzie treaded water and stared across the pool into a far corner of the yard.

Todd sat, surrounded by some of the basketball players, three girls Lizzie didn't know, and Volleyball Girl. Lizzie could only surmise that they were discussing anatomy because the girls were touching each guy's arms and chest, clearly making comparisons. One girl's hands lingered on Todd's shoulders, caressing playfully.

Jealousy dug its claws into Lizzie. A second too late, she remembered to keep herself fully afloat, and water seeped into her open mouth. She sputtered and grabbed hold of the chaise.

For the last hour, she'd tried to ignore her nerves, worrying whether Todd was going to say anything to her or if she should approach him. Staying in the pool racing had helped, especially winning every round. But any time there'd been a lull in activity, she slyly searched for Todd. For the last twenty minutes, he'd been in that same corner chatting away.

The starting line for the race was on the shallow end, right where Todd sat. Lizzie couldn't be certain, but she thought she'd heard Vollyball Girl (Cassie) say, "Isn't that your girlfriend right there?"

Lizzie assumed she was talking to Todd and wondered—was she asking because Todd denied having a girlfriend? Or was she simply asking as a point of clarification?

Lizzie never heard the answer. Jake had blown the whistle to start the race. Lizzie had never swum so hard and so furiously in her life. In the seconds it took to get to the deep end, she'd already imagined Todd and the leggy brunette holding hands and laughing at how crazy Lizzie was to let something as minor as a little nude wrestling break them up.

Are we broken up? she wondered.

Todd had barely spoken a dozen words to her since Wednesday.

Now he and Vollyball Girl were talking privately, still part of the larger group, yet obviously having a side convo. Todd must have said something funny—typical—because she threw her head back and laughed. She ran her fingers through her lush hair, pushing it off her face. Folding her long legs demurely, she sat up, leaning into the conversation. It was more than Lizzie could take.

"Mike, I'm going to get out for a little bit," she said. She massaged her sore arms. "I'm *so* paying for all these athletics tomorrow."

Mike nodded knowingly. "Yeah. Go talk to him, Liz."

With some effort, Lizzie climbed the ladder out of the pool. The night's chill pricked her skin, and goose bumps raced, covering every inch of her body. She waddled over to her clothes and dried off as quickly as possible, wrapping a blue beach towel around her. Still damp, she slipped her shorts on, then unraveled the towel, moving it from her body to her hair in a turban. A second too late, she realized it would be impossible to get her shirt on over the turban.

She sat down heavily on a nearby chair, glaring over at Todd and massaging her sore, and now cold, arms. She watched him, now once more entertaining the gaggle of girls, his nervous hair sweep disappearing as the girls' laughter grew, and he became the hot surfer boy everyone else seemed to notice instantly.

Why didn't he come talk to her?

Her eyes scanned the yard, searching for the clique—neither Kelly nor Jacinta were there yet—before automatically rising toward Brian's window.

Was Mina bold enough to sneak off to Brian's room with his parents in the house?

The thought made her stomach clench. Out of fear for Mina getting caught or the thought that she was the only one not bold enough to keep taking chances, Lizzie wasn't sure.

Sitting there alone, her boyfriend off having his shoulders rubbed by an athletic Amazon, Lizzie felt utterly elementary.

Tears burned her eyes. She reached hurriedly into her bag and grabbed her shades. Wearing shades at night was way movie starish, but it beat sitting in the dark, crying like a dork. She wiped the tear track from her face and pretended to be engrossed in searching for something in her bag. It nearly flew out of her hand when a shadow fell over her, blocking the swath of light illuminating her little corner of the pool.

"Hey," Todd said simply.

"Hey." A thrill shivered down Lizzie's back, and she cringed at being so happy that Todd had come over.

Todd pushed a mass of tee shirts and shorts off a nearby table and sat on its edge, his long legs splayed in front of him. His eyes skated across the landscape, looking over Lizzie's head toward the basketball court. After a few seconds, they finally settled their nervous dance, but still refused to connect with Lizzie's. She looked up at him as he cleared his throat, shifted on the table, and clasped his hands behind his neck.

"Liz, I—"

"I'm sorry," Lizzie said. She hadn't had any intention of apologizing. But it had come out, and she quickly explained herself. "I mean, I'm not sorry about making the pact with Kelly. But . . ." Lizzie fiddled with the towel, and it slumped in a pile from her head. She busied herself folding it while she spoke. "I am sorry that I didn't . . . you know, tell you."

Todd got a funny look on his face. He opened his mouth to say something, and Lizzie thought he was about to make a joke, but instead, he blew out an explosive breath. "Dude, this sucks."

"I know," Lizzie said.

"Look, don't take this wrong. You're cool, Liz." Todd's words came out in a rush. "I love kicking it with you and all. But it's like, this whole abstinence thing is too weird for me."

"How is it weird?" Lizzie scowled.

"Man, 'cause I thought we were tighter than that." Todd paused as one of the varsity players walked up and gave him a pound. Once the guy passed, Todd continued, his voice low. "It's like you don't trust me or something."

"It's just something I want to do." Lizzie frowned, confused. "What does trust have to do with it?"

"Everything." Todd threw up his hands as if the conversation was hopeless. "So basically, you don't trust that I'll respect you saying no? What am I, a total dickhead?" His eyes rolled. "Totally no pun intended. But so you had to go all, 'I pledge never to let Todd touch me,' on me?"

Lizzie peered at him to see if he was joking. But Todd's blue eyes were flat. She'd never seen them so devoid of humor. It left her speechless.

Todd's words poured as if he'd saved up every thought he'd had for tonight.

"And you don't get it. Just a few seconds ago, you said you were sorry for not *telling* me about the pact." His mouth turned up in disgust.

"But I am," Lizzie said.

What was wrong with that? she wondered. She felt like she was losing her mind.

"Sorry for not telling me. But not sorry that you never asked me how I felt about you even wanting to take a pledge?" For the first time, his eyes locked on hers. "It can work both ways, you know? If I was like"—Todd's voice took on a doofy country drawl—"'Yeah, Lizzie, I decided I want us to have sex. Let's do it.'—I'd be a sleaze. Am I right?"

"Well—" Lizzie stopped and thought about it. She'd never thought about it that way. Todd had never forced her to go any further than she wanted. The desperation she felt, wanting to say the right thing to Todd sat heavily on her chest. At this point, she was ready to apologize for the hole in the ozone layer if it meant squashing the argument and moving on. "So you're mad because I didn't tell you?"

"Dude, I have an older sister. I so don't mind bossy chicks." He chuckled bitterly. "Telling me we have zero chance of hooking up is bad enough. But it's like you decided it with all your girls first and then sent me a written notice about your chastity vow." Todd snorted. "It's not cool, Liz."

As Todd's voice got louder and more animated, Lizzie head checked to see if they were making a scene. But the party went on, unfazed.

"Are we going to compromise or something?" Lizzie asked quietly.

"How?" Todd threw his arms up, and they came down on his board shorts with a dull smack. "You've already taken the oath, right?"

"Yeah. No. I mean . . . I don't know," Lizzie said, wishing he'd follow her lead and speak lower.

Todd stood up. He looked to the corner where he'd come from. Volleyball Girl was still there. Lizzie followed his gaze, and her mouth went dry. She was an A student, but it didn't take book smarts to figure out what was about to happen.

Her heart froze, and she switched gears, preparing for the boom.

Fine, let it be over, she thought.

Part of her almost wanted that. Wanted it over so she could go back to thinking with all of her brain instead of half of it. She didn't need someone having that much control over her.

But the part of her that went mushy inside when he called or walked her to class wouldn't go without a fight.

"If I had talked to you first and said I wanted to take the pact—" Lizzie stopped and waited for him to fill in the blanks.

Todd turned back to her. Some of the sparkle was back in his eyes and voice. "I don't know. Buy stock in Vaseline, I guess." He chuckled under his breath.

Neither of them said anything for a few minutes, and for a second, Lizzie held out hope that Todd would say something Todd-goofy, like, "Alright, well, dude, next time just let me know what's up first." But he didn't. His eyes did their nervous dance again, glancing over her head, then back to the ground. His foot kicked at the concrete as if he was trying to remove a stain. He looked back over at the basketball court, then finally at her. When he spoke, he coughed up the words as if someone had whacked him on the back, helping him spit them out.

"Guess this is going to majorly fug up our friendship, huh?"

This.

Lizzie knew what this was. And she wasn't sure what hurt more, that Todd was breaking up with her or that he'd informed her that they were breaking up by telling her how much the breakup was going to suck.

She peered up at his hurt face. He looked as if he didn't really want to do this. And Lizzie wanted to scream, then why are you? But she knew why. And that sucked, too. Realizing he was waiting for an answer, she shook her head no, too choked up to speak.

"No?" Todd peered down at her. Lizzie heard hope in his voice, but she didn't have the strength to reassure him again.

"But I'm a lame, right?" Todd asked, sounding sad about it.

Lizzie managed a thin smile. "Majorly," she squeaked.

The tears were coming soon. She wanted (needed) him to leave. She wasn't going to cry in front of him even though her ducts were flooding. Thankfully, Todd stood up.

"See you around?" He asked, hope in his voice.

Lizzie nodded. She held her breath. The effort kept the tears at bay until Todd finally walked off.

Dividing Lines

"You coulda been more involved but no,
I'm not the girl that you knew before."
—Tiffany Evans ft. Bow Wow, "I'm Grown"

At eleven o'clock on the dot, Brian's parents swooped in and cleared out the backyard like a duo of riot cops. Everyone respectfully vacated the yard, streaming into the front yard and to their cars, talking, some making plans for the hour until their license dictated it was time to head home. Mina gave Brian a quick kiss on the lips and searched the yard for Lizzie, figuring they'd walk to her house since Kelly and Jacinta hadn't shown up.

It was only as Mina stood in the front yard saying good-bye to Sara that she saw the girls. Lizzie, Kelly, and Jacinta stood by Kelly's car, talking to JZ. When Mina walked over, they all wordlessly got in the car.

Mina eyed JZ quizzically.

He shrugged. "Rough night, I guess."

The ride from Brian's house to Mina's was a short one, but long enough for Mina to know something was wrong.

The girls' footsteps echoed on the hardwood floors of the silent house as they filed inside. Mina's parents, no longer on twenty-four/seven chauffeur duty, were now enjoying their own newfound freedom.

Mina plucked a note from atop the counter informing her they'd be home by midnight.

"Hey, we still have forty minutes. Afterparty," Mina declared giddily. "Let's call the guys and invite them over."

She was greeted with silence.

"Okay, that was a joke." Mina frowned and eyed her friends. Jacinta gave her a shrug. "What's wrong?"

She flipped the light on in the sunroom and plopped on the large sectional sofa. Jacinta sat on one side of her, Kelly the other. Lizzie pulled up an ottoman, facing them. Her eyes were red-rimmed.

"I'm not really up for a sleepover tonight," she said.

"Why not? Todd's going to be with Brian in DC all day tomorrow. We may as well do the girls' thing," Mina said.

Lizzie's lips pursed. "Is that the only reason you had us over? Because the guys already have plans tomorrow?"

Mina's eyebrow jumped, but her voice was calm. "Hello, we've had tonight planned for two weeks." She tugged at her spiky ponytail. "Y'all were supposed to be trying new do's on me."

"Your hair's too short now to do anything with," Lizzie said, her voice heavy. Her fingers fiddled with her own hair, flowing just past her shoulders.

"Liz, what's wrong?" Mina looked from Kelly to Jacinta. "What did I miss?"

Jacinta's eyebrows shrugged.

"Todd broke up with me tonight." Lizzie sat up, cross-legged, on the ottoman and straightened her back.

"Lizzie, no," Mina said. She scooted off the sofa and sat beside Lizzie. "Why didn't you come find me?"

"Why didn't you come find *me?*" Lizzie said. Her voice broke, and she cleared her throat, swiping at a random tear. Her eyebrow steepled. "Did you and Brian sneak off to his room?"

Jacinta chuckled. "Quickie," she sang.

Mina shook her head. "Okay not. His parents were there." She furrowed her eyebrows at Lizzie as she moved back to the sofa so they were facing one another. "We dipped out for like fifteen minutes to his room, but not for that. It was only so he could apologize. Why are you acting like every time I'm with him, we're sexin' or something?"

"Because you're obsessed with Brian," Lizzie said, thrusting her lip out in a stubborn pout. "And I'm so over it."

Mina scowled. "You're over it. What does that mean?"

"That I'm sick of being the sidekick when Brian's too busy or Jacinta's with Raheem," Lizzie snapped.

Mina's jaw clenched. It worked itself loose as she spoke, her voice low and calm. "I know you're upset about Todd, but don't take it out on me."

"Even if I did, you wouldn't notice, Mina." Lizzie rolled her eyes, and fresh tears fell. "You don't notice anything that doesn't have to do with prom, Durham, or being with Brian."

"That's not fair," Mina said. Her pout matched Lizzie's.

Jacinta slid to the edge of the couch, making her body a shield between Mina and Lizzie. "Come on, y'all. Don't fight."

Kelly mirrored Jacinta's movement so that the four of them were in a huddle. She patted Lizzie's knee. "I agree with Cinny." She tittered nervously. "That's a first, huh?"

Lizzie went on, ignoring them. "Okay, if you answer this one question right, I'll take back what I said." She wiped her nose with the back of her hand as she eyed Mina.

"What question?" Mina scowled before reining in her anger. She breathed in slowly through her nose and let it out, determined not to take the attack personally.

She had gone looking for Lizzie earlier. There'd been a whole flock of theatre uppers hanging out by Lila, the Bay Dra-da President. Lila's bright strawberry-blond hair must have served as a beacon because nearly every theatre hound was gathered around her by the tiki bar. Mina hadn't seen Lizzie, but she'd assumed she was in the mix somewhere. So she'd ended up near the basketball court talking to Sara, watching Brian and some other guys play ball.

She started to mention it, but decided against it—for once, exercising silence.

Finally, with tears leaking but her voice strong, Lizzie asked, "How did Kelly and Greg's date go tonight?"

Mina squinted. "Huh?"

Kelly flinched slightly, her eyes darting from Lizzie to Mina.

"How did Kelly and Greg's date go tonight?" Lizzie asked again. Her back straightened another half inch, and Mina caught the smug glint in her eye.

"Seriously?" Mina said. "Lizzie, how would I know? Kelly . . ."

"You'd know because we're girls, Mina. We're best friends." Lizzie's eyebrows rose. "We share everything, remember? The second it happens, we're right there sharing." Her back slumped as she leaned in. The sarcasm was thick as she snapped, "Right? So how did her date go?"

"Dag, she called you out," Jacinta said. She shook her head.

"Okay, well, the first time I even saw Kelly was on our way home," Mina said. Her head swiveled from Kelly to Lizzie. "Nobody said a word in the car. How am I supposed to know . . ."

"You didn't ask," Lizzie said.

"I didn't ask what?" Mina sputtered, growing defensive.

"You didn't ask Kelly how it went when we got in the car."

Mina frowned. "I figured she was going to dish when we got back here."

"Yeah, okay." Lizzie's jaw clenched. She folded her arms. "Mina, you're my best friend. But I'm tired of waiting for you to care about me or what's going on in my life. We all are."

"Woah. Hold up, Lizzie," Jacinta said. "Don't speak for all of us."

"Oh, my bad. Of course." She thrust her chin in the air. She clenched two fingers together. "You guys are likethis."

Mina's head shook from side to side slowly. She eyed Lizzie wearily. "Why are you so mad with me? Are you blaming me for you and Todd breaking up?"

Lizzie threw her head back and sighed explosively. "God. No, Mina. This isn't about Todd or Brian or Raheem or whoever," she shouted, arms flailing. "Everything is not about the guys. Look, never mind."

"Lizzie, I'm trying to understand," Mina said. Her chest tightened. She wanted to lash out at Lizzie, but didn't dare.

"So *now* you're trying to understand?" Lizzie spat.

"Kelly, do you agree with Liz?" Mina asked. Her eyes laser-beamed through Kelly. "I never care about what's going on with you guys?" Unable to help herself, she added, with emphasis, *"Ever?"*

"I . . ." Kelly looked from Lizzie to Mina. Her eyes were deer-in-the-headlight large as she shook her head from side to side. "I'm not . . . taking sides. I just . . . you guys need to talk."

"Kelly, it's cool if you don't want to take sides," Lizzie said. She fixed Mina with a look. "But I'm not scared to say it. I didn't say never. But lately, yeah, you don't seem to care about anything else but Brian."

"Fine." Mina sat back against the sofa with a thump. "Fine. I'm the world's worst best friend then. I can't believe you're giving me grief. In a few months, he'll be gone and . . ."

"Yes, we *know*, Mina. Like you'd ever let us forget," Lizzie snapped.

"Just be real about it, Lizzie," Mina said. Anger trembled in her throat. "What are you really pissed about? Because it's one thing if I'm your punching bag 'cause Todd's not around. If that's it, cool, I'll take it." Her shoulders hitched. "You know, that's what girls are for. But you're bringing up stuff like this has been on your chest for a minute. So be real."

"Kelly and Greg broke up before they could ever get together because Angel showed up tonight," Lizzie said. A sneer crossed her face at the look of surprise on Mina's face. "Oh, but see, Angel showed up because he asked Kelly to the prom, but she said no." Lizzie's voice was sarcastic and cutting. "So Kelly's date didn't go real well tonight. You didn't know that because it just happened. But you didn't know about the prom thing, either, and that's old news." She snorted. "By the looks on Jacinta's face, she knew. So you're the only one, Mina. How come you didn't know?"

Mina's eyes welled. "Kelly didn't tell me."

"Not like you asked," Lizzie said.

"How can I ask about something I didn't know about?" Mina said, tears falling. The smothering feeling from the weekend before wrapped itself around her neck.

"You don't ask about anything anymore," Lizzie said softly.

"That's not true," Mina said weakly. She turned to Jacinta for some sort of confirmation or denial that she was as bad as Lizzie said, but Jacinta's face was as perplexed as Mina felt. "Is this because of Todd? Or because I didn't take the pact?"

Lizzie chuckled bitterly. "Even though you didn't have my back with it, the pact is so . . . whatever."

Mina's eyebrows caterpillared into a unibrow. "Didn't have your back?"

"Uh-oh," Jacinta said. She slid back an inch.

"Come on, you guys already settled that," Kelly said, forcing brightness into her voice. "I'm down with you on the pact, Lizzie."

"Thanks," Lizzie said.

Mina winced at the small, but genuine smile Lizzie flashed at Kelly.

"If you had told me sooner . . ." Mina started.

"What? You would have taken it with us?" Lizzie said, a look of total disbelief in her eyes. She and Mina stared at one another until finally, Mina looked down. Lizzie snorted. "Yup, exactly."

Guy Time

"Man for real? You broke up with her?" JZ stopped midroll. The wall he was painting was massive. They'd been there all morning and were still only on the first coat of paint.

Paint dripped down his roller onto the wall in thin, blobby peach streaks.

"Son, come on. My aunt gonna kill me if this room looks all streaky," Brian hollered over.

JZ rolled it down, absorbing the drips. He talked over his shoulder to Todd, whose face was now a dark crimson. "T, son, that's . . . man, that's not right. Even I'm not that cold."

"I didn't break up because of the pact," Todd said.

"Yeah, you did," Brian said, laughing.

JZ laughed, too. But he turned serious again. "Then why did you?"

"Dude, 'cause she played me," Todd said.

JZ's eyes popped. "Lizzie? Come on, T. You know Lizzie's not like that."

"Alright, check this." Todd stopped painting. He put his roll down into the pan and looked from JZ to Brian. His voice echoed in the big, empty room. "If you were me, you're saying you wouldn't have broken it off? She said she's taking the pact for a year."

JZ smirked. "Man, ain't no girl gonna take that kind of pact when she's with the kid."

Todd's eyes rolled. Secretly, he admired how smooth JZ was with girls. But he didn't harbor any delusions that he would ever have that same ease. Humor was his thing, and he was comfortable in his own awkward, comedic way. But everybody acted as if nice guys like him were also suckers. That's how Lizzie making the pact made him feel, and he admitted it. "Whatever, Jay, dude. It's like Lizzie thought I was such a sucker that she figured it didn't matter how she came at me with this whole pact thing." He turned back to his roller, letting it glide through the thick peach paint until it was sopping. He placed it on the wall with a thump and let the paint drip before outracing it with the roller to soak it back up. "I'm a nice guy, but I'm not a sucker."

JZ shook his head. "But you like her, right?"

"Yeah, I like her. Lizzie is chill."

"Shoot, then find a couple of . . ." JZ faked clearing his throat. ". . . chicks who down with being the jump off." He shrugged. "Then keep Lizzie as your main girl."

"Man, come on. That's wack, too," Brian said.

"What? You're not going to do that when you leave for school?" Todd asked. He squinted over at Brian.

Brian put his free hand up as if he was taking an oath. "I plead the Fifth."

"I'm gonna make pretend I didn't hear that," JZ said.

"Me, too," Todd said.

"Naw, I'm joking. I don't know what's gonna happen when I leave." Brian's shoulders shrugged. "I'm just going to cross that bridge when—"

"Until you see how fine the dimes are at Duke?" JZ asked. His eyebrows stretched knowingly. "Righ', righ'. I hear that."

"It's not even like that," Brian said. He pointed his roller at Todd. "I thought we were talking about dude and Lizzie?"

"Alright, T, I'm just saying," JZ said. "If Lizzie not down, some other girl might be without wanting to be all girlfriend with you."

Todd's head shook no. He cracked a smile. "That sounds like your style, playa. Not the T-man."

"Well, if the T-man trying to be all hemmed up with one girl, he needs to go ahead and get with her," JZ said. He stopped painting and turned around. "T, for real, man, if you really don't care about getting the goodies, just tell her you were rummin' and want to get back." He jabbed his paint roller toward Brian, spilling paint on the sheet covering the floors. "Everybody can't be as lucky as this fool. Got his girl just down the street, on tap and whatnot." JZ took his empty hand and tapped it to his own beat against the palm of the hand holding the roller. He sang out. "Smack that . . . all on the floor."

Brian laughed. "Go 'head with that, man."

JZ chuckled. "I'm just joking. That's my girl."

They grew silent until JZ muttered. "Y'all can have that relationship stuff. I do enough work in class; brother don't need to work at pleasure, too."

They shared a boyish chuckle before going back to slathering the walls in peach passion paint.

Real Talk

"I'm the only one that looks out for me, can be me, . . ."
—Emily King, "Walk in My Shoes"

Who cares more than me? Mina thought, frowning down at the piece of paper she held.

In her hand, was her last Pop Life column for the year, due by the end of the period. She'd been proofing it. But her mind kept drifting back to the disastrous weekend.

Lizzie and Kelly leaving early on Saturday.

Mina trying to play referee by calling Todd and getting blown off.

The weekend had been a roller coaster of drama.

For a second, the words on the paper were nothing more than a blur as she stared so hard her eyes went out of focus. She shook off the haze and thoughts of the weekend, bringing herself back to the column.

It was a tribute to some of the seniors going off, doing big things. Of course, her baby boo was one of the people mentioned. But no matter how badly she wanted to throw in smiley faces and hearts after his name, she'd made sure to keep her journalistic integrity in check by sticking to the facts: *Brian James's impact on the DRB Blue Devils basketball team will be sorely missed. But he'll be taking his twenty-five points and fifteen assists per game to another famed Blue Devil team—*

the Duke University Blue Devils. We know Brian will keep things poppin'
as a freshman starter in Durham.

The End.

She smiled down at the paragraph, letting the silence of the empty journalism classroom float around her. She was the sole *Bugle* staffer in the last period class today. Ms. Dunkirk, their advisor, had gone with several staff members to the Principal's office; the photographers were off in the darkroom; and the other three writers had gone on a print check, code word for legal pass to cut class. It was the generic term all staff members used when they were on official school paper business.

James, Erica, and Beth were probably sitting at McDonald's, Starbucks, or somewhere at the mall under the guise that they were talking with businesses that had taken an ad out in the paper.

As this could be done over the phone or via email, Mina wondered why Ms. Dunkirk still allowed print checks. But it was one of the most popular privileges of being on the paper, and since print checks had to be done within the journalism class period, it wasn't like the students ever had time to go too far.

Mina had gone on a few print checks. Though, now that she thought about it, a lot of her print checks were actually real work—interviewing some student or faculty member during her class period. But she'd had her fair share of goofing off. Once she'd ended up at the Blarney Bean gossiping with Erica, and another time, she and Beth had gone to the mall for some window shopping at Forever 21.

She'd passed on today's because school work had been the last thing on her mind lately. Her column had been among the neglected victims. The quiet classroom had cleared her mind and allowed her to zip off the article in no time.

She sat back in the seat, luxuriating in the silence. The only other classroom nearby was the music room, and it was soundproofed.

Some days being here alone or with only one other person was eerie. But not today.

Mina's eyes were drawn to Brian's name in the article.

What was life going to be like dating a Duke baller? How weird was it going to be to watch Brian playing on television?

Her arm broke out in chills.

Then, images of Brian's popularity at DRB High multiplied times twenty flashed in front of her: girls from Duke knowing him, hanging out in his dorm room, chilling on the quad with him. Girls from all over the country saying, "Oooh, girl, look at number 20. He's cute."

Blasting the images, she forced happier pictures into her mind.

Prom night, they were riding in a Hummer limo with several other couples, including JZ and his date. For some reason Mina refused to understand, the older girls could not get enough of JZ. This was his second year going to prom.

It was going to be a crazy night.

Yeah, let's think about that, Mina said to herself, the tension ebbing. She circled Brian's name on the draft and made a tiny heart next to it.

"What's up, girl?" Brian's voice whispered from the entrance of the classroom.

Mina jumped up, leaving the paper behind, and trotted over. He was looking senior casual in a blue DRB senior class shirt, jeans, and a fresh pair of Jordans.

She answered his silent question as his eyes scanned the room. "I'm here by myself. Well, the paparazzi are in the darkroom. They won't be out 'til the bell rings."

Brian's brown eyes smiled at her.

Mina could stare into his big brown eyes with those long, curly lashes all day. Standing on her toes, she pushed her face toward his. He brought his face closer, and they kissed, a peck at first, then more.

She pulled away, her chest rising softly, excited at being so bold in school. She leaned against the entryway.

"What are you doing out of class?"

"It's not like we're really doing anything until exams," Brian said. "But officially, I'm running an errand for Ms. McCord."

Mina's phone vibrated in her pocket, and she jumped. She flipped it open and read the text from Jacinta.

"Cinny said, can you stop her to the store on the way home?" Mina asked.

Brian pursed his lips. "There y'all go, wanting me to chauffeur."

Mina put her hand on her hip. "Okay, it's not like you're not already giving her a ride home."

"How are y'all gonna get around next year?" He folded his arms, eyebrows arched.

"JZ, Michael, Lizzie . . . shoot, even I'll be driving by then." Mina laughed.

"Oh, so that's all I'm good for, *and* I'm that easily replaced?" Brian pretended to walk off.

Mina pulled his arm, easily dragging him back into the classroom.

"Just jokes, baby boy."

Their hands fell into a light clasp.

"What store?" Brian asked.

Mina deftly typed out the message with only one hand. The phone buzzed back almost immediately.

"A Rite Aid or something," Mina reported. She typed back yes, without waiting for Brian's official answer.

"Alright. So what's that you owe me now? Five favors?" He cut his eyes at her. His fingers ticked off the list as he called it aloud. "Michael using my truck. Taking Cinny to the store. Me taking the blame for that party . . ."

Mina played along. "I may need reinforcements to help me pay back all that. Maybe you should call Golden Girl."

Brian snorted. "Oh, I can call her if you want."

Mina pouted. She tried to let her hand fall from his. But Brian chuckled and held on.

"Now see, how come you can say it and be joking? But I can't?" he asked.

"Um–eh, date rule, I guess. I can joke about your ex, but you can't," Mina said with a straight face. She walked to a nearby desk and sat atop it. Brian sat in the desk's chair.

"And does the rule roll both ways?" His eyebrows arched. "Can I talk about your ex?"

"Nope," Mina said, keeping a smile at bay.

"Man, who made up that wack rule?" Brian grumbled playfully as Mina raised her hand. "Figures."

They sat in silence for a few seconds, Mina's legs dangling, kicking softly at the air, Brian's tall frame upright at the smallish desk. He batted at her swinging feet. Mina cocked her head to the side, breathed in and out through her nose deeply once, and opened her mouth to speak when Brian said, "Uh-oh."

"What?" Her eyebrows furrowed.

"That's your 'I was thinking' intro."

"My what?"

"Whenever you're ready to talk about something that's been on your mind for a minute, you do that." Brian pointed at her face. "You turn your head a certain way. Breathe in and out just one time, like you sucking in the air you need to say what it is, and then you say, 'I was thinking.'"

"I do not," Mina said. "And for the record, your imitation of me sucks."

Brian leaned back in the chair, lifting the front legs off the floor. "Oh, my bad." He raised his eyebrows, openly sarcastic. "What were you gonna say then?"

Mina hesitated for a beat, grinned, and said, "I was wondering . . ."

Brian laughed. "Okay, this time you're wondering. Usually you're thinking."

"Point is, you were wrong."

Brian rested the chair back on the floor. "What's up, toughie?" His toffee face grinned up at her. He tugged on her leg, and Mina turned so her feet were on his lap, enjoying the calf massage. "What are you wondering? Whose house we should dip to after school today?"

"Actually, I was wondering whose house you dipped to before . . . you know, last Friday." She scratched her head, then smoothed the hair down, trying to keep her voice casual and unsqueaky. "Before last Friday, when was the last time you . . . you know?"

She could see the thoughts churning in Brian's head, and he admitted as much when he asked, "Is this one of those trick questions? Like some test from a magazine you're trying on me?"

"No," Mina said. She leaned back on her hands. "I'm just curious."

"For the record, I'm crazy for answering this." Brian rocked the chair back again. "It was right before we started going out."

"Like right, right before? As in days?" Mina crossed her legs. "Or right before, like months?"

Brian had a look on his face like he couldn't believe he was having this conversation with her, but he answered. "Like, I don't know . . . a few weeks."

Mina's nose wrinkled. "Eww, so you had sex with somebody and then was all up on me kissing and stuff?"

Brian got up and circled the desk, arms waving. "Danger, danger, abort really awkward conversation with crazy girlfriend. Abort."

Mina chuckled, but maintained her serious tone. "You're crazy."

He stopped his race around the desk. "True dat. If I wasn't, I would have never answered you."

"Was it with Golden Girl or somebody else?" Mina asked, too curious to stop herself.

Brian clamped his hands together and set them on top of his head. "Serious?"

"I mean, what's wrong with me knowing?"

He scowled. "Why do you want to know?"

"So it *was* Golden Girl?"

He shook his head. "No. It was just this random chick I used to holler at sometimes."

Mina squinted in concentration, thinking back two Decembers ago. "But you had been trying to holler at me. Why did you—"

Brian brought his arms down, the smile gone. "And you had a boyfriend. Guess we were both wildin' out."

Mina nodded slowly. She heard in his voice that he wasn't going to answer any more questions about it. But she had so many more.

How could he have sex with some "random" girl at the same time he was obviously trying to get with her? *Hello, where's the love?*

Was it that same weekend he asked her out? *If so, EWW!*

Would he be doing that at college? *Please, please, no.*

Then she thought of one for herself—if he did do that at college, would she care as long as he came back home her boyfriend?

A silvery bitter taste filled her mouth as she accidentally bit down on her tongue.

She wasn't ready to answer that one.

"Let me get back before Ms. McCord send the dogs after me," Brian said, bringing Mina out of her fog. "See you in a little bit."

He started past her, and Mina grabbed his hand. A sliver of joyful warmth ran up her arm when he palmed her hand back. He stood in front of the desk, looming over her.

She stretched her eyes up to his mass of black hair, thick on top, shorter on the sides, just the way she liked it. "What are you doing with that curly nest for prom?"

"I thought I'd cut it down real low." He winked. "Just like you like it."

Mina grimaced. Brian looked insanely young when he cut his hair low, like an oversized, very tall ten-year-old, in Mina's opinion. Well, an oversized, very tall, *fine* ten-year-old, but a ten-year-old all the same.

"You better not," she warned.

"Why? Don't I look cute with it short?" He struck a pose.

"Then our kids will look back on our prom pictures and be like, 'Mommy, I didn't know you could go to prom in fifth grade.'"

Mina nearly slipped off the desk from laughing so hard.

"See, then I'll have to break it down and be like, 'naw, son, I wasn't in fifth grade. Just ask you mother what we did after prom.'" He wrapped his arms in the classic breaker pose, starting them both up laughing harder.

"I'm not messing with you no more, toughie," Brian said through snorts. "Let me dip."

He moved in for a quick kiss. Mina responded eagerly, and it turned into a longer, more involved one. He pulled away first, and they shared a private, knowing glance before he rushed off. Any tension her nosy question had brought on was melted.

Not long after, the bell rang, ending the school day.

Mina filed down the crowded hallway. The buzz, as the school year's end loomed one day nearer, was deafening. She jockeyed for position at her locker, dumping everything. With her column done and in the midst of a cease-fire on regular homework, there was very little she needed to take home. Not that finals weren't around the corner. But she'd be lying to herself if she claimed she would get any studying done this week.

It's prom week, baby, she thought with a grin.

She mentally leapt ahead, visualizing her entire summer calendar, some events happy, others not so much. With a slam of her locker door, she grinned when Jacinta's voice scolded, "So you're not even going to pretend to study this week, huh?"

"Nope."

"What is Momma Mooney gonna say about that?" Jacinta crossed her arms, mock disapproval on her face.

Mina linked arms with her, and they walked. "Are you excited about prom?"

"Truth?" Jacinta stopped in the middle of the hall, forcing people to flow around them. "Not really."

"Did you . . . you know take the test?"

"I'm going to get one when we stop today."

"Want me to go in with you?" Mina asked.

Jacinta chuckled. "Of course. Why would I do it without my sidekick?" She started walking again.

Mina smiled, then stopped abruptly. "Hey. How come I'm the sidekick?"

They giggled all the way to the car where Brian was holding court, running his mouth with a crowd of guys. JZ was already in the truck, riding shotgun, elbow hanging out of the window as he talked. He answered Mina's "what's up?" eye with a nonchalant, "To the back today, shorty. I get tired of being all cramped up back there."

Mina knocked his elbow off the window ledge as she passed.

She and Jacinta hopped in the back. Soon the boy chatter broke off, and Brian slowly maneuvered the truck through the clusters of people congregating in the senior lot. When they got to the Stop sign at the end of the lot, he looked in his mirror. "What store you want to go to, Cinny?"

Jacinta cleared her throat. "Umm, can you take me to the Walgreens?"

"Walgreens?" JZ and Brian chorused.

Brian scowled. "The one up by Bailey's Landing?"

"It's a CVS right on the main strip on the way home," JZ said. He turned to look at Jacinta.

Jacinta looked over at Mina, her eyes silently pleading for backup.

"Well, the CVS never has what I'm looking for." Mina said. She chattered on purposefully. "I love that lip luster stuff from Revlon. They never have it, though."

JZ's eyes rolled. "I know you not making us drive all the way to Walgreens for no lip gloss."

"Who is *us?*" Mina pushed the back of JZ's head, the one benefit of sitting in the backseat. "Brian's the one driving."

"Man, drop these dudes off at CVS and make 'em walk the rest of the way home," JZ said, posturing.

"I'd like to think he would," Mina said. She gave Brian her best nagging girlfriend look.

He ignored it, instead checking his mirror and the growing line of cars behind him.

"Look, before people start giving me the horn—seriously, you want to go to Walgreens?" Brian asked. He eased the truck out a little more, pointing it north.

"Please." Jacinta flashed Brian an angelic smile, sending Mina and JZ into a fit of laughing.

"Man, go ahead. I can count on one hand how many times Cinny been sweet," JZ said. "That must be some good ass lip gloss."

Mina and Jacinta shared a smile as the truck made a hard left.

With all the windows down and the radio blasting, they headed away from the neighborhoods that housed their Blue Devils peers and into northern Del Rio Bay, home of the Northern DRB High Wranglers. What Northern Del Rio lacked in tony, suburban posh like the cliques' neighborhoods and pseudourban hipness (the city of Del Rio Bay), it made up for in pure practical functionality. The truck made its way past houses that grew smaller and plainer. In between large pockets of trees were large, sprawling strip malls with every conceivable chain and discount store known to man.

When they finally arrived at the large Walgreens, which stood alone on an island in a busy intersection, Brian cut the engine. No one moved. He raised his palms as if to say, "what now?" and that got Mina moving.

"Come on, Cinny." She opened her door, scuttling out.

Jacinta followed reluctantly.

JZ hollered out the window. "Don't be all day."

"Are you alright?" Mina whispered once they got in the store. Jacinta's face was ashen and scared in the bright fluorescent lighting.

She gnawed at her bottom lip. "I just don't want to do this."

"Well, has it come on?" Mina asked. Her shoulders hitched at Jacinta's "what do you think?" look. She took another step, trying to prod Jacinta along. But Jacinta stayed put. They stood in the middle of the seasonal aisle. Among the cookout paraphernalia were a few early Fourth of July decorations.

"My heart is saying I'm not pregnant," Jacinta said, almost as if she was talking to herself. Her breath streamed in a deflating hiss. "I wish my stupid body would listen."

Mina rubbed Jacinta's shoulder. "Maybe you're not. But wouldn't it be better to just know for sure?"

Jacinta winced. "Not really."

Mina walked, and this time Jacinta followed. They rounded a corner and found their way to the feminine hygiene products.

Jacinta's mouth curled in a scowl–grimace. "Is it me? Or is it kind of stupid to put the pregnancy tests next to the pads and stuff?" She picked up a pack of sanitary napkins. Her eyes lingered on the package wistfully. "It's like saying, na-na-na-na-na, you don't need these."

Mina's shoulders shook as she laughed. "Okay, don't take this the wrong way. But umm, most people are glad they're pregnant." She snorted as she added, "Maybe the people getting the tests are saying that to the people whose period did come on?"

They snickered as they gazed over the selection of pregnancy tests.

When a few seconds had passed with Jacinta doing nothing, Mina nudged shoulders with her. "I don't think the test can walk to you."

"Good. Maybe when the technology becomes that smart, I'll take it," Jacinta said, turning to leave.

Mina caught her arm. "Come on, Cinny. I know this sucks, but . . .

let's do it Band-Aid style. Just pick a test, any test, roll to the counter, and dip."

Jacinta allowed herself to be pulled back. With her mouth set in a grim line of concentration, she scanned the aisle. "So is everybody talking about how the hood chick managed to get knocked up?"

"No one is talking about it . . . well, not to me," Mina said. "Shoot, me and Lizzie barely talking at all. And Kelly's been too busy . . . making pacts with Lizzie."

Jacinta glanced over at her. "Yeah, they're growing close. You chill with that?"

"I'm not jealous or anything." Mina stroked the long part of her hair, curling the ends with her finger, thinking aloud. "But Lizzie's acting like Kelly is a better friend to her just because she took the pact and I didn't." Her voice took on a sarcastic nag. "Look at me going on about myself again." She smiled when Jacinta chuckled. "I guess I'm chill with them hanging out. Just wish it wasn't 'cause she thinks I'm a flake."

Jacinta nodded as she finally picked up one of the tests. She read the front aloud. "Ninety-nine percent accurate. No pregnancy test can detect pregnancy at conception." Her eyebrows knitted. "Okay, what? It's nearly a hundred percent accurate, but it can't detect it?"

Mina read over her shoulder. She tossed the words around in her head, trying to redefine them. "Maybe it's just how they cover themselves. So like, if it says you're not pregnant but you are, you can't sue 'em."

"I like that idea." Jacinta grinned. "Suing the company, like it's their fault and not Raheem's."

"I know Raheem would be mad if he heard you say it was his fault," Mina said. "I mean, you were there, too."

"That's the thing." Jacinta grew serious. "Is it anybody's fault? Or am I just cursed? I'm on the pill, Mi. So why am I standing here looking at stupid pregnancy tests?" She leaned her head back and sighed up at the ceiling. Her voice trembled on the edge of crying.

"I thought I was doing things right, and still I'm like thisclose to being just another hood rat, pregnant at sixteen."

Mina felt like she should turn away from Jacinta's uncharacteristic show of vulnerability. But instead, she linked arms again and gave Jacinta's a reassuring squeeze.

"You're not a hood rat."

Tears clung to Jacinta's eyelashes. She wiped at them as she chuckled. "No. But I am very close to becoming a bobblehead 'burb girl. Look at me crying in the damn Walgreens. No harm, Mi. I love you to death, but I think you're rubbing off on me."

Mina beamed. "I'm gonna take that as a compliment whether you meant it that way or not."

Jacinta held up the blue and white box, read it again. She turned it toward Mina. "This one?"

Mina nodded, and they took it to the counter. Under the circumstances, Mina thought Jacinta did well. Mina knew she would have been a puddle of tears in the aisle and then had a panic attack, to boot, once at checkout.

The clerk, a forty-something white woman with a snaggle tooth, didn't raise an eyebrow at their purchase, and Jacinta managed to look nonchalant, bored even, as she handed over the cash. Mina couldn't help looking back at the cashier before they went out the door. The woman had already gone back to reading a magazine, as if teens came in buying early detection pregnancy tests every day.

On the Rebound Tip

"Baby, seasons change, but people don't."
—Fall Out Boy, "The take Over The Break's Over"

Sitting in the library, waiting on Greg to show for their tutoring session, Kelly had the speech–apology all ready in her head:

Greg, I'm sorry about what happened on Friday. Angel's this guy I dated for a few months. We've been over for, like, a year. But he's sort of pushy and cocky. I hope that you didn't get the wrong impression, like I asked him to stop by or anything, because I didn't. I would have explained sooner, but it was awkward, and I was embarrassed. But I told him it's over. Like really over.

Kelly bit her lip, thinking over that last line. It felt a little like overkill, especially since she'd told Angel no such thing on Friday. She'd have to think about that, maybe throw it in last minute if Greg didn't accept her apology.

If she got to apologize, that was.

She double checked the time on her Sidekick.

2:40.

Greg was ten minutes late.

It would be crazy to blow off our session over Friday night, espcially with finals around the corner, Kelly thought.

As she looked around the quiet, near empty library, ten minutes turned to twelve, and the worry that Greg might not show turned into embarrassment and a certainty that he wasn't coming. Still, she waited—shuffling papers around, trying to make herself look busy instead of stood up. Not that the librarian, the two students shelving books to earn community service hours, and the two teachers whisper talking near the door—the entire population of the library—noticed.

At fifteen minutes, a fierce debate broke out between Kelly's ego and her conscience.

Who was Greg to judge her?

True, Angel had been wrong, bursting into the Ria like he owned it. But it wasn't like *she'd* done anything wrong, like gush over Angel. All she'd done was listen, and if Greg had stayed at the table the whole time instead of walking off, he would have . . .

He would have what? Kelly wondered. She stared at the door to the library as if it held answers.

He would have shown Angel I was his, she answered herself.

Okay, "his" wasn't the best description of what Kelly was to Greg. But all Greg had to do Friday was stand his ground. Angel was the kind of guy who could smell fear. He took some sort of weird pleasure in making people uncomfortable. Greg should have been stronger, that was all. It wasn't her fault he'd walked off.

Kelly blinked hard, shaking off the daze just as her Sidekick vibrated noisily against the table. She snatched it up and pretended not to see the librarian's pinched annoyance at the rattling. It was a text from Greg.

Nt cmg

That was it. No reason. No nothing.

Just: Nt cmg.

Kelly threw the Sidekick into her purse and quickly gathered her books, her breath icy hot in her chest. She made tracks to the door just as the first wave of tears blurred her vision.

Maybe she deserved to be stood up. But it ate at her that Greg was writing her off, not giving her a chance to explain Friday's fiasco. *And by the way, how are you going to do on finals next week without me, Mr. Canon?* she thought, her steps a hollow clunk on the hallway's linoleum.

Swiping at the tears that managed to escape, Kelly took another deep breath before bursting through the main doors to the front courtyard. She gave the small clusters of people dotting the front campus a wide berth, not wanting to run into anyone who might question her tear-streaked face, and made a beeline for the sidewalk that led to the main road and her neighborhood.

Angel's call came as she stood at the crosswalk, waiting for the light to change.

She pressed the phone against her ear in time to hear his, "'Sup, ma?"

"Nothing," Kelly said. With the phone to her ear and her tote bag weighing down her shoulder, she was forced to slow down crossing the street. A large truck and a string of cars passing by drowned out Angel's voice. Kelly said "Huh?" three times before the right mix of low traffic noise and Angel's shouting got through.

"I said, what's wrong? You sound upset," he said.

"Did you honestly call to chitchat, Angel?" Kelly asked, scowling at the phone.

His ironic "yeah, I'm busted" chuckle came through loud and clear.

"You know why I'm calling," he said. "But for real, you sound like something wrong."

"Not like you care, but the guy I was with on Friday just stood me up," Kelly said. She took her time with the short distance, blending in with the light bustle of moms walking their kids or dogs, students walking home—just another person yapping on her phone as she went about her day.

"Awww, he left you sitting at the pizza place by yourself," Angel teased.

"I'm his tutor," Kelly said, wondering why she was explaining.

"Oh, then what you care? That's his grade, not yours," Angel said. "So you was tutoring him on Friday?"

"No. It was a date. Are you jealous?" Kelly said, meaning it in a sarcastic way.

But Angel surprised her, coming back in his soft but tough way with, "Yeah, I am."

There was an awkward pause, long enough for Kelly to exit the main street and get through the gates of her neighborhood, where the quiet settled around her, allowing her to hear Angel crystal clear.

"I'm still feeling you. Is that a crime? Look, stop making me look like some sort of old punk," Angel said with an embarrassed chuckle. "I'm not asking you be my girl or nothing. But I do want to take you to prom."

"Why? Did your other girlfriend turn you down? I don't want to be your second choice," Kelly said, not believing for a minute that she was. No way Angel asked other girls, and they said no. He was too persistent and fine for that. But having the upper hand, even for a second, was nice.

Silence came from the other end of the phone. Kelly thought he hadn't heard her, so she started to ask him again just as he finally spoke up. His voice was so low, even in the quiet, she had to smash the phone to her ear to hear him.

"Kelly, you barely let me say ten words to you since last March. Every time I thought you might be ready to talk to me, I'd drop over Jacinta's with Raheem when I knew you was gonna be there. And you cold shouldered a dude." He snorted. "So I didn't ask."

"Well, why now then?" Kelly asked in hushed suspense.

"Real talk, I was gonna blow through prom solo. But Raheem kept riding me about how stupid that was when it was plenty shorties I could ask." Kelly could practically see Angel winking at her as he said, sweetly "But I wanted to go with you, nenesita."

"You were going to go alone?" Kelly whispered, completely taken in by Angel's admission.

Mr. Tough came out as Angel bragged, "Well, I was gonna take two honeys, but they won't let you buy more than two tickets. So that messed a brother's game up."

Kelly looked at the phone as if it had bitten her, then she heard Angel laughing.

"I'm playing, ma. I'm saying, real talk, I didn't ask no other shorty to go with me." His voice went silky smooth as he said in Spanish, "Only you."

Kelly stopped in front of her house.

Aww, only me? she thought, breaking out in a smile.

The words were good balm for a wounded and recently stood up tutor, even if her mind was already weighing the baggage that went along with seeing Angel—explaining this last minute invite to Grand, Angel's hustling, his uncanny knack for talking her into things she thought she didn't want to do.

She looked up at the big estate—the sprawling yard, tennis courts off to the side, the pool and studio in the back. Angel was probably home in the small row house he shared with his uncle in his perpetually darkened room, walls covered with posters of near naked models, boxes of sneakers piled high.

Everything about her and Angel were different. And she could say no on that alone. They'd tried it: it didn't work. Let's be friends, it's not you, it's me, and all that great breakup talk.

It was easy to say no to Angel bursting into the Ria, confident that he could sweep her off her feet. And she should have because saying no to the quiet, sincere Angel was a different story.

"Come on, ma, you know I'm gonna show you a good time," Angel said. Sensing her silence was in his favor, he added one last gentle ego stroke. "For real, I been missing you."

And there it was, the boost she needed. One minute, she was scampering away from campus, her ego busted. The next she was telling Angel yes, her mind already calculating how she was going to do this without Grand knowing.

She hung up with Angel, dashed into the house, her mind already concocting a plan, Operation Take That, Greg—a tag she planned to share with no one.

And by the way, Greg who? she thought, standing in the middle of her closet, which was the size of most people's bedroom.

She took inventory of a section vibrant with colorful party dresses. Thanks to Grand, she had enough dresses to attend fifteen proms, if she wanted.

She plucked a pink strapless, tea-length dress from a cushiony satin hanger and held it up to her in front of the floor-length mirror. With her free hand, she pulled her thick, chestnut hair back into a messy updo. She admired her image and realized her heart was racing.

Dropping the bundled hair, she placed the dress on a peg and busied herself looking for accessories. The puzzle of the sudden date came together in her mind.

It made no sense to grieve over a missed tutoring session. Like Angel said, it was Greg's exam grade. They'd only had one date. It hardly made them soul mates. Going out with Angel, if nothing else, would be an unpredictable good time.

And Jacinta would be there, so she wouldn't be totally alone with him.

With a push of a button, a panel opened, revealing the cubbies holding her shoes. She grabbed a pair of crystal heel sandals and slipped them on. The entire outfit was coming together well. And the best part was she wouldn't have to even tell Grand she was going.

Kevin was leaving to fly to Los Angeles after school on Friday to spend time with their parents. He was only in middle school—all he'd miss the last week of school was rented DVDs and lame games disguised as learning.

Grand was seeing Kevin off, then going to dinner and a movie with some friends. Kelly would simply be home before her grandmother.

Nope, no sense in telling Grand about this. It was really only another date, anyway.

Angel had said he didn't want anything more. But if he did . . .

Kicking off the crystal heel sandals, Kelly scrambled for her purse and fished out the Sidekick. She plopped down in the middle of the closet and texted Lizzie, the one person who would be honest with her.

Lizzie was having a great day.

She'd gone through the entire school day without a single thought about Todd. Well, there was that little fleeting thought in second period when she'd opened her Chem book and a note from Todd had fallen out and she'd teared up a little before her Chem partner, Tabby, thrust a beaker full of something bubbling toward her.

Okay, it wasn't great. But Lizzie was having a good day.

She'd changed every single one of her regular routes to class—routes that had been originally chosen for their proximity to Todd's routes so they'd catch one another in the halls a few times a day. It worked. She hadn't run into Todd once until . . .

She was standing in front of the auditorium, talking to Mr. Collins. He was going on about the annual end of the year Role Reversal night Bay Dra-Da held with The Players. "I know it falls on prom night." His hairy brown mustache wriggled in disapproval. "So that means none of my seniors are going. But I hope to see you there, Elizabeth. Remember, it's for charity."

"Well, I . . ." Lizzie started when she got an eyeful of Todd and Volleyball Girl rounding the corner.

Unable to break eye contact, she took in every detail of their body language. They were walking side by side with barely an inch between them. Of course, Volleyball Girl was laughing like an idiot, and Todd's mouth was moving, so he was telling some sort of joke, Lizzie figured.

Her eyes bucked in surprise, and Mr. Collins instinctively turned his head to see what she was gaping at. Seeing only two students walking down the hall toward them, he cleared his throat.

"Elizabeth, you were saying?"

Her mouth moved in automatic answer, but her eyes stayed locked on Todd as he moved her way. "Well, I was going to be helping my friend get ready for prom but . . ."

Mr. Collins cut her off with an exasperated sigh. "Oh, no. Don't tell me you're going to prom, too. I'm going to have to talk to Madame Zorba about this and make sure it doesn't fall on the same date as prom next year. I really need some of my best students to show."

"No, I'm not *going* to prom," Lizzie said, watching as Todd finally saw her watching him. Emotion flickered in his eyes—guilt, in Lizzie's opinion—then he forced a smile on his face. He threw up a weak, obligatory wave.

Lizzie's eyes fluttered away. She clamped her mouth shut against the trembling in her jaw.

"Oh, good. So you'll be there," Mr. Collins said expectantly.

"Yes," Lizzie whispered huskily.

"Well, don't sound so excited about it," Mr. Collins said, accompanied by his customary ha, ha, ha laugh.

"Oh, I didn't mean . . . no, I'm excited about it," Lizzie said.

Mr. Collins patted her shoulder. "Good. Good. See you then."

He walked off, leaving Lizzie in the hallway alone.

Her neck ached as she fought against turning to see where Todd and Volleyball Girl had gone. She was relieved when her phone beeped, signaling a text, saving her from her own impulses.

She pulled open the door to the auditorium and escaped into its cool dimness. The stage was dark, the room still. The only sound, the occasional rumbling of the AC, which spewed cold air into the vast space. Walking into the auditorium brought her bigtime stress during audition time. But today, it was her hiding place. She turned her phone to vibrate so it wouldn't disturb the silence.

She slunk down into a seat, resting her shins on the seat in front of her, and read Kelly's message:

Gotta ask u smthng. Pls b honest w/me. Pls!

Lizzie typed back "ok" and waited.

Her eyes popped at Kelly's response.

Greg ditched our tutoring session. Guess he's through w/me. But jus fnshd tlkg 2 angel. He asked me 2 prom agn n I said yes. Am I cr8z?

Lizzie sat upright, folding her legs beneath her. She wasn't even sure how to respond because the truth was, Kelly and Angel were finished before they started. Though she'd done a good job giving him the cold shoulder for the last twelve months—Kelly, being Kelly, was too sweet to cut him off completely forever. So Lizzie wasn't all that surprised he'd slipped back into the picture.

Her phone buzzed:

u still there? Rmbr b honest! Am I cr8z to say yes?

Lizzie thought crazy was an understatement. But then again, her opinions on dating were 180 degrees different from her friends, and look where that had gotten her with Todd or for that matter, with her own best friend. She threw Kelly her support.

Crzy yes bt its jus 1 nt, rt?

Lizzie detected a definite tone from Kelly's response—relief.

See thts wht I thght 2! Jus 1 nt. Not lke he'll gt the goodies ☺

Lizzie chuckled low in her throat so the sound wouldn't bounce off the walls.

Extly, she typed back.

It seemed like Kelly wouldn't really be rid of Angel until he graduated. If all it took was a prom date from her so he could move on, Lizzie was all about that for her friend, though she wasn't about to put it that way to Kelly.

She hugged her knees to her chest, holding the phone near her temple as if attempting to relay her thoughts to Kelly telepathically. Obviously, she was the only one who couldn't just go with the flow, so Todd had found someone who would. Hadn't everyone been saying that all along?

A hundred clichés filled her head.

If you can't beat 'em, join 'em.

When in Rome, do as the Romans.

When you're up the creek without a paddle, jump in and swim back downstream.

She'd made up that last one. But it was the one she preferred over the others because she wasn't going to just give in completely. There had to be a way to compromise with Todd. If he'd let her.

The phone buzzed urgently in her hand, the vibration tickling her temple. Seeing another text from Kelly, she slid the smooth, cool phone to her ear and decided to call her back. She needed some help of her own.

Compromising Positions

"You ain't going nowhere, I know because I told you so."
—Young Buck, "U Ain't Goin No Where"

With Kelly's easygoing but practical advice ("Liz, just tell him the truth") still ringing in her ears, the plan was simple—Lizzie was going to tell Todd how much she really liked him, apologize for not trusting their relationship to run its course, and ask for another chance.

Used to Mina's more involved schemes for keeping things on track, Kelly's so straightforward, it might work suggestion was just crazy enough to get Lizzie her boyfriend back.

Lizzie hoped.

She strode into school the next morning, heading toward Todd's locker, determined. "Todd, I didn't mean to be such a dweeb about it," she muttered under her breath, practicing as if she was running lines. Two steps from Todd's locker, she looked up through the crowding hallway and saw Volleyball Girl, spring fresh in a yellow and blue plaid mini and a matching yellow polo that highlighted her tan, heading her way.

Was she coming to wait by Todd's locker, too?

Lizzie didn't want to find out. In a panic, she sped up and veered to the left, colliding with Mina.

"Ow." Mina rubbed her collarbone. "I was trying to run into you today, but not literally." A tiny smile lit up her brown sugar face. It grew larger when Lizzie smiled back. "Where are you dipping to so fast?"

The hallway filled quickly. People bumped the girls, forcing them to squeeze together to hold their spot. Lizzie glanced back among the crowd, and Mina followed her gaze to Volleyball Girl at Todd's locker, running her fingers through her lush brunette curls, head cocked to the side as she peered down the jam-packed hallway.

"What's wrong?" Mina asked.

Lizzie swallowed hard. She was not going to cry. She was not, was not, was not going to be one of those girls who cried at school because of boy problems. Not today, not . . .

"I hate crushes," Lizzie said before she began blubbering.

Mina's eyes narrowed in confusion, but she immediately put an arm around Lizzie and walked her to the only quiet place around, the girls' restroom. They stood in the empty lavatory for a few seconds while Lizzie sniffled and hitched. Mina waited patiently, handing Lizzie tissues until the tears stopped.

"I was going to apologize to Todd this morning and ask if there was any chance we could try again but . . ." Lizzie slumped against the sink. She shrugged her shoulders heavily. "I think he's already moved on."

"Who, Cassie?" Mina asked.

Lizzie nodded, not surprised that if there was any gossip going around about her and Todd's weekend breakup, Mina would already know.

"Yeah, she's totally trying to get with Todd." Mina dismissed it with a hip nudge and smile before leaning against the sink with Lizzie. "But I haven't heard anything about him trying back."

"He sure looked like he was trying yesterday. I saw them together after school," Lizzie said. She turned and stared at her glossy, red-rimmed eyes in the smeared mirror.

"Well, too bad. The statute of limitations isn't up on your breakup window," Mina said. "Shoot, Friday to Tuesday is barely a break, much less a breakup."

Lizzie's laughter boomed in the small, cavelike bathroom. It had been a while since she'd heard one of Mina's made-up, nonsensical life rules, rules that only applied in Mina's world. The absurd idea that there was actually some sort of time limit where a breakup could be reversed tickled Lizzie and reminded her of a hundred other Minaisms created for the sole purpose of making them feel better about situations that sucked.

Her shoulders shook with the last remnants of laughter, then her green eyes grew somber. "Sorry I went off on you on Friday."

"Breakup stress. It's cool," Mina said. She shrugged, but relief flooded her face.

A warm joy spread through Lizzie's heart. They both knew some of the things she'd said went beyond any sort of temporary insanity outburst. But she loved Mina for saying so. It was just the thing she needed to hear right now.

"I should have told you about the pact when I first thought about it. At least you would have known how much I wanted us to do it together," Lizzie said.

Mina nodded. "Be honest. Do you think I'm some sort of sex-crazed bimbette because me and Brian did it?"

Her eyes, crinkled with worry, pierced Lizzie's, relaxing only after Lizzie shook her head vehemently. "No, not at all. I didn't want you to take the pact because I have anything against . . ." Lizzie's eyes fluttered in a nervous tic. "Doing It. Just seems like we're both so caught up in the guys, and the pact seemed like a way to help us . . ." She frowned, concentrating hard on finding the right words before deciding on, "Take a step back."

"I don't mean to obsess about Brian so much," Mina admitted sheepishly. She crossed her fingers. "Scout's honor that I'll probably, definitely, maybe work on doing better."

Both she and Lizzie laughed at the noncommitment commitment.

"I won't hold my breath," Lizzie said.

"I never meant to put him before our friendship. . . . Is that what you thought I was doing?"

Lizzie shook her head, meaning it. Brian wasn't really the issue. It was the whole invisible tug-of-war with Jacinta, the reality that Mina and Jacinta could now trade stories about contraception and a million other things they might now have in common that Lizzie didn't want to think about.

She pushed away the image of her once more standing on the outside, looking in on her friendship with Mina. They were making up. She wasn't going to add fuel to a dying fire. She'd have to find her own way around that hurdle, for now. She forced nonchalance into her voice.

"So, how was It?" Lizzie winced. She sounded like some little kid in awe of her older sib. But once again, thank goodness, Mina's reaction was the Mina she'd always known.

She grew thoughtful for a few seconds, then spoke in a rambling confession.

"It was . . . weird. But not like bad weird . . . just like, oh, my God, I'm naked in front of him weird." She paused long enough to smile at Lizzie's chuckle before going on. "My stomach was cramped for, like, two days afterward. I would get sort of nauseous whenever I thought about it. What's been cool, though, is that Brian's been so . . . so normal about it. I thought he was going to change. Like maybe start throwing shade, trying to play hard or something." She shrugged as if asking, then answering a question in her head. "But he didn't. It's . . . I feel closer to him. And I think he feels the same way . . . I hope." She smiled weakly. "That's not good, is it? Since he's leaving soon. I guess you owe me a told-you-so."

Lizzie shook her head. "I'll pass."

They smiled at one another, letting the silence speak for them.

"Have you guys done it since?" Lizzie said, struggling to shrug off the younger sibling worship feel of her questions.

Mina's eyes lowered for a fleeting second before meeting Lizzie's. "Yeah. But it wasn't at the pool party. For real."

A thick, awkward pause sat between them, neither of them sure where to take the conversation.

Lizzie took a quick internal breath and hoped like heck what she was about to say would come off as light and corny as she meant it because she couldn't live with her friendship with Mina turning into a constant tutorial on dating, sex, and making out—like it sometimes felt with Jacinta. She needed to feel like she could say anything to Mina without feeling like such a kid, so she dove in.

"Condom?"

Mina's eyebrow hitched. Her answer was a hesitant, "Yeah."

Lizzie folded her arms in mock consternation. "What kind?"

Mina's eyebrows knitted. "No idea."

"Flavored?" Lizzie smiled broadly. She breathed a quiet sigh of relief when Mina smiled, then chuckled.

"Okay, eww. No," Mina said. She covered her eyes, then turned her back. "This is me while he was doing all that."

Lizzie laughed. "How come I can *so* see you doing that?"

"Because I did. I was completely weirded out about it."

They muffled their laughter in case a passing teacher decided to inspect the noise. But there was no need—the sounds of the hallway, rowdy when they'd ducked into the bathroom, had dwindled as people made their way to class. On cue, the muted chime of the first bell accompanied the dying noise.

After a few seconds, Mina took a deep breath and sighed. "Are we really cool now?"

"Totally," Lizzie said.

"Then, come on. Let's go talk to Todd."

Lizzie frowned. "The second bell is about to ring. He's probably already gone."

Mina pulled out her phone and texted a message. "Well, wherever he was, he'll meet us at his locker now. Come on."

"I should just wait," Lizzie said. Her stomach tightened. She and Mina were good now, but one step at a time. Maybe she and Todd would be fine as just friends, anyway. She wasn't up to this. Not now.

Mina wrapped her arms around Lizzie in a tight hug, then twirled her until she was facing the door. "Nope."

"We'll be late," Lizzie said weakly.

Mina laughed. "Like that matters to me and Todd. I have like five tardies this year. And you know Todd—he's chronic."

Lizzie pleaded. "I don't want to get in trouble."

Mina gave her a playful shove in the back. "It'll be your first time ever late, Miss A Plus. You can afford it."

They burst into the quieter, less hectic hallway. A few stragglers wandered by, and a teacher's voice boomed from the opposite end that people should be moving along.

When they turned the bend, Todd stood at his locker, talking to Volleyball Girl.

"No, I'll talk to him later," Lizzie said, her eyes begging Mina to let it go.

But Mina's footsteps were hurried. She was at Todd's locker in seven steps, leaving Lizzie to her snail's pace.

"Hey, Cassie," Mina said in her best "I love everybody" cheerleader voice. She talked through Volleyball Girl's hello. "Hey, T."

"What's up, Mina?" Todd said.

Obviously in no hurry, his long body leaned casually on the locker.

Mina spoke toward Lizzie, trying to hurry her with a loud, "Can me and Lizzie holler at you for a second?"

Cassie took the hint. "So, Todd, let me know about Friday, okay?" she said. "Bye, Mina."

Lizzie timed her steps perfectly to step into the spot Cassie had vacated. Once at the locker, she wriggled nervously, her shoulders popping as if she was trying to scratch an itch without the aid of her hands. "Hi," she said in a library-quiet voice.

"Hey, Lizzie," Todd said. His cheeks grew a dull pink, and he quickly began a marathon hair-pushing session as he looked from Lizzie to Mina. "You guys gonna jump me? Should I call my boys for backup?"

Mina put up her hands in surrender. "I come in peace, dude." She gave Lizzie a good luck eyebrow shrug and a quick "See y'all later," before scurrying down the hall.

"Hey, what happened to you not caring if you were late," Lizzie shouted after her.

Mina laughed. "This is your first late, not mine. I gotta dip."

Lizzie chuckled harder than necessary, giving her confidence time to make an appearance. But with the bell seconds away, there was no time. She squared her shoulders and went on without it.

"I'm really, really bad with this kind of thing," she admitted, remembering that Kelly had said to be honest. Todd's eyes clouded with confusion, pushing her on. "Crushes and relationships, I mean."

"Ohhh." He shrugged. "No worries."

"If I said that I really like you and that part of the reason I needed to take the pact is because I'm completely freaked out by how much I like you, would that make sense to you?" Lizzie looked up into Todd's blue eyes. She expected him to make a joke, and she wasn't sure how she felt about that. She needed him to be serious right now. Her heart leapt happily when he nodded. Her shoulders relaxed, and her legs did, too, a little too much. There was a very real chance her rubbery knees were about to give out. She propped herself up against the locker.

"So basically, you like me so much you *don't* want to have sex with me," Todd said. His eyes glinted playfully.

The second bell rang, announcing that they were officially late.

There was so much Lizzie wanted to say, to get out in the open now while she still had the nerve (well, some nerve). But she was only willing to be so late to class. She stood upright. Her legs were once more solid underneath her, now that she'd broken the ice. She walked as she talked.

"That's one way to look at it." She stopped after a few steps and faced Todd. "Look, if we're just going to be friends . . . I think I can be okay with that. But I know the way I dropped the whole thing on you was lame. I'm sorry. I just wanted you to know that."

Sorry, Kelly. I'm too chicken to ask for a second chance, she thought.

"Are you still planning on doing the pact?" Todd asked.

Lizzie wished she could reward the hope in his voice, but she told the truth, "Yeah."

He looked over her head, staring down the empty hallway for a few seconds. Not wanting to be impolite, Lizzie slyly checked the hall clock over his shoulder. She was officially two minutes late. Her class was only a few doors down. She needed to get going, but the invisible draw she felt for Todd kept her rooted in the hallway. Finally, he draped his arm around her shoulder, guiding her toward her class.

"So, okay . . ." He furrowed his brow in concentration. "Define sex for me. I mean, what's off-limits? What's allowed?"

This time, it was Lizzie's turn to feel hope. She dare not think too far ahead about what Todd meant. The old Lizzie would have. But the new going-with-the-flow Lizzie was going to ride this current and see where it took her.

Confessions

"And your heart no longer pledge allegiance to me."
—Jay-Z, "I Know"

Thursdays were reserved for balling at JZ's house. Except this Thursday.

Tomorrow was prom night, and everyone was involved in some sort of last minute prom chore, except JZ. Earlier that day, his mom had taken him to get his tux. After establishing that, indeed, he was one handsome devil in the designer monkey suit, pink vest to match his date's gown, that was all the prom to-doing he had on his list. So he found himself alone on a Thursday for the first time in two months.

His phone buzzed, and without looking, he knew who it was. He smirked down at the message from Jacinta:

Yall ballin 2day?

He typed back, Naw Y? u cmg over? and hit "Send."

He knew the answer would be yes, and it was.

The first time Cinny had texted him and then come over, he'd been surprised since the little flirt thing they'd had going on since meeting had cooled off once Raheem blew his top at Nationals. They'd sat downstairs watching videos and talking, mostly about the madness of the booty-shaking in them (JZ was decidedly for it, Jacinta against), as JZ waited for Jacinta to 'fess up about why she was there. An hour into it, he not only realized that Jacinta just wanted to chill, but also that he enjoyed hanging with her.

There was a dull chime of the doorbell, followed by the murmur of his mother greeting Cinny. By the time she came downstairs, JZ was shooting pool.

He looked up from the table. "What's up, girl?"

Jacinta sat on one corner of the pool table. "Nothing."

JZ's eyes caressed the fullness of Jacinta's bottom, covered by tight jeans, spilling over onto the table and blocking the corner pocket. He purposely shot his ball her way. It bounced off her butt and rolled slowly back toward him.

"Wanna play?" he said.

Jacinta went and picked up a cue stick in response. She chalked it, making JZ smile. Cinny was about the worst pool player, second only to Mina. But she was getting better. JZ respected that she attempted to take playing seriously.

He racked the balls, easily breaking them with his first shot. The solid yellow went in a corner pocket, and he played on. He talked casually, his eyes on the game. "Alright, not that I want to hear anymore about your *cycle*." JZ's eyebrows raised in a high arch before slinking back to rest. "But how'd that whole missed period work out?"

He was relieved when Jacinta smiled. He'd been reluctant to make light, but he and Jacinta had that kind of easy bond. It would be fake if he hadn't poked fun.

"Still missing." Jacinta plopped back down in her spot on the table's corner.

"There you go, cheating, blocking my shot." JZ scowled.

Jacinta waved him off. "Like you not gonna win anyway."

JZ maneuvered around the table, setting up his next shot. He overshot by an inch when Jacinta said, "On a scale of one to ten, how wack is it to break up with somebody on prom night?"

JZ snorted. "Eleven."

Jacinta's scowl turned into deep thought. "I thought so."

JZ moved a step back from the table so Jacinta could take a shot. "So why you talking about breaking up when y'all ready to . . . I mean, when you're—"

"When I'm what?" Jacinta's eyes rolled. She bent over, aiming at the blue and white striped ball.

JZ arched his hand from his chest to the bottom of his stomach to mime a pregnant belly. "You know . . . with child."

Jacinta cackled. "With child? Who are you? Shakespeare?" She reared her stick back, barely connecting with the ball on the shot, then stood up and leaned against her stick. "Whether I am or not, me and Raheem . . . we're . . ." Her head shook slowly side to side like she couldn't find the words.

JZ's mouth upturned in a skeptical grimace. "Yeah, yeah. Don't even say y'all over, Cinny. Heard that before. You rummin'."

"I'm serious, Jay." Jacinta's face lay on her hands against the stick. She swayed slightly side to side against it as she confessed. "Things haven't been right between us since we got back together. It was okay the first few months. But it's like since Christmas, when he committed to GU, he's acting like—" Jacinta frowned, concentrating. "Like that made it official that I'm his wifey or something. Like I'm not going anywhere, ever, unless it's me and him."

"Shoot, aren't you?" JZ's bitterness took him by surprise. He masked it with more light sarcasm. "I'm saying, if you're not his wifey after three years of going out, then what are you?"

He made a mental note that it was right after the Christmas break that Jacinta had first begun calling for her pop in visits. But he didn't have much time to process the thought.

"Just because we've been together for a minute doesn't mean it's forever." Jacinta's voice rose. "And when we got back together, I did it 'cause I believed him that things were gonna be different."

"They weren't?" JZ went back to focusing on the game.

Jacinta's shoulders hiccupped. "Sort of. He did stop tripping so hard about what I do when he's not with me. But I don't know . . . he started talking more about us getting married when he goes pro. Always talking real permanent. He never did that before." Her sigh filtered out in a low hiss. "At first, I played along. I figured him going to school was going to be a break. You know? And whatever happened after he went off to school happened." She chuckled bitterly. "Shoot, you just don't know how disappointed I was when he picked Georgetown over Syracuse. And you know why he picked it, Jay?" She waited for JZ to look up at her before she answered. "Because it's closer to home. So then, every time we're together, he's talking about how I can come visit him any time I want. And during the off-season how he's gonna come home on weekends to see me." She threw up one hand and let it come down in a floppy slap on her leg, the words pouring. "I just kept telling myself, 'get through summer, Cinny. Just get through summer, and then he'll be at school. Once he's there, he'll have classes and basketball. So we'll have space. And once we get some space, I'll probably miss him. . . . ' You know? I'll probably want to see him." She rocked slightly, swaying with the cue stick as she hugged it. Her voice lowered. "But Georgetown is so close to the DRB. And he reminds me how close every time, talking about how much we can still see each other."

"And that's a bad thing?" JZ said, meaning it as a joke. But Jacinta glared at him.

"Yeah. Yeah, JZ, it's bad." She sat down heavily on the table's corner. "Every time I think I have this worked out, shit happens. I break up with him. He follows me down to O.C. begging to get back. So we get back. We agree to respect each other's space." Her voice rose higher as she ranted. "Well, that worked fine until every other conversation became about 'the future' and how often he's gonna drive from DC to see me." She raised her arms for another shrug, and the stick tumbled out of her hand, hitting the carpet with a dull thud. "Stupid me. I figured, well, once he's at school, he won't be pressed

about me. Then my stupid period doesn't come on. I can't win, Jay."
She whispered again. "I can't win."

JZ hit in his last ball. He thought about making a crack about
winning, but Jacinta was lost in thought, staring down at the floor.
He racked the balls, keeping busy. He wasn't good at the sappy stuff.
Michael could give advice without blinking, but that wasn't JZ's
style.

He forced himself to walk around to face Jacinta. Squatting, he
picked up her stick. His heart raced as he fought all the silly, smart-
alecky one-liners rising up in his throat. He laid the stick on the
table, then sat beside Jacinta, his long legs stretched out next to her
short, dangling ones.

He cleared his throat. "You think if you break up, he's gonna go
psycho or something?"

Jacinta sighed as if she weren't so sure, but her response indicated
otherwise. "No. I don't think he's that pressed. But it feels like he'll
keep . . . I don't know, trying to convince me we can make it work.
It's like he acts like, well, we love each other, so of course, we can
work it out."

"Can you?" JZ asked.

"I guess. But don't both of us gotta want that?"

Jacinta's eyes were heavy with sadness. She looked at JZ as if he
might have the answer, making his heart thump against his rib cage.
He wanted to say the right thing, but wasn't sure what that was.

Finally, he asked, "You really don't want it?"

Jacinta stared off across the room for a few seconds before answering. "I'm always gonna love Raheem . . . I mean, I hope we're
always gonna be friends. But I don't want to be . . . *with* him anymore."

Her shoulders relaxed as if she'd dumped a load off them.

"Maybe you're saying that 'cause . . . you know, the whole
missed period thing. You know y'all girls get mad at us like it's our

fault." He cut his eyes toward Jacinta playfully, but she wasn't smiling, so he grew serious again. "I'm saying, maybe once you get through all this, you'll feel different."

Jacinta's head ticktocked. "No. I felt like this before, Jay. For a while now. I'm just scared to tell him."

Scenes from a Prom: Act One, Scene One

"Party like a rock star. Party like a rock star."
—Shop Boyz, "Party Like a Rock Star"

Prom preparation was in full swing at the Mooney's house early Friday evening.

Between her mom, Lizzie's mother, and Mina's Granny J, Mina could barely breathe. The three women mother henned her, pulling, tugging and fluffing at her hair and dress.

This must be how a mannequin feels, Mina thought as Mrs. O'Reilly whacked softly at invisible lint at the hem of Mina's dress.

Mina made WTF? eyes at Lizzie, and they giggled softly.

The older women hadn't given Lizzie much chance to help, so she'd long given up and sentenced herself to a nearby corner of the Mooneys' master suite, the only room large enough for all three ladies to have sufficient room to fuss over Mina.

When Granny J went to smooth Mina's hair for the tenth time, Mina had a mini meltdown. "Granny, are we done yet?"

Miss Jenna, Mariah's mom, was a petite woman with smooth, flawless brown sugar skin. She was to Mariah what Mariah was to Mina—a look into the future. They were three generations of the same wide brown eyes, small ears, and pouty mouth.

"I know *you're* not tired of somebody making over you?" Granny J put her hands on her hips and fixed Mina with a look. She chuckled softly and went back to her fussing, ignoring her granddaughter's exasperated hiss.

"Brian's here," Mina's dad bellowed from downstairs.

The announcement sent the women into a frenzy of hair patting, strap fixing, and face powdering.

Seeing that she wasn't going to be let go that easily, Mina hollered over to Liz. "Can you go get my handbag, please? It's in my room, sitting on my dresser."

Glad to finally have a task, Lizzie bolted.

The sea of activity finally ceased. The women stepped back and admired their work.

Mina was a vision of brown skin swathed in satiny, sapphire blue. The dress hung perfectly on her compact frame, hugging at the top and swaying softly through her hips, kissing the middle of her thighs. She'd wisely gone with her mom's suggestion and worn her hair in a simple sleek wrap. Bent slightly at the ends, the longer hair reached out as if trying to lick her cheek. The one-inch heel sandals showed off her pedi—pearly sapphire polish to match the dress and a tiny flower encrusted with a single crystal on the big toe.

"She's gorgeous," Lizzie's mom said, proud.

Too choked up to speak, Mina's mom nodded.

"Well, let me go meet this boy, see what all the fuss is about," Granny J said with mock gruffness. She swatted Mina on the butt and kissed her cheek before heading downstairs.

Lizzie's mom hugged Mina. "Let me go get the camera ready. Have fun tonight, sweetie."

Finally able to breathe, Mina walked over to the full-length mirror. She grinned at her image. All the fuss had been worth it.

"Ooh, I look so cute."

Wiping at tears, her mom chuckled. "Well, thank God you're not vain." She stood beside Mina in the mirror and put her arm around her daughter's waist. "I can't believe you're going to prom. Wasn't it just yesterday that you and Lizzie played dress up in my closet, flopping around in my heels?"

"Actually, it probably was. I borrowed a pair of your shoes and wore them to school the other day."

Mariah squeezed Mina's waist. The tears leaked uncontrollably through her smile.

Mina dabbed at her own eyes. "Mommy, you're going to get me crying. And I do *not* want y'all to have to redo my makeup."

"I know, right?" Mariah laughed. She wiped her eyes to staunch the leaking. "Have fun and be good tonight." She hesitated, her mouth ajar as if she wanted to say more. Instead, she sniffed and smiled.

"Mariah, come on now," Mina's dad yelled.

"Let me get down there." Before leaving, Mariah pecked Mina on the lips. "Have fun, baby girl."

Mina twirled around once, winked at herself, and headed out. She nearly collided with Lizzie, who held the crystal bag out to her.

"Thanks, Liz." Mina started for the steps, then stopped. "Oh, wait. I forgot something."

She and Lizzie walked to her bedroom.

Mina rummaged through a tiny, silver star-shaped jewelry box and pulled out the ring from Brian.

"I figured you never took it off," Lizzie joked.

"It was getting icky from lotion and stuff." Mina slid the ring on her left pinky. She shrugged her shoulders. "How do I look?"

"Adorable," Lizzie said with a warm smile.

"Thanks for helping me get ready," Mina said.

"Yeah. I'm not sure I was much help." Lizzie's eyes rolled. "Our moms were like Nascar prom dressers."

"I know that's right." Mina walked over and gave Lizzie a tight hug. "I'm glad you're here, though."

"Would I ever miss it?" Lizzie asked.

Mina couldn't answer over the lump in her throat. She shook her head really hard in answer and gave Lizzie an extra squeeze.

When she let go, she looked around the room, double-checking for forgotten accessories.

"Mina," her dad yelled, the irritation in his voice clear as a bell.

"Am I forgetting something?" Mina asked, more to herself than Lizzie. "I'm forgetting something, aren't I?"

Lizzie's and Mina's heads swiveled from left to right. They searched the room, neither sure what they were looking for.

"You have your lip gloss? Cell phone?" Lizzie asked.

Mina nodded. That was pretty much all that fit in the handbag, anyway. Still, it nagged at her that within the tornado that was her getting ready, something had gotten caught in the storm and been forgotten.

The feeling kept her rooted in her room a few seconds longer until she heard her father's footsteps approaching the stairs.

"Okay, let's go," she said, scurrying out.

Scenes from a Prom:
Act One, Scene Two

"I'm insane, I need a shrink."
—DJ Khaled ft. Lil Wayne, "We Taking Over"

On the other side of Del Rio Bay, Jacinta was in a bad mood.

Everything and everyone was getting on her nerves.

One, she felt nauseous—head tripping, stomach woozy nauseous. The feeling had started when she was in the hair salon. All the smelly holding spray and spritzes had turned her stomach sour. The feeling lingered, rising and falling in waves that made her dizzy. She felt like lying down and staying 'sleep until Raheem went off to school.

And Raheem was another thing.

She'd told him that she wanted to get dressed at her Aunt Jacqi's. The house was bigger and Aunt Jacqi's yard had a nicer background for pictures. She hadn't told him that second part. It would have only meant a lecture about her acting boogee. Raheem had gone down the litany of reasons why it made sense to leave from The Cove: it was closer to the hotel where the prom was being held. It made no sense for him to drive over to The Woods and then back to Del Rio Bay proper. Most of both their families lived in Pirates Cove, so who would drive everybody over to The Woods, blah, blah, blah—he had a million and one reasons why it made more sense, and Jacinta had nothing to match, except she didn't want to get dressed in The Cove.

So she'd lost that battle.

And here she stood in the tiny room she shared with her sister on the weekends she visited home, in only a strapless bra and panties. The room felt smaller than usual because her aunt Jacqi and her younger sister, Jamila, kept coming in with new questions, "Where did you say you put those heels?" "Cinny, can I try this lip gloss on?"

The urge to slam the door shut and lock herself in was so strong Jacinta had actually gotten as far as shutting it quietly when Jacqi burst in, practically taking Jacinta's toe off in the process.

"Girl, come on. Raheem is going to be here in a few minutes." Jacqi held Jacinta's dress in her hand. It was still on the hanger under a clear plastic covering, like it had just come from the dry cleaners. She placed it on the sill above the door, her hands pushing up the plastic in a hurry. Within seconds, she had it off the hanger and was holding it out for Jacinta to pull on over her head. She frowned, her eyes questioning Jacinta. "Cinny? Come on."

Jacinta lifted her arms slowly, like they weighed two tons.

Jacqi draped the dress over her arm. "What's wrong?"

"Nothing." Jacinta's voice was flat. She let her arms fall.

"Are you and Raheem arguing or something?"

"No."

Jacqi put her free hand on her hip. "Then what? I thought you'd be dressed and standing on the corner waiting for Raheem for this night." Caught up in her own memories, she rambled on, "The way you always trailed after Raheem and Angel being a tomboy, first, I thought you were going to end up one of the boys. Then after y'all started going out, I thought we were gonna have to lock your butt in because you always wanted to be with him." She held the dress up again. "Shoot, this is almost like a wedding day for you two."

Jacinta winced at the comparison.

"That was only a joke, Miss Jacinta Renee Phillips." Jacqi shook the dress at her. "Come on."

Jacinta's arms went up again, and Jacqi helped her pull the dress on and over her curves.

Jacqi fluttered about, walking around Jacinta, making sure the dress had fallen correctly. She buzzed on, more excited about the night every second. "Is your father letting you head to O.C. with Raheem tomorrow? I can remember going after my own prom. It was the craziest weekend ever." She shook her head.

"I don't think I'll be going back to O.C. until *my* senior year," Jacinta said.

Jacqi laughed. "That's right. Still on probation. Is that why you upset? Is Raheem rolling down there with his boys without you?"

"Him and Angel might go. They said they weren't sure yet . . . something about crashing with some of the basketball players."

Jacqi stood back, giving Jacinta the once-over.

"Aww, my niece looks so cute." Her eyebrows arched. "Grown. But cute."

"Aunt Jacqi, can you see if my father has any stomach stuff?" Jacinta asked.

"Stomach stuff like . . . what? Pepto-Bismol?"

"Anything. My stomach hurts."

"It's probably just nerves," Jacqi said. She put in Jacinta's left earring. "Is it cramps? Is your period coming on?"

"I wish," Jacinta said under her breath.

Jacqi's head popped up from scooping up the second earring. Still standing right beside Jacinta, she was quiet for a full second. Slowly, she inserted the second earring.

"Cinny, are you late?" she whispered.

Jacinta took her time swallowing, counting the seconds it took to push the moisture down her throat. One and a half. She swallowed three more times before nodding slowly.

Jacqi pulled out the lone chair in the room and sat down.

"How late?"

"Fourteen days." Jacinta felt like a little girl, looking down at her aunt in the chair for a reprimand. Her face was hot with embarrassment and shame.

"You know for sure if you are or not?"

"I was hoping it would come on," Jacinta said as if that answered the question. She didn't want to mention that she had the test. That it was hidden at the bottom of her drawer beneath a stack of winter clothes that she'd never put in her storage trunk. That every night she prayed she wouldn't need to take it. And that every morning she woke up both angry and determined that it would come on tomorrow.

Jacqi rubbed her eyes hard as if trying to erase a bad image. She took a deep breath, exhaled, then stood up. "Take a test tomorrow. I'll get you one tonight."

"I have one already," Jacinta said, her voice barely audible.

Jacqi's eyes popped slightly, but so fast Jacinta would have missed it if she hadn't been staring her aunt in the face. The take charge tone in her voice remained firm. "Fine. Take it tomorrow morning. We'll . . ."

There was a knock at the door, and they both jumped.

"What in the world are y'all doing?" Jacinta's father's voice said from the other side. "As teeny as that dress is, no way it should take this long to get it on."

"We're coming, Jamal," Jacqi said.

"Well, can I see before she comes downstairs?"

"Tomorrow," Jacqi whispered to Jacinta. In two steps, she was across the room, opening the door.

Jacinta's dad beamed at the sight of Jacinta in her brown and yellow-printed slip dress. If he had any concerns about its length or lack of material, they were gone now.

"Look at you, baby girl." He opened his arms for a hug.

Jacinta willingly went into the embrace. The warmth and strength of it made her want to blurt the truth to him, telling him so he could fix it like he'd always fixed things for their family. But the voice in the back of her mind screamed, no, loud enough to overpower the vulnerability she felt. She listened to it, even as she held on, crushed in her father's strong hold.

Prom Nightus Interruptus

"You take my hand and say you've changed."
—Jo Jo, "Too Little Too Late"

I did this wrong, Kelly thought.

She ran the flat iron over her hair one last time, pressing every single natural wave out of her thick, chestnut hair. Normally, her hair, tight with waves and curls, was right above her shoulder. With it flat ironed, it was every bit of three inches longer. It was shiny and sleek and gave Kelly an entirely different look.

The problem was, in her anxiety and rush to get ready the second Grand walked out the door, she'd started on her hair before her shower. It had taken her nearly an hour to flatiron her entire head of hair. Getting it all into a shower cap was going to be a chore. And even with a cap on, it would likely frizz. Not totally, but enough that she might have to run the flatiron over parts again.

Getting dressed for a date wasn't rocket science, but that's what mothers, grandmothers, and girlfriends were for—to help you get ready in an orderly and logical fashion. Now, she was stuck in a baby doll tee with the day's musk settling over her.

Staring blankly at the mirror, she ran through her options. Angel would be here in another forty minutes. She didn't have time to flatiron again, not even just a few segments.

She lifted her right arm and sniffed toward the pit.

She'd showered this morning. She hadn't had gym. Maybe . . .

She lifted her left arm and sniffed.

It was fine.

Thank God she'd shaved this morning.

She spoke aloud to her image in the mirror. "This will be our little secret, okay, nenesita?"

Without waiting for the image to reply, she unplugged the flat iron and reached for her makeup bag, sorting through the items she wanted. She wasn't big on wearing makeup, a little eyeliner, maybe mascara and lip gloss—done. Even wearing that little bit had practically taken a presidential pardon when she'd approached Grand about it last year.

Kelly had to admit she'd been a bookworm, stay-at-home kind of gal all her life until her freshman year. Dating, wearing makeup, sleepovers every other weekend hadn't just been a shock to Grand; it had been like Kelly was abducted by aliens and returned a new person.

Most days, Grand was happy with the new Kelly. Others, completely confounded.

Kelly didn't feel different. She still enjoyed curling up with a book on the weekends she wasn't with the clique. And wearing makeup was strictly a special occasion thing. As far as dating, beyond talking on the phone with Angel a lot and hanging out with him all of half a dozen times, Kelly wasn't going to be anyone's dating tutor any time soon.

She frowned, leaning her head to the right. She thought she'd heard the chime of the doorbell. Her suite was in the back of the house—it wasn't unusual for her not to hear the doorbell or to mistake some other sound for it. But the house was completely quiet until she heard it again.

It was definitely the doorbell.

Angel was early.

That didn't surprise her. She'd told Angel her grandmother was gone for the evening. Knowing him, he'd come over early thinking maybe he'd sweet-talk her into a little making out.

The thought angered Kelly.

She threw the tube of mascara down and hurried down the long hall and the spiral staircase to the front door. She snatched the heavy door open, ready to scold Angel, the words right on the tip of her tongue, and came face-to-face with Greg.

Their eyes were a matching pair. His bucked at the door's sudden opening, hers widened at seeing him instead of Angel.

"Oh . . . hey, Greg." Kelly looked beyond him, somehow convinced that Angel was still somewhere nearby.

"Hey. Sorry to bust in like this. You got a minute?" Greg shoved his hand in his jeans pocket. He rocked back and forth slightly.

Kelly stepped back so he could come in. Eyebrows furrowed, her eyes skated across the landscape of her front yard as if they sought proof that Greg, not Angel, had ended up at the door. She closed the door behind them and walked Greg into the kitchen.

"Your hair looks really nice like that," Greg said as he took a seat at the counter.

Kelly's hand flew to her head, smoothing down the already flat hair. So used to feeling swirls, the straight hair felt odd under her fingers. "Thanks."

"I'm not really as big a lame as you might think," Greg blurted. He chuckled nervously. "Sorry I flaked on our tutoring session the other day."

"We still have one more before your final," she reminded him, hoping her voice didn't betray her disappointment.

Greg had only come to apologize about ditching their session? It was as if she'd imagined their date at the Ria. Like it had never happened.

Greg cleared his throat noisily. "So was that dude your ex or something?"

The tension in his voice made Kelly smile.

She was so used to being the timid, nervous one in the boy–girl dating scenario that it felt deliciously awesome to know she wasn't the only one who felt that way. Plus, if this were only about tutor-ing, why would Greg care who Angel was. She regrouped quickly, answering immediately.

"Ex, yes. I'm sorry he crashed our date like that."

"I've never seen him before. Is he from around here?"

Kelly's head shook. "No. He lives across the bridge in Pirates Cove."

Greg's eyebrows arched, then came down quickly.

"Are you guys getting back together?"

For a second, the image of her answering the door in a prom dress flitted through Kelly's mind.

"Why, no, Greg, we're not getting back together. I'm just going to prom with him," she saw herself saying.

It was so absurd it made her want to giggle.

"No, we're not," she said aloud.

She walked over to the counter and stood in front of Greg, her emotions playing leapfrog—happy, embarrassed, excited.

Where would she even start explaining had she answered the door in a prom dress?

"Well, we broke up sort of abruptly," she said, wanting to be hon-est without getting into the nitty-gritty. She didn't want the boy running out of here screaming. "Friday was the first time we'd spo-ken in a long time. Guess you can say we had some unresolved is-sues."

Greg snorted. "Just a few."

"I wanted to let you know all that, but you know . . . the date sort of fizzled after that." Kelly's shoulders hiccupped. "Then you didn't show the other day . . . ."

"Yeah, I shouldn't have ditched our session." He wiped his hands on his jeans, rubbing them back and forth, then stood up suddenly. "Well, I was on my way to Jake's house, and I remembered you lived over here. That's why I stopped. But I didn't mean to get all stalker on you."

They stood only inches apart.

Mmm . . . he must have changed his shirt before coming out, Kelly thought. She could smell the detergent in his clothes. The scent was so ordinary and normal it helped center her thoughts.

"Are you mad at me?" she asked.

"I was. But it was our first date; it's not like we're . . . you know, exclusive." Greg's Adam's apple went up and down nervously. He stood still as a tree, not moving an inch. One step forward would take him right into Kelly. "That's why I stopped, I guess. To let you know it was cool and that if you still wanted to tutor me, I wouldn't flake on our next session."

The more nervous Greg became, the more confident Kelly grew. She giggled softly as she teased. "You could have just called me."

Greg grinned. "True. But you know . . . Jake lives just down the street. So . . ."

Kelly knew it was a gamble Greg may not even understand her. But she bit the bullet and asked in Spanish, "Do you want to go out again?"

His eyes rolled up and to the left as he worked to pull the meaning of her words from his brain. Finally, a smile spread across his face. "Si." He shoved one hand in his pocket; the other he ran across his low cut hair. "What about tonight? A bunch of us are going bowling. I was going to be the fifth wheel. The lame without a date. So . . ."

He looked expectantly at Kelly, his boyish face both nervous and hopeful.

For the first time since Greg had walked in, Kelly got her own case of the nerves. A bolt of panic struck her in the chest. If she said no, Greg might think she was teasing or leading him on. Plus, he seemed so nervous Kelly thought a no might send him scrambling.

She forced a smile on her face. "Hold on for a minute. I need to check with my grandmother."

She hurried away, taking the steps two at a time as she raced to her bedroom. Once there, she paced between the love seat in her sitting room and the door.

Just say no. You can't go. Angel's on his way, she told herself.

Exactly, he's on his way. How can he be your ex if he's on his way, her brain reminded her sarcastically. Try explaining that.

She paused at the love seat, gripping it tightly to get her thoughts to slow down.

"I can't go. Just tell him Grand said no," Kelly said to the empty room.

More lies. She didn't want to tell any more lies.

No more.

She raced to the bathroom, picked up her Sidekick, making her fingers fly so she wouldn't change her mind. She pulled up Angel's number and typed in a short, simple text: I cnt go 2nite

She hit "Send" so hard she jammed her finger.

Angel was going to blow up her Sidekick—that much she knew. And when he did, she'd tell him the truth—she couldn't go out with him. They were over. She was wrong for saying yes in the first place.

That was the truth.

Her throat tightened.

A fine mess you've gotten yourself into, Miss Kelly, she thought.

A fine mess.

She grabbed her purse, dropped the Sidekick into it, and went back downstairs.

"Can you go?" Greg asked, his face bright with anticipation.

As long as I let myself, I can, Kelly thought. She smiled. "Yup."

Scenes from a Prom:
Act One, Scene Three

"If you didn't know, you're the
only thing that's on my mind."
—Usher, "Love in This Club"

As much fun as taking pictures had been, Mina found herself anxious to get on with the night. She had flash fatigue five minutes into picture taking and was distracted by how good Brian looked in his tux, to boot. His sapphire blue vest matched her dress to a tee, bringing the phrase perfect couple to mind.

They made their way to the huge Hummer limo six separate times before being called back for another picture. Once by Brian's mother, twice by Mina's, once by her dad, once by Michael, and the last by Lizzie. Mina sent her a silent "Not you, too?" look.

Lizzie smiled sheepishly. Then Todd muttered a joke about how they really should take after photos when everyone was looking a hot mess from dancing and other extracurricular prom activities. That got Mina laughing, and the last photo had captured that.

The limo ride was surreal. For some inexplicable reason, Stefan had brought a pair of dice. Brian, JZ, Stefan, and Wade immediately squared off on the floor of the limo, shooting craps, hollering and fussing about shots being messed up by the carpet. Mina and the guys' dates grumbled about it a little, but then quickly fell into conversation about how nice everyone looked, who had gotten their hair done where, and plans for afterparties. By the time Wade pulled out the tiny bottle of Hennessy, which he proceeded to mix with a

Coke, the limo noise was at its peak. Mina and JZ's date passed on sipping Wade's concoction, but everyone else took a sip.

Secretly, Mina was surprised that Brian took a hit from the can. Not that she'd never seen him drink, but it was rare enough that each time jolted her a little. She was pleased when Brian passed once Wade produced yet another miniature and grabbed a second can of Coke from the limo's well-stocked soda bar.

Instead, he came over, sat beside her, his arm around her shoulder. "What's up, toughie? You good?"

"I'm good," she said, angling her mouth toward his ear so she wouldn't have to yell over everyone else's talking.

He rubbed a small piece of her dress between his fingers. "Silky. You look nice tonight." His hands flirted with her thighs. "So, what do you have on underneath that?"

"Wouldn't you like to know?" Mina teased.

He nuzzled her ear with his mouth. "Absolutely."

Mina grew warm with him so near. She sank into the seat closer to him.

"When do I get my surprise?"

Brian squinted, then shrugged, pretending he didn't know what she was talking about. Mina shoved his leg. "Don't play."

He grinned as he moved his face in and kissed her. Mina kissed back shyly, not used to being so open in public. Just then the limo stopped, delivering them to their destination, a waterfront hotel overlooking the Del Rio Bay.

The hotel was the premier spot for proms. Every year, there was mad schedule juggling so that Sam-Well and DRB High had their proms on different weekends. That way, both schools would get the opportunity to use the venue. This year, the scheduling hadn't worked. Both schools scheduled prom the same weekend, and DRB High had swooped in and reserved the date first.

The four couples filed out of the limo, joining a large stream of promgoers doing the same. Seeing everyone so formal and coupled up made Mina feel very adult. She expected, at any moment, for someone to start talking about their stocks or work stress. They all resembled very young-looking adults.

Brian held her hand, and she followed obediently behind him. Even though all the guys looked identical in their black tuxes, people were somehow still able to recognize one another. With his free hand, Brain dapped up, gave pounds, and shook hands with a dozen guys as they made their way inside.

Mina managed a few of her own hello as she floated along with him.

Her breath caught in her throat when they finally walked into the main room. The prom's theme was "Big Things Poppin'." In honor of that, hundreds of silver stars hung from fishing line in the ceiling. In large glow-penned letters were the names of each senior and where they were headed after graduation. Some had the names of a college, others boasted simply a city, and others listed an occupation, like music producer or model. The committee had really worked hard to ensure that each senior answered the questionnaire so there would be at least one star for everyone in attendance. Mina's neck craned upward as she read the stars.

It was apparent the committee was well-organized. The stars were clustered for easy identification. She recognized the batch of stars above her immediately. They were for the basketball team.

Mina squealed. "Ooh, look, there's yours." She tugged Brian's hand and pointed out several stars. One had his name and Duke University, another said his name and Durham, NC, and another had Duke Starter on it.

"Remind me to snatch 'em down before we go," Brian said.

Mina nodded and let herself be pulled away.

In no time, they'd found their table, a prime spot near a window with a view of the Bay. But the spectacular scenery didn't keep them still long. First, they headed to the section for pictures, wanting to get them done early before Mina's hair sweated out. Then she and

Brian were on the dance floor any time the DJ spun a hip-hop track. Every time they headed back to the table, Wade and Stefan were a little more drunk, their dates equally as tipsy. JZ and his date had gotten themselves lost in the crowd and only came back to the table to eat the unexciting entrée of chicken and rice pilaf.

It didn't take long for Mina's feet to begin howling. The heel sandals were only an inch high, but walking out in them was not for the timid. When the DJ went from T.I. to a Foo Fighters song, she practically raced back to the table to sit down.

Their table was blessedly empty. Last she'd seen them, Stefan and Wade were close to pissy drunk. Mina had grown tired of their antics an hour ago. It was a wonder an administrator hadn't caught up with them and sent them home. She pulled up the chair closest to the window and stretched her legs into the chair beside it. Brian lifted her legs, sat down in the chair, and dropped them gently back into his lap. He massaged her calves, his eyes teasing.

"Can't hang, huh?"

"I sure can't," Mina said, still trying to catch her breath from the four-song set they'd danced to. She moaned softly. "That feels so good." She lectured him affectionately. "Shoot, you try grooving with heels on."

Brian plucked her tiny sandal off and held it up. "This little thing? How does this thing hurt your feet?"

Mina's eyes rolled. "Okay, little. Keep rubbing, please."

Brian's hands kneaded her calves. "I'm not touching your cheesy toes, though."

Mina lifted her leg as far as she dared in a dress, toward his face. "Boy, I just got my toes done. These toes are clean enough to eat off."

He pushed her leg down and scowled. "Man, whatever."

Their laughter was lost in the crashing of the Foo Fighters. The song blended into a Justin Timberlake track, and the roar of approval from the crowd thundered.

"That's your boy, ain't it?" Brian said.

"Um-huh. But I gotta pass this time."

"Good. How I look dancing to some Justin Timberlake?" Brian's eyes rolled.

Mina's head shook as she scolded him. "Oh, my God, you are so lucky my feet hurt. I'd make you dance just for saying that."

"You ready?" Brian asked.

"To go?" Mina asked, surprised. She opened her hand bag and looked at her cell phone. It was only ten. Prom still had another hour and a half. And her parents had said she could stay out until one. She was going to soak up every second.

Brian slipped Mina's shoe back on. "Yeah. Come on. I told you I had a surprise for you." He held his hand out and helped her up. "Besides, if we leave now, we get the limo to ourselves. Unless you want to share a ride with Stefan and Wade."

That put pep in Mina's step. "Un-ah. Let's dip. But how's everybody getting home?"

"I already told them I was rolling out early. The limo's just gonna come back for them after it drops us off."

Mina followed Brian as they zigzagged their way between tables and then through gyrating bodies on the dance floor. When they got to the door, she pulled away. "Hold up. Your stars." Brian followed her back to the section where she'd seen his name. The stars were dangling above a dangerously crowded segment of the dance floor. "Can you reach them?"

As if the bodies weren't there at all, Brian reached up and yanked the stars. With some effort, they finally came down.

Mina tittered. "What if you're not supposed to take them?"

"This is just three less stars they need to take down when they clean up."

He grabbed the last one, took her hand, and led her out.

As if by some Jedi mind trick, the limo was there waiting for them at the hotel's entrance. They climbed in, and it slowly pulled off.

The Hummer limo with just the two of them in it felt ridiculously empty. Mina plopped down in a middle seat, and Brian sat beside her.

She looked around at the luxe black leather interior. A television set was built into the bar, and as if he was reading her mind, Brian leaned up, plucked the remote from the bar, and turned it on. They were greeted with static.

"Guess we didn't pay for the deluxe cable package," Brian joked. He turned it back off.

"Are you going to give me a hint about this surprise?" Mina asked.

Brian's head shook vehemently. He switched the subject as if she hadn't spoken. "So, you all set to leave for O.C. tomorrow morning, right?

"Yeah. My bag is packed and everything."

Mina's parents were letting her go reluctantly. But once Mr. and Mrs. James had stopped over and assured them the foursome would either be on the beach or on the boardwalk—translation, no alone time for the young lovers—her parents had relented. Not without a major lecture about trust, of course.

Mina had to actually remind herself that she hadn't been the one to sneak to O.C. last year. It had been Cinny, Lizzie, and Kelly. She hadn't even known they were coming. But the sins of her friends had left an impression on her parents. Under the circumstances with them letting her go, Mina didn't think it wise to point out that she'd personally not broken any rules or trust, a fact that hadn't stopped them from punishing her last year for harboring the secret that the girls had come down to O.C.

"Are we riding with your parents or are you driving, too?" Mina asked. She sat cross-legged on the large, plush bench.

"We're riding with them."

"Do they have an itinerary to make sure we don't spend a second alone together?" Mina's eyebrows steepled. "I know my mother would."

Brian laughed. "I don't think so. But then again, it wouldn't be nothing for my mom to whip out a schedule full of minigolf, parasailing and water aerobics."

"Water aerobics?" Mina scowled.

"Okay, not saying I've ever taken water aerobics." Brian's eyes stretched mischievously, making it clear he absolutely had.

Mina teased him until he wrestled her onto his lap.

"Okay, that's enough of that." He kissed her, preventing any further ribbing. They remained tangled, lips locked until the limo door opened, ushering in a whirl of fresh, cool air.

The air had the proper effect, bringing them both back to the present.

"Alright, ready?" Brian backed out of the limo. He took her hand. "Keep your eyes closed until you get out."

Mina did as she was told, stumbling as she made her way out of the limo. She heard the limo door shut and Brian instruct the driver about heading back to the hotel for the others. The sensation of movement overtook her as the limo pulled off. Brian steadied her when she wobbled.

He took her hand in his and said, "Open your eyes."

Mina eagerly popped her eyes open. The light in her eyes dimmed. They were standing in front of Brian's darkened house.

Scenes from a Prom: Act One, Scene Four

"Almost heard ya sayin' you were finally free."
—Brandy, "Almost Doesn't Count"

A good night can go bad easily.

Jacinta had been the unfortunate victim of such a phenomenon more than she cared to remember.

But a bad night getting worse—that was a new one.

Having Aunt Jacqi in on her secret had eased Jacinta's mind a little. No longer carrying the burden alone had made it easier to smile through the pictures. She was even feeling a little guilty about yesterday's dish session with JZ.

Raheem looked handsome in his tux, and everyone was so excited for them, from his mom to her little brothers, that thoughts of breaking up with him slowly faded. She'd stick with her original plan, let him go off to school, and let things happen as they may.

But it wasn't in the stars for things to work out, at least not for the night. She knew it the second Angel muttered, "Man, what's wrong with this chick?"

He cursed in Spanish.

Jacinta looked up from the complicated console of the totally pimped out, silver Benz E-Class, a rental, forgetting for a minute that she was trying to decipher how to turn down the radio.

"What?" Raheem looked in his rearview mirror. He wheeled the Benz to the stop sign at the entrance to Pirates Cove.

Jacinta turned in the seat. Angel's face was contorted in an angry scowl.

"Kelly just texted that she can't go," Angel said, his thumb madly scrambling over the phone to respond.

Jacinta's already nauseous stomach flipped. She felt the immediate anger and tension seeping from Raheem and wasn't surprised when he snapped, "What's up with your girl, Cinny?" As if she was to blame.

Jacinta rolled her eyes. "How would I know? She didn't even tell me she was going until yesterday."

Her short conversation with Kelly ran through her head like a movie trailer.

Kelly had been timid, almost embarrassed for accepting Angel's prom invitation, and that was a red flag to Jacinta. But she hadn't had the energy to question. She'd said only one thing to Kelly, "Don't play with Angel, Kelly. It could get ugly." The warning had sent Kelly sputtering into explanations about how she was going only as Angel's friend, feeling sorry for him, blah, blah. Jacinta hadn't bothered to inform Kelly that Angel was completely open over her, that he took any sign Kelly gave as hope they'd be more than friends. She hadn't bothered because it was becoming the same old, same old with those two, and Jacinta was sick of being in the middle. Yet here she was.

Raheem's angry voice reminded her of that. "I always knew she was a no-good trick. Just 'cause she boogee don't mean she ain't a trick."

Jacinta automatically defended her friend, realizing it was fuel to a growing fire the second she spoke. "She's not a trick, Heem."

Raheem fixed his mouth to argue, but was interrupted by Angel's surprised exclamation. "Ain't this a bitch? She not texting me back. Man, drive me over there."

"No!" Jacinta yelled so loud both boys stared at her, wide-eyed. "Look, Angel, I'm not trying to rub it in. But how many times have I told you to let that go? Kelly moved on. You need to."

"Then why she say she'd go?" Angel's voice brimmed with controlled fury. A small vein rose on his left temple, the only flaw on his smooth caramel-complexion face.

What he kept in check, Raheem let go with flourish. "'Cause she a dicktease." He continued to rail against Kelly as he pulled the car over to the side, to let other cars pass. "Angel, man, forget her. Taquila going to prom stag with Jolene. She be glad to see you solo." His chuckle had a nasty edge to it, making Jacinta's stomach knot. "And besides, she probably give a little brain. You know Kelly ain't."

Jacinta tried to hide her disgust at Raheem's snide comment. She reasoned once more, "Angel, I think she only said yes because she felt . . . pressured."

Angel and Raheem jumped all over that notion, talking at once.

"How she pressured just from a call?" Raheem rolled his eyes.

"She could have said no. It would have been swazy," Angel protested.

This time, Jacinta's eyes widened with skepticism. "Real talk, y'all." She looked between the two of them, then stared Angel in the eye. "How many times did you ask her before she finally said yes?"

"Once," Angel said, furrowing his brows in a challenge.

Jacinta's eyebrows rose. "Angel, okay, you're lying. Are you saying that last week when you made me tell you where the girl was on a date, you didn't mention prom?"

"He ain't force her," Raheem insisted.

"Heem, having your ex show up while you on a date to ask you to his prom might as well be force," Jacinta said. "And obviously, he called her after that, too."

"Whatever. She could have said no," Raheem said.

Angel's silence was enough for Jacinta. She knew Angel, and she knew he hadn't just simply asked and taken no for an answer. If he had, Kelly probably would have never said yes. Still, she clammed up. She wasn't going to win this in Raheem's eyes.

"Call her," Angel said quietly.

"Huh? Why?" Jacinta asked exasperated.

"Call her." Angel sat back calmly as if he were a celeb directing one of his personal assistants to pick all the green M&M's out of the packet. "Look, she's not answering my calls. She'll answer if you call from your phone."

"Angel," Jacinta pleaded.

"Cinny, just call her," Raheem pressed firmly but softly. "Just do Angel a solid, and ask Kelly why she flaking?"

Jacinta's fingers trembled from anger as she dialed. It always amazed her that Raheem could get mad at her about things that went down between Kelly and Angel. She felt bad for Angel, but he was the one refusing to let the girl go. He . . .

"Hello," Kelly's voice said.

"Kelly, hey. It's Cinny." Jacinta hunched her shoulders at Angel as if to ask, now what?

"Ask her what's up," Angel said, sitting up expectantly.

"Look, Angel wanna know why you flaking." Jacinta sighed, eyes rolling.

Kelly's voice lowered. "Can you hold on for a second?"

There was silence for a few seconds. Jacinta wondered if Kelly were by her grandmother or maybe someone else she didn't want hearing.

"What she say?" Angel barked.

Jacinta sucked her teeth, shushing him. She put her finger over the phone's tiny speaker. "Hold on."

When Kelly came back on, she spoke in her normal tone. Her words gushed out as if she didn't have a lot of time to go into details. "Cinny, I shouldn't have told him I'd go. I feel bad, but I feel worse because I was wrong for accepting anyway. I was hurt that Greg stood me up the other day. And when Angel called, I . . . I let him saying how much he wanted me to go to prom with him stroke me too much."

"What she saying?" Angel barked again.

"That she should have never said yes," Jacinta said, a clear "I told you" in her voice. She smashed the phone up to her ear to hear Kelly over Angel's mutterings.

"Tell her we coming over," Angel said, determined. He nodded at Raheem, and Raheem pulled the car into traffic.

"Kelly, look, Angel wants to come see you. Please talk to him and set things right," Jacinta said. Without waiting for an answer, she passed Angel the phone.

"Why you playing games?" Angel blared into the phone.

The car was silent as he listened to Kelly's response.

"Heem," Jacinta whispered. "Don't drive all the way over there. She said no; Angel needs to respect that."

"Cinny, don't sit here and talk about respect. What Kelly did is straight disrespectful." Raheem's nose flared. He kept the car heading toward the 'burbs of Del Rio Bay.

"What is going to her house gonna change?" Jacinta's voice calmly pleaded. "What if her grandmother's home? What? Are y'all gonna force the girl into the car and take her to prom?"

On her last sentence, Jacinta's voice rose, near hysterics.

Raheem glanced over at her, alarm on his face. For the first time, he seemed to process the begging in Cinny's eyes. He pulled the car into a grocery store parking lot, the last retail stop before going over the DRB Bridge.

Jacinta's heart slowed, grateful for the relief.

"Kelly, you act like I asked you run off cross-country with me," Angel was saying, his tone softened but still angry. "It's one night. Why you change your mind? Or did somebody change it for you?" Angel pulled the phone away from his ear. "Man, what you doing?" He put the phone back up to his head. "Naw, I'm talking to Raheem."

"Man, go 'head and handle your business," Raheem said. He turned the car off. "Me and Cinny wait outside."

Once they got out, Raheem leaned against the door, then remembering he was dressed to the nines, stood back up. Jacinta stood beside him, her dress blowing in the light breeze, tickling her thighs.

"Thank you," she said.

Raheem snorted, but his voice had lost a lot of its venom. "Like you said, it's not like Angel can make her go." He admired the car, his eyes soaking up the rims and high dollar paint job. "Man, this the kind of whip we gon' push when I go pro."

At the word we, Jacinta's relief morphed into dread. A boa constrictor squeezing her heart in its coils.

Raheem reached out and pulled her into an embrace. "You take the pregnancy test yet?"

She shook her head no against his chest.

"Why not?"

"I'm taking it tomorrow," Jacinta said.

"Well, we already know what we gonna name it if it's a boy. But what kind of girl names you like?" He chuckled. "We could mix our names together and call her Rahcinta."

Jacinta's heart galloped so fast she was surprised Raheem couldn't feel it. But he was lost in his name game.

"'Cause Jaheim is a boy's name . . . like the singer."

Jacinta kept her voice as neutral and soft as possible. "Can we talk about it later?" Feeling Raheem's body tense, she added quickly, "I haven't felt well all day. And this whole Kelly thing gave me a headache. I don't feel like thinking about anything, especially not baby names."

Raheem's eyes narrowed in that half closed way, but he nodded okay.

There was a knock on the window as Angel beckoned them back in.

When they were inside, he handed Jacinta her phone.

"So, what's up?" Raheem asked.

Jacinta put the passenger side mirror down to put on more lip gloss. She slyly watched Angel in the back. His shoulders hitched as he sat back, melting into the seat. He cocked one arm up over the empty seat beside him and put on what Jacinta knew was his hard face.

"Ay, I ain't chasing her," Angel said. "I already texted Taquila and told her keep that phat ass hot for me."

Raheem put his fist out for a pound. "I know that's right."

Even as Angel gave Raheem's fist a tap, Jacinta saw that his eyes were sad. Obviously, he'd had high expectations for tonight. Maybe some of them Taquila Gordon could satisfy, but not all of them. She felt bad for Angel. But mostly, she felt envy.

Kelly had cut Angel loose, and even though she'd almost gotten caught up in his web again, almost didn't count.

Tears stung Jacinta's eyes. She batted her eyelashes, fighting the flow furiously until they retreated.

The L Word

"Just let me set the mood right.
Let me make you feel alright."
—Justin Timberlake,
"Set the Mood Prelude/Until the End of Time"

"So is the surprise—that this cul-de-sac is hella scary when yours and JZ's houses are dark?" Mina said. "Because I already knew that." She hid her disappointment behind the joke.

Brian pulled her along by the hand. "Yeah, that's it."

Mina tipped slowly, her feet still sore. She looked wistfully down the dark road, wondering if the limo was too far gone to catch.

All the plucking and fluffing she'd endured was for what? For them to stay at prom for two hours and then come here?

She felt like crying.

What about all the afterparties they'd talked about in the weeks leading up to prom? Brian knew how badly she'd wanted to head to Kim's lakehouse luau.

They stepped into the empty house, and Brian keyed in the code to cut off the alarm. He walked back to Mina and wrapped his arms around her. She involuntarily sniffed in the last remnants of his cologne, a light nutty scent, as her head lay on his chest. Usually, she loved being so near him. But she was too irritated to feel soothed by his embrace.

Seething, Mina blurted, "This is the surprise? For real?" She stepped out of his hug, glaring. "We could chill here anytime, Brian. I wanted to roll through Kim's party."

The smile winked out of Brian's eyes like someone had snuffed out a candle.

"Hey, Mina, do you ever think sometimes you talk too much?" he asked, his voice flat.

"I'm just saying. It's prom night, and you know my parents are never gonna extend my curfew again." She rolled her eyes. "Not 'til my own prom, probably. I thought we were gonna flow all night?"

"You want me to call the limo back?" He pouted.

"If this is the surprise"—Mina's eyebrows arched—"yeah, call him back."

"Cool, then you ride back to the hotel and hang out with Wade and Stefan." He snorted. "I'm sure they hurling by now."

"Eww, you didn't have to say all that. And why would I go by myself?" Mina gestured to her dress, the hemline swaying with the movement. "I didn't go through all this to sit at your house. Or to go stag to the afterparties."

"Yup, you're right. I'll call him back." Brian slipped his cell out of his pocket and cruised through his numbers. He sounded like he did on the nights Mina only went ninety-nine percent of the way— pissed but trying to act like he wasn't. "Oh, go up to my room. You left your little white sweater here. You gon' need it if *you* chilling at Kim's."

"Well, are you coming with me?" Mina peered at him.

"Why would I? It's right on the door," Brian said. He turned his back and talked to the limo driver. "Ay, man, sorry 'bout this. But can you roll back over to the 371 Dogwood address?"

Mina stomped upstairs. Brian knew good and well what she'd meant when she'd asked was he going with her. This was stupid.

An argument on prom night. All because she wanted to hang out more. What was wrong with . . .

Her mouth fell open when she opened the door to Brian's room, which was aglow in shiny, bright glitter. At least it looked like glitter. But it was really reflections from the sparkly lamp, a squat, spaceship lamp with soft, white, iridescent plastic strawlike tentacles. It made shapes and soft colors on the walls like a disco ball, only less cheesy.

On a table set up in front of the window that overlooked the backyard, was a big bouquet of silver and sapphire balloons. A panda bear with I Love You in red letters sat up against the base of the balloons.

Mina walked to the table, mouth still gaping. A bowl of blue and silver M&M's were next to the bear. She peered closer. She'd never seen M&M's that color. She grinned at the writing. They said Mina and Brian on one side.

She jumped as Brian said, "So, *do* you ever get tired of being wrong?"

There was a smile in his voice.

"When did you do all this?" she asked, her eyes glued to the table of goodies. The lights swirled around them, giving the room a life of its own.

"It wasn't easy. My parents kept wanting to get a picture of me getting into the limo. I had to damn near beg them to meet me at your house so I could set this up." Brian laughed softly at the memory. "You should have seen me trying to hide those balloons in my closet. I got it done right before the limo came and got me."

"I love the M&M's," Mina gushed.

Brian plugged in his iPod, and soft music came from several speakers throughout the room.

"So you still wanna party hop?" Brian was behind her, his hands on her waist.

"Is the limo guy going to kill you for calling again?" Mina asked sheepishly.

"Nope. 'Cause I never called him." Brian dodged Mina's elbow aiming for his stomach. "But I will if you want. I just thought it would be nice to chillax alone. Not like we're really going to get that chance in O.C."

Mina nodded as she turned around and threw her arms around his neck.

"So, do you mean it?" she asked.

"That I'd call the limo guy if you wanna roll? Yeah."

Mina giggled. "No. This." She leaned over and picked up the panda, waving it in his face.

A tiny smiled played at the corner of Brian's mouth. "Well, *he* means it." He tapped the bear's tummy. "He loves you."

Mina elbowed Brian again, this time connecting, as she laid the bear gently back down on the table.

"Ow, those bony things hurt." Brian grabbed her elbow, slid his hand down her arm, and wrapped her arms around his waist. "Yeah, I mean it. I love you, toughie." He grinned down at her upturned face, then frowned. "What? A brotha gotta ask if you love him back?"

"No. I do love you," Mina said, her voice strong and certain. Liking the way the words rolled off her tongue, she said them again. "I love you."

Their lips met, parted, then met again over and over. Each time, the kiss was more drawn out, the pauses short and urgent as if they breathed better with their lips locked. Mina clung to Brian. Thanks to the heels, she didn't have to tiptoe to hug him around his neck. Her mind whispered that this time next year, he'd be at school, and she clung harder.

The Aftermath

"You got your eyes on me, I feel you watchin' me."
—Jay-Z, "The Watcher 2"

Later, she and Brian sat outside her house in his truck, talking, letting the minutes to her curfew tick slowly toward them.

He lifted her left hand and wiggled her pinky. "You flossin your ring?"

"Now, you know I'm not flashy." Mina grinned devilishly.

"Yeah, true. That's why I saw on your Facebook three different pictures of you posing so that it was dead in the camera. One of 'em had 'I'm so icy' as the caption."

They shared a laugh over that as Mina glanced at the clock.

She cracked her door open. "Alright. I'll see you in the morning." She leaned over, kissed Brian primly on the lips, and dashed.

When she opened the door and stepped inside the house, the shadow of Brian's headlights backing away sliced into the house's darkness. Minus a small light on in the kitchen, the house was in sleep mode.

Mina slipped her shoes off. She tiptoed lightly across the hardwood floors in her bare feet, marveling at how odd it was to walk into the house with her parents deep in slumber. At her normal curfew of 11:45, her parents were either still out themselves or up watching TV and talking. She'd usually spend a few minutes giving them a vague update—"we had fun tonight"—or sharing the less incriminating bits and pieces of some of the more outrageous stories.

But tonight, they'd kept the light on for her and moved on. Mina stood on the bottom step for a second, soaking in how it felt to be walking into the house at one AM. It was the next day, and she was just getting in.

Weird.

Humming quietly to herself, she eased into her room, which was aglow from her computer screen. She thought she'd turned it off before leaving. Frowing, she walked over to her desk to cut off the monitor when her mother's voice came from out of nowhere.

"Did you all have fun?"

A shot of pure terror zigzagged through Mina's heart.

The sandals fell from her hand and thumped to the floor.

"Oh, my God, Ma, you scared me." She bent to pick up the shoes with one hand, holding the other to her chest. Her mom sat on the bed, her back against the wall, her legs crossed at the feet. In the ghostly glow of the monitor, her mom's face looked angry.

Mina squinted, trying to focus, as she walked over to the bed. Turning off the monitor was forgotten. "We had a ball." Mina kept her voice hushed, not wanting her voice to carry and awaken her father. She plopped on the bed beside her mom and crossed her legs, glad for someone to share her prom details with. "They had the ballroom decorated really nice." She handed over one of the glowing stars to her mom. "Aren't these cute?"

Her mom glanced down at it before thrusting it back. "Um-huh."

Mina talked through the weird vibe coming from her mother. "It was ridiculous, Ma. Stefan and Wade got so drunk. And . . ."

"Were you and Brian drinking?" Her mother asked, never changing positions, tone, or facial expression.

Mina shifted uncomfortably. "No. It was just them, and their dates had a little."

"Did you and Brian stay at the prom the whole time?"

Mina's mind raced. Where was this going? Her mom knew they were going to a few afterparties, but since they hadn't gone, Mina wasn't sure how to answer. The spit in her mouth went MIA.

"No. We . . ." Her tongue made a strange clacking sound as she sputtered, "I mean Kim had her party and . . ."

"So you went to Kim's?" Mariah Mooney's eyebrow arched so tightly Mina dared not lie.

"No, not exactly," Mina said. Fear slowly oozed from her. Her mouth worked in an attempt to moisten her tongue. She plucked at her dress, unraveling a small thread. She twirled it between her fingers as her mother's tight voice lectured.

"Amina, you know nothing pisses me off more than a lie. If I ask you again, 'were you at prom the whole time?' you better be ready to answer with the full truth or say good-bye to your summer."

Mina swallowed hard. Her heart skittered erratically, one second thumping heavily, the next racing like a stone skipping over water.

"Now, I'm going to help you out." Mina's mom pushed herself off the bed. She walked over, shut the bedroom door, then sat at Mina's desk. "Let's start from the beginning. Are you and Brian sexually active?"

Mina's ears rang as if someone had boxed them.

Her mom's mouth moved, but Mina didn't hear a word. She put her right hand out and steadied herself on the bed, coming to when her mother said, "Did you hear me?"

Unable to find her voice, Mina merely shook her head no in admission.

She watched her mother squash a baleful glare. Within seconds, she'd gained enough patience to speak. Her voice was calm, but just short of "I want to wring your neck" anger. Mina knew the voice well. "I said I already know the answer to my question. Because of this."

Mariah swiveled around and pointed to the monitor. And that's when Mina saw it. She didn't even have to ask what it was or what it said. It was the thing she'd forgotten, the thing she knew she had to do before rushing off to prom that night.

An IM exchange between her and Brian.

What were the odds? What were the odds that she'd forgotten to exit out of the instant message? She never did that. Always, always after she'd finished a conversation, she exited. It was habit. A habit she'd gotten herself into because she'd heard too many horror stories from other people about getting busted that way.

Stupid.

It was stupid, stupid, stupid.

Worse, Brian should have been getting dressed instead of dallying around with her online. And that was Mina's fault—she had forgotten to turn on her Away message. The IM exchange should have never taken place. It was the perfect storm of idiotic mistakes.

From where she sat on the bed, she could see but not read the message. She didn't need to. She knew what it said:

BJBBoy: so do I gt 2 tap tht 2nite?

BubbliMi: crude much?

BJBBoy: my bad cn I put u 2 bed?

BubbliMi: LOL ok cn we be mre cliché? Sex on prom nt?! Very hallmark movieish

BJBBoy: naw cliché is 1st time on prom nt

BubbliMi: Aww gee, my mom wld b so prd 2 knw I'm not a cliché

BJBBoy: Proud mght b pshg it!

BubbliMi: 4 real! Go get dressed Mr. Nasty Talk. I'm bng summoned to gt my dress on

BJBBoy: gt a surprise 4 u 2nite

BubbliMi: I <3 surprises!!

BJBBoy: ur boy gon hook u up

BubbliMi: cnt w8

BJBBoy: L8r

Mina's body trembled lightly, and goose bumps broke out on her bare arms. Her mother's voice, choked with tears, made her rip her eyes away from the screen.

"How long have you guys been having sex?"

Mina's stomach roiled. She felt decidedly gross having this conversation. Still, she answered, knowing to be silent meant her mom's wrath or worse, her dad waking up and asking about the hubbub. "The first time was two weeks ago."

Her mother sighed. Mina couldn't tell if it was relief or resignation.

Mariah swiveled the desk chair away from the monitor and faced the bed. The anger that had been etched on her face was gone. But Mina wished it was back. She hated the utter sadness that had replaced it. Or maybe it was disappointment. There wasn't much difference at this point.

Her mom leaned over, resting her elbows on her thighs. The tears were gone from her face, but there was a sadness that threatened to break into tears at any second. Her voice was just above a whisper. "Maybe this is a foolish question, but why didn't you come and tell me?"

Mina looked at her as if she'd just asked how come Mina didn't place her hand in a roaring fire. "Ma, how was I supposed to tell you? Ooh, good news, me and Brian . . ." She shuddered, unable to finish.

"I meant, why didn't you tell me before it all happened? Let me know you were thinking of having sex with him?" Mina's mom snorted. "You can't even say the words 'had sex' out loud to me. If you're that embarrassed to talk about it, how in the world are you able to do it?" Her eyebrows did another sharp arch. "Or are you more comfortable having this talk with Brian?"

"It's not like we really talked about it," Mina mumbled. "It just happened."

Her mom's head shook vigorously. "No. These things don't just happen. And you're my child. I know you. You analyze just about everything, even if it's whether you're in the mood for pepperoni versus sausage on a pizza." She wagged her finger at Mina. "You didn't just do it. You might *believe* that it just happened. But you thought about it. Whether it was a few days, weeks, or months . . . you thought about it before it happened."

Mina kept her face blank, hating when her mother pulled the "I know you" card.

"We talk about a lot of stuff, Mina. Why not this?" Her mom's voice hitched again. "I always thought that I made it clear the door was open for us to talk about anything."

Mina uncrossed her legs and sat on the edge of the bed so she and her mother were only two feet apart. "If I had . . . I mean, you would have probably made me stop seeing Brian."

Mariah's shoulders heaved in a slow motion rise, then an abrupt fall. "You don't know that, Mina. I wouldn't have been happy, no. And I would have probably tried to talk you out of it. Brian's leaving soon. Even if he did give you that friendship ring, three hundred miles apart for days and months at a time is hard on a relationship. I would have told you that ring or not, there's no guarantee that you'll stay together. And yes, I would have said sex would only bind you up emotionally and make life harder for you." Mariah shook her head. "I like Brian. But, honey, once he's in school . . . he's going to live his life. And you should live yours."

Bile rose, hot and bitter, in Mina's throat. Tears streamed down her face. She wanted to cover her ears, make her mom go to bed, beg to have this discussion another time or never. But her tears brought on the tears her mother had been holding back, prolonging the conversation.

Mariah got up and sat beside Mina on the bed. She wrapped her arms around Mina, engulfing her in a hug, stroking her hair gently as she spoke. "I didn't mean to ruin your night with this talk. I knew we'd have it at some point . . . but I really thought you'd come and tell me before . . ."

"Are you going to tell Daddy?" Mina asked, the thought making her heart race. She kept her head on her mom's chest, listening to the answer in stereo as her mom's voice vibrated in her ear and above her head.

"Honey, I have to."

Mina's head shot up. "Mommy, no." Her tears poured. "Why?"

"Two reasons." Mariah tugged her back down gently, resuming her hair stroking. "One, because this isn't something I want to keep from your father. It could have all sort of ugly repercussions if he ever found out because of . . ." There was a frown in her voice. "Well, if something else led to him finding out. And second, because I'm not letting you go to O.C., and your father's going to want to know why."

Mina's head popped up again. She stared in her mother's eyes, mute.

The question at the tip of her tongue, the one she dare not ask was, "Am I being punished for having sex? Or because I didn't tell you?"

Her emotions clamored inside—anger at her mom, at herself. She was grossed out at the thought of her father knowing she'd had sex and scared for what this meant for her and Brian over the summer.

Mariah met Mina's angry, hurt gaze.

"Just so there's no question—if you had come to me and told me you were thinking about having sex, I would have tried to talk you out of it. But I'm not stupid, Mina. The decision is . . . was yours to make. But I would have also made sure you were protected against disease and pregnancy." Her eyes pierced Mina's as if she was trying to see into her head. "You all did use protection, right? And please don't lie."

Mina nodded, and this time her mom did sigh with obvious relief. Her eyes crinkled slightly in a weak smile.

"Well, there's that, huh?" she said, a bitter edge to her words.
Dabbing at her eyes, she held Mina's gaze. "You've put me in a bad
position, Mina. I don't want to feel like I can't trust leaving you and
Brian alone. But I don't want you to miss out on the last two months
he has before school. What do you think your punishment should
be?"

Mina's eyes narrowed with confusion. "For not telling or having
sex?"

Mariah chuckled wryly. "Let's just say for making an adult decision but for not being adult enough to face the issue with me."

Mina's shoulders popped. She picked at the unraveled thread in
her dress. Michael was going to kill her when he saw that.

"Do you and Brian need a chaperone every time you're together
now?" Mariah narrowed her eyes.

Mina had no answer. She felt sick. *Just do whatever. I don't even care
anymore,* she wanted to say. But she said simply, "I don't know. I
mean, I don't know what my punishment should be."

"What if I said not to do it anymore?" Mariah appraised her,
watching Mina's actions carefully. There was a chuckle in her voice,
like she knew this was the wackiest of all the options.

"I guess, if we're not allowed to see each other, that's about the
same thing," Mina said, pouting.

Mariah stood up. She opened her arms and waited until Mina
begrudgingly stood up and walked into them. Mariah hugged with
a vengeance. First, Mina only stood there. But soon, she wrapped her
arms around her mother, squeezing. The tears, from shame and relief, flowed again.

"Well, for now, the trip to O.C. is off. We'll discuss the rest later,"
her mom said.

"I'm sorry," Mina said.

Her mom quipped Mina's dad's favorite line, "For having sex or getting caught?"

"For getting caught," Mina admitted.

Her mom laughed softly. But Mina didn't. She held on to her mom, wondering how the night's vibe had changed so fast.

Consequences and Repercussions

"Nobody wanna see us together, but it don't matter."
—Akon, "Don't Matter"

Once her mom went to bed, Mina set her phone to silent and went on a texting spree.

For a spirit lift, she texted Lizzie first:

totally busted, my mom knows me n' Brian did it. Think lock-down infinity!

Next, she texted Brian:

cnt go 2mrrw ttly busted!

Then she texted Jacinta:

hope ur nite was bttr than mine

She sat on her bed, wrapped in a blanket cradling the phone; huddled over it in the pitch blackness of her room, gazing down, waiting for its backlight to shine, indicating a new message had come in.

OMG, so sorry. How'd she find out?????

From Lizzie.

Aww day-um. Call me

from Brian.
Mina typed back furiously.

cnt, house 2 quiet. It sux but basically I 4got to close out our IM frm earlier. Hmm . . . ur fault.

She chuckled at Jacinta's message:

Kelly stood up Angel, Angel tried to OD on phat azz, I wasn't in da mood 4 dancing n' Raheem hates Kelly said she ruined nght 4 ev'bdy. Top that!

She could top it, in her opinion. But she felt bad for Jacinta all the same. It was one thing to have a bad after prom night, but a bad prom night was the worst. She decided not to one-up Jacinta. Instead, she wrote back:

well looks like I'll b home w/u guys this wkend while Brian is in OC. Long story, tell u l8r.

Her phone glowed brightly in the night as the messages poured in. From Brian:

So I'm toast in the mooney household rt abt now, huh?

Jacinta:

how bout movie n' a preggers test? I'm taking it 2morrow. Cn u come over?

Mina zipped off her answer to Brian:

Oh yeah, totally toast. No worries I'll probably b punished til u graduate from Duke, by then they'll have 4gotten!

And to Jacinta:

if the 'rents let me. Yeah I'll definitely cme over.

She was surprised when Jacinta's response was:

see if Liz n' Kell will come 2. need girl power support!

Mina rubbed at her eyes. The words blurred on the tiny screen. She'd been up since six AM, and the day was finally coming down on her. She typed back to Jacinta that she'd hook up an afternoon pow-wow before bowing out of the exchange.

She quickly texted Lizzie the short version of being busted and was glad Lizzie never "I told you so'ed" her. Instead, Lizzie sent a long message:

bright sidin it 4 ya—the wrse tht cld hapn did. & rmbr u did 6 wks pnshment stdg on ur head lst yr. wht cld they thrw at u? summers only 8 wks. CAKE WALK

Mina smiled at Lizzie's philosophy, even though the thought of being punished all summer made her feel like she'd been fed through a paper shredder. Pretty appropriate since something told her her social life would be nothing but bits of confetti by August. Still, she made fun of herself in her message back to Lizzie:

the good news is, they probly will let me keep my phone and talk over the PC since phoneIM sex is better than real sex.

She and Lizzie exchanged a few bawdy jokes before Mina wrapped up the convo, asking Lizzie about meeting her at Jacinta's tomorrow around noon. Assured that Lizzie would call Kelly, she said her good nights and settled in for a final exchange with Brian.

Wht r u going 2 tell ur parents abt me not going now? She typed.

Keeping the phone cradled near her face, she lay down on the bed and closed her eyes a few seconds. The thought of facing her father in the morning and then one day having to face Brian's parents was the final gut punch, depressing her. Her eyes fluttered open in time to see the phone light up with Brian's response:

IDK u think ur mom will call mine?

Mina bolted upright. She hoped not. But she wasn't sure. Her mind was too tired to process it. She wrote back:

IDK jus tell 'em I got sick

She chuckled at his answer:

that beats telln' the truth. I'll think of something

The battery light on the phone blinked urgently. She wearily retrieved the charger from her desk and plugged it in just in time for Brian's last message.

Luv u, Toughie.

She texted back, I love u too. ttyl, then scrolled back to his last message, staring at it until her eyes refused to stay open.

At eleven the next morning, she awoke reluctantly. Sunlight streamed into her room, bouncing off her yellow walls, preventing any more sleep. She sat on the edge of her bed, smoothing down her bedhead, then crept to her door, opening it quietly.

She closed it again as the faint sound of her parents talking wafted up the steps.

The prospect of spending the entire day (weekend, even) in her room seemed the best option. Simply hide out until her parents had forgotten all about her devirginization. She dropped back down into bed and pulled the covers up to her chin, settling in for the long haul until her cell phone chirped.

"Hey," Mina said. She melted into the pillow, ready for girltalk.

"I can't do this by myself," Jacinta blurted.

Mina sat upright. "What?"

"This stupid test. Can y'all come over now while I take it?"

"Now?" Mina asked. Jacinta sounded distant, as if she wasn't holding the phone all the way to her mouth. Mina had to squash the phone to her ear. Even then, she could hear the desperation in Jacinta's voice.

"Yeah. Did you ask Kelly and Lizzie already?"

"Yeah. But I need to let them know you want us over now." Mina kicked the covers off. "Let me call them. We'll be over soon."

She hung up, then hastily three-wayed the girls. They promised to meet at Jacinta's within the hour. Mina grabbed a retro brown Scooby Doo tee shirt and brown and pink plaid Bermudas. She slapped her hair into the Pomeranian ponytail and headed to the bathroom. She spent the better half of thirty minutes, lathering slowly, working up the nerve to face her father.

After giving herself a pep talk—you can face him, you can do it. He's always the good cop, remember? You've been through the worst with the late-night mom lecture—she headed down the stairs cautiously, as if expecting someone to pounce on her at the bottom.

Sounds of the TV coming from the sunroom floated inside the empty kitchen. She took a deep breath, crossed herself, and walked on unsteady legs into the sunroom.

Her parents sat on the large sectional, the daily newspaper spread out everywhere around them. She swallowed hard, cleared herself a spot, and sat down between them.

"Well, good morning. The dead has risen," her father said. He leaned his cheek in for a kiss, and Mina obliged. "Good time last night?"

Mina nodded. She waited, bracing herself for her dad to say something about virginity, disappointment, or punishment for life. But he went back to watching sports highlights.

Mina cleared her throat. "Can I go see Cinny?"

Her father's eyes stayed on the TV, but she saw his eyebrows rise. He remained silent.

"For what?" her mom asked, bringing the paper down from her face long enough to give Mina a look that spoke volumes.

"She's . . . prom wasn't . . . she and Raheem are having problems, and she's . . . she could really use a friend right now." Mina cracked her knuckles. "She called and asked if me, Kelly, and Lizzie could come over."

"Just the girls?" her dad asked. "Or is this one of those the-boys-plan-to-drop-in-later things?"

Mina shook her head. "No. She sounded really sad on the phone. I think she needs someone to talk to."

Mariah's eyebrows neared their arch of disapproval. She muttered, "Too many boyfriend problems for me," before folding the paper. "Jack, can you turn the TV off for a second?"

Her husband obliged.

Here it comes, Mina thought. A thick patch of heat moved from her face to her neck. She looked straight ahead at the now black TV.

"Remember we talked about you getting a job when you got your license?" her mom asked.

Mina scowled, trying to connect the odd question to her pending punishment.

"Well, now's a good time as any to get one. Your father and I think, once school's out, you need to go ahead and start working," Mariah said.

"But I thought you wanted me to wait until September so I could drive myself," Mina said. "You said you didn't feel like having one more thing to schlep me to."

"Well, we drive you to everything else," her father said gruffly. "This won't be any more driving than usual."

"We don't want you spending the whole summer sitting around the house or thinking you're going to be out every day at one of your friends," her mom said.

Or having sex with Brian, Mina added silently.

She'd known she was going to have to work this school year. Had even picked out where she was going to apply, Seventh Heaven. But that was fall, when any employer would have to work around her school and cheer-other activities schedule. If she got a job this summer, she'd likely be working every weekend, all the sucky late shifts during the week and never getting to . . . see Brian. Which was the point, of course.

My punishment, she thought with glum realization.

She slumped down in the sofa. She wanted to scream, "It's not fair, it's not fair. You said September."

She couldn't believe her parents were actually willing to go against their own adamant ruling just to keep her and Brian apart.

"What? Is it not fair that you have to give up your summer to work?" her dad asked, reading her mind. He stared her in the eye. And for the first time since she'd sat down, Mina saw the same disappointment in his eyes she'd seen in her mom's.

She squirmed. "No. I just . . . this was going to be my last summer off. I didn't think I'd have to work."

"Yeah, well, we didn't think we'd have to help fill your time," Mina's mom snapped. Her voice softened. "You were going to be working by September anyway. So it's not totally out of the blue."

Yeah, right, Mina thought, nodding in response.

"I'll go apply at Seventh Heaven, if someone takes me. Sara said they're hiring now." Mina looked from one parent to the other as they nodded approval. She waited a few minutes, letting the silence of the room serve as a subject-changing pause, then said, "Can I go see Cinny?"

"Yes," her mom said. She picked the newspaper back up, then brought it down with a rattle. "Keep your phone on. We'll probably head out to eat or something later."

"Okay," Mina said, feeling like a chastised child. So this is what it was going to be like—them dictating her every movement, scheduling her every second, at least until Brian was off to Durham.

She pushed herself off the sofa, anxious to make her exit. If energy was a physical thing, the energy in the sunroom was swirling angrily above their heads now, threatening to crack into a T-storm at any minute.

Her father was acting normal, but not normal. Her mom's tone and facial expressions kept changing from neutrally pleasant to near anger. It was as if they were struggling not to mention the virginity thing while also being clear she was being punished for it. It was all very "he who must not be named" making for a thick, bewildering tension.

Tears itched her eyes. She turned to scramble away when her father, being normal again, caught her by the wrist. "No kiss?" His thick eyebrows arched softly, giving his maple syrup-complexioned face the look of a friendly grizzly bear.

In that instant, the tension melted once more. Mina leaned in and pecked him on the lips. Smiling, he popped her on the butt with the remote and flicked the TV back on. Mina walked over, planted a kiss on her mom, then made her getaway.

Positively Negative

"The monkey on your back is the latest trend."
—The Moldy Peaches, "Anyone Else but You"

The girls crammed into the hall bathroom at Jacinta's. The bathroom wouldn't have fit another person in it if they had tried.

Jacinta sat in the tub.

Lizzie sat on the commode, a picture of patience, as Mina stood behind her, curling her hair. Kelly sat cross-legged on the floor, a large bin in her lap, its contents of hair products spilled all over the floor. A curler warmer sat in the middle of the floor. Its cord snaked up toward the sole outlet behind the sink.

Mina slid the curler to the very end of Lizzie's hair, then swiftly rolled the huge, bristly cylinder into place, patting it to double-check it would stay put. She held her hand out, and Kelly laid another warm curler in her hand.

She went about the business of curling Lizzie's hair like someone with a lot of experience, instead of someone simply trying to take her mind off real life.

There was no evidence that anything other than a girly gathering was taking place, unless Jacinta, sitting in the tub, hugging her knees to her chest, staring down at a little plastic wand that looked like a thermometer, counted.

She'd been staring down at the test for twenty minutes.

Mina glanced over at Jacinta, biting the urge to scream, "Just take it. Take it."

Her hands shook, making the curler lopsided. She rerolled it once, twice, five times before it was straight, then took a calming breath to slow the tremor in her fingers. Sliding the tail of the comb through Lizzie's hair, she took a thin segment of blond hair, combed it more than it needed, and let the movement relax her.

Her hands slowed down, and her mind followed.

"Kell, did you and Greg have fun bowling last night?" she asked.

"Yeah. It was a bunch of us. How'd you know?"

Lizzie raised her hand.

"I can't believe you went straight cold turkey on Angel," Mina said, no judgment in her tone.

Kelly's face, lips tight, eyes soft, was a mix of regret and relief. She pulled out a large curler and handed it to Mina. "I have a hundred text messages from him just from last night."

"Shoot, only a hundred?" Jacinta muttered.

Mina shook her head. "A hundred? Good thing you have unlimited."

They tittered nervously.

"Kelly, don't be offended," Lizzie said. She turned her head slightly and glanced over and down at Kelly until Mina nudged her head back the right direction. "But this time, stay broken up."

"I feel like crap that I stood him up, but . . ." Kelly cut her eyes nervously to Jacinta in the tub. "It felt so nice hanging out with Greg. Am I a bad person because I kind of like a guy who doesn't come with so much . . ."

"Drama," Mina said.

"Baggage," Lizzie piped in.

"Stress?" Jacinta looked at Kelly's head, nodding to all three answers. "The way you flaked yesterday was bad. But I'd be lying if I said I was mad. You did the right thing."

"If Greg hadn't shown up, would you have gone?" Mina asked.

She patted at the curlers that made Lizzie's head three times bigger than normal.

"Probably," Kelly said. "And I would have ended up—"

"Like me," Jacinta said. She scowled at their surprised faces and waved the plastic wand. "I didn't mean sitting here, holding a pregnancy test."

They giggled nervously at the mention of the reason they were there.

"I just meant trapped," Jacinta said.

"You feel trapped with Raheem?" Lizzie asked. "Then break up . . . I mean, for good this time."

Jacinta placed her chin in her knee. "I know it sounds like it's that easy, but it doesn't feel like it. I mean, I already broke up once, and . . . even when he leaves for school, if I'm . . ." She waved the wand again. "It's like no matter what, we're Raheem and Cinny. Cinny and Raheem."

Her voice lowered, forcing the girls to lean in to hear.

"Maybe we *are* just meant to be together. And I'm fighting a losing battle." She flipped the wand in the air lightly and caught it with one hand. "Maybe this is a sign."

Lizzie's eyebrows knitted into a unibrow. "Cinny, it doesn't mean that. I know Mina is all fanatical about signs." Her heavy head wobbled as she turned around and smiled at Mina. "Not saying that's wrong, Mi. But everything isn't a sign. Your period's late or missing or whatever. But that doesn't mean you're supposed to be with Raheem *forever.*"

The girls jumped, gasping when Jacqi, standing in the hallway, said, "Jacinta, this is only a sign that you guys were careless or used faulty contraception." She moved to the doorway, closing in the already crowded bathroom. "Stop all this madness. Go into my bathroom, and take the test. I let you wait for your friends. They're here. Now go."

The girls went back to their hair curling, averting their eyes.

They weren't used to anyone cowing Jacinta. It was like watching a heavyweight fighter take a good hit to the chin.

Jacinta stood up, her face stoic, and stepped out of the tub. She climbed over Kelly. Her Aunt Jacqi took a step back and let her pass.

A few seconds later, a door down the hall shut, and the house grew silent.

"Miss Jacqi?" Mina said. She finally gave up cramming more curlers onto Lizzie's head and leaned up against the sink. "Cinny said she's on the pill. So how . . . I mean, when you said faulty contraception, do you think that's what happened? The pills were bad?"

Jacqi folded her arms. She stared down the hall at the closed door as she talked. "I don't know. More than likely, Jacinta skipped some and got thrown off."

"I'm sorry, but that freaks me out," Lizzie said. She stood up and had to get help from Mina for balance. "Pregnant on the pill?" She shuddered.

"I guess if she is, the baby will have lots of aunties," Mina said thoughtfully, looking from Lizzie to Kelly.

Jacqi snorted. "And I'll be sure to call one of y'all when the baby is crying at three AM."

She took a few steps toward her bedroom. The girls jumped at her voice, shrill with anxiety, "Cinny, you're not still just staring at that thing, are you?"

Jacinta's voice came back muffled. "No."

"Well, then come on. What does it say?" Jacqi said.

Her nervous energy infected the girls.

Kelly stood up, gathering hair products. A can of hair spray fell out of her full hands and hit the ceramic floor with a clatter.

"Sorry," Kelly said, scrambling to pick up the can and mistakenly overturning the bin of hair accessories.

Mina bent over, picking up the scattered curlers, pins, and rubber bands, and bumped into Lizzie, who lost her balance and nearly fell over the toilet.

Jacqi shook her head at their bumbling.

"You girls—" she started but abruptly trailed off when Jacinta appeared at her side in the bathroom doorway.

Jacinta stepped into the crowded bathroom and threw the plastic wand onto the basin. "Well, that's that," she said, leaning against the wall.

Mina moved and sat on the tub. She patted the empty spot by her side. Jacinta joined her.

The four girls sat in a square, Lizzie's knees practically touching Mina's, all three of them looming over Kelly as she remained on the floor.

Jacqi stared at the basin from the doorway.

"Well?" Lizzie asked.

Jacinta flipped open her cell phone. "I'll know in exactly two minutes."

"Okay, seriously, why do these things take so long?" Mina whined.

Lizzie chuckled. "Mi, three minutes isn't long."

"I don't care if it's positive or not. I'm not going to lose my mind over this," Jacinta said. She looked up at her aunt for reassurance. Jacqi gave her a thin smile before resuming her stare off with the sink.

Jacinta followed her gaze. She eyed the basin wearily, then recoiled slightly as if expecting a snake to slither its way out of it. She kept talking, never taking her eyes off the basin. "I'm just not. I know three girls from The Cove who got pregnant when they were only thirteen." She chuckled wryly. "I'm a late bloomer compared to them."

No one shared in her laughter, and the silence broke her resolve momentarily. "What? I wasn't even gonna take this test except my aunt made me. I told you." She looked at Mina. "I don't feel pregnant. I'm *not* pregnant."

Her voice cracked. She took a deep breath and closed her eyes. When she opened them again, for a second, the normal Cinny shone through as she jokingly chastised the girls. "And no matter what the test says, don't go getting all dramatic on me, bobblehead 'burb girls. Seriously."

"Well, it wouldn't be the end of the world," Jacqi said robotically. She frowned as if realizing she'd spoken aloud.

Lizzie shot a look at Mina, her crinkled brow saying what she didn't: "Yeah, it would be."

Jacinta closed her eyes again, seeming to gather strength in the darkness of her mind.

"Is it time yet?" Mina asked. She stood up, reaching over Lizzie to get the test from the basin. It slid into the sink. "Oh, my God. I'm sorry, Cinny."

Mina tripped over Kelly and a stray jar of hair gel getting to the sink. She plucked the test gently from the sink, holding it between her fingers like it was a delicate instrument.

"Don't worry, Princess. You won't get pregnant just from touching it," Jacinta said.

Mina snorted. "I hope me knocking it off didn't mess up the results."

Jacinta held out her hand. "Don't think it works like that."

Mina dropped it into Jacinta's palm, then sat back on the tub, asking again, "Is it time yet?"

Jacinta looked down at her cell phone. She nodded that it was time.

"Okay, on the count of three, let's all look at it together," Mina said, seeing terror in Jacinta's face.

Jacqi watched the girls' ritual from the door, her brown face a rubbery look of pained anxiety.

"Why three?" Jacinta asked. The test, facedown, was pinched between her fingers like the world's fattest needle.

"Five then," Kelly said, leaning in.

"Five, three, let's just count." Mina scowled down at the test.

"Three," Lizzie said primly. "Ready?"

Jacinta nodded. She closed her eyes and let out another deep breath.

"Ready."

"One," Lizzie started. She looked at Mina and Kelly, beckoning them to join.

"Two . . . three," they chorused.

Jacinta turned the test over, and all eyes stared at the results window.

A distant humming came from the kitchen as the bathroom grew silent.

Jacinta's eyebrows furrowed. She looked up at her aunt. "What does it mean if the line is sort of visible? I mean, it's not one hundred percent there, but you can see a shadow almost." She looked expectantly at Jacqi. "It means negative, right? Because you can barely see it. It's not a solid line."

The anxiety on Jacqi's face crumbled into worry creases, making her face even more masklike.

"But it's hardly there. See." Jacinta leaned up and shoved the wand over to her aunt.

The girls stared at Jacqi, waiting for an answer. Lizzie grabbed the test's directions off the sink and translated them aloud. "It says even if the indicator line is faint, you could be pregnant . . ." Her voice fell, disappointed, as she finished. "And to take again."

"No, but I mean, look at this line." Jacinta got up, stumbled over Kelly, and pointed at the test. She was pleading, near tears. "I mean it's barely there. Right? That doesn't count as an actual line."

"Let's just make you a doctor's appointment. Okay?" Jacqi handed Jacinta the test back. She put her arm around Jacinta's shoulders and gave her a squeeze. "I'll call first thing Monday."

Jacqi headed back downstairs, leaving bewildered silence in her wake.

Jacinta slumped against the wall in the hallway and slid into a sitting position. Her eyes remained glued to the plastic wand.

The girls finished cleaning up quietly, at a loss for words.

Epilogue:
Blessings & Curses

"Damn all these beautiful girls,
they only want to do your dirt."
—Sean Kingston, "Beautiful Girls"

It would be another two weeks before a doctor confirmed what Jacinta knew (hoped-prayed)—she wasn't pregnant. She waited a grand total of five minutes after walking out of the doctor's office before she started her told you so's, texting Raheem and the clique to announce that she'd been right all along. The whole thing was some mishap with her birth control. The doctor prescribed her a new one, mandated condom use, and sent her on her way.

Her grin covered her entire face. She leaned her head back on the seat and breathed in the freedom of summer, of the tests results, of the countdown before Raheem headed to Georgetown University. She closed her eyes, letting the hot sun bake her honey skin golden.

As soon as she got home, she was heading to JZ's. He was teaching her how to swim, even had her getting up at the crack of dawn to condition with him some mornings.

Her smile broadened.

It was hard for anyone, including her, to believe she was giving up her summer mornings to exercise. But she loved every painful minute of it.

Because she'd dodged a bullet. She knew it, felt it in every pore.

She was getting a second chance to do things right, to choose a path for herself.

And she wasn't going to waste it holding on to old fears.

"Well, somebody's happy," her aunt Jacqi said.

Jacinta nodded, not wanting to break the spell of the sun's warmth on her closed lids. But her aunt broke it for her.

"So, we need to tell your father."

Jacinta's eyes flew open. "Why? I wasn't pregnant. Why do we have to tell him?"

She breathed a sigh of relief when her aunt said, "We don't *have* to tell him." And she was about to thank her when Aunt Jacqi finished, "But we're *gonna* tell him."

Jacinta stared at her aunt as if she'd just proclaimed herself Queen of England. Her mouth worked soundlessly as her thoughts raced, refusing to come together in a coherent plea.

"This little scare took place while you were living with me. I'm not hiding it, or he might take it wrong," her aunt said. She glanced away from the road and over at Jacinta. "And also, you and Raheem need a little break. Maybe Jamila and the boys can come visit you at my place on weekends for a while. I think you have too much idle time when you go home."

Jacinta snorted softly. "That's cool with me."

She gazed away from her aunt's surprised expression and out the window.

"Technically, this is just like female stuff, Aunt Jacqi," Jacinta said. She kept the panic at bay by speaking quietly and calmly. "It wasn't even like I was pregnant. It was the pills."

She found herself nodding along with her aunt's bobbing head, pleased they agreed. Her heart slowed its gallop.

"You're right, and that's what you can tell your father," her aunt said matter-of-factly. "When you tell him."

★ ★ ★

One hundred twenty.

Kelly looked down at the text from Angel, the one hundred twentieth text from him today. It was only eleven o'clock in the morning.

He's just getting started, Kelly thought bitterly.

"Who dat?" Greg quizzed her playfully. He touched her knee lightly, grinning, his eyes hidden behind a pair of Aviators.

"One of those stupid service texts," she said, lying easily and feeling bad for it.

But Angel wasn't going to mess this up for her, even though his presence slithered around Kelly, waiting for just the right moment to squeeze. She turned the phone to silent, determined to be done with Angel's text assault but unsure how.

The night she and Greg became an official couple, she'd 'fessed up about prom night. He'd forgiven her when she promised that was the end, said he wasn't worried about her past.

Kelly wanted to feel the same way. But the past wouldn't stay there if Angel could help it.

She hadn't told anyone, not even the girls, that Angel continued to text her hundreds of times a day. The messages bounced between pleading and abusive, then apologetic and confused as to why Kelly was being such a "bitch."

No amount of apologies or reasoning from Kelly penetrated Angel's agitation.

Nothing she said convinced him that her saying yes had been nothing more than a terrible lapse in judgment.

Nothing.

Most days she left the phone home, pleading forgetfulness when Grand or the clique reamed her out for not answering their calls. She glanced down at the phone as it lit up, another message from Angel.

"I'm going to the concession stand. Want something?" Greg asked.

Kelly shook her head. She waited until Greg hotfooted it across the burning sands of Cimara beach before snatching the phone up and glaring at it. The backlight continued to blaze as another message came in.

At that moment she hated the phone passionately, as if it were Angel himself.

She wondered briefly if the incoming call was Mina. She was supposed to call when the clique was on their way. But all Kelly saw was Angel's messages, his number time after time. Even if Mina called, her missed call would be buried by his.

She hugged her knees to her chest, gripping the phone. She gazed around the crowded beach, wanting the frivolity of the beachgoers to inject her with some happiness. But the phone sat in her hand like a lead weight, forcing her deep into the throes of anger and frustration.

As if sensing it, she looked down just in time to see another message from Angel. Her eyes scurried away but not fast enough. She'd read it.

Kelly 4real just let me holler at u for a minute. Don't do me like this.

She shot up off the beach blanket and ran across the hot sand to the water's edge.

Tears stung her eyes, making her feel like she was underwater. She gripped the phone tightly, feeling her pulse beating against it. The phone felt alive. Her stomach rolled.

With as much force as she could muster, she pitched the phone deep into the Del Rio Bay. And watched, willing the phone to float away, go away, leave her alone. The waves sucked it in. It disappeared for a second, then reappeared atop the crest of a wave before plopping back under, gone for good.

She swiped at the tears, drying her eyes, and forced a smile on her face.

She was starting over.

It was gone. He was gone. She was starting over.

Mina eyed the clock on the cash register with suspicion. No way it was only eight-thirty. That's what time it had been when she'd last checked, and that was at least five minutes ago. At least.

She pushed the sleeves of her light blue Henley up to her elbow and grabbed the vacuum, determined to force the time to move. She rolled it to the front of the store, staking out a spot in the middle of the entrance, the better to see the happs in the rest of the mall, what little there was to see in the night's dwindling traffic. There were a few women, probably in their thirties, heading into Victoria's Secret—hot night out lingere shopping—and an older couple window-shopping for shoes next door.

In contrast to the quiet scene of the corridor, music thumped powerfully from the DJ stationed in Seventh Heaven's front window. Meant to create a club atmosphere and keep customers pumping out the cash as the music bumped in their chests, at eight-thirty on a Friday in June, the teen girls who would normally storm Seventh Heaven were at beachside bonfires, swim parties, or sharing a slice of pizza at Rio's Ria. Vic, the DJ, was as lonely as Mina, but not nearly as bored. His long, lean body twisted and popped to the beat, his head perpetually bent into the right headphone so he could hear his mixes. When boredom set in, he challenged himself to change up the beat, keeping the store alive with rhythm, even when it was empty.

Vic, never Victor, was a junior hottie from Sam-Well. Every other Friday and Saturday, when he spun records at Seventh Heaven, he became DJ V. Mina had always figured it stood for Vic, but he said it was for Vanish because his mixes were so smooth, the transition from one song to the next was nearly invisible. She'd found that out on a Friday, of course. Shift supervisors always got to pick their crew, and any time Jessica Johnson worked a Friday, Mina worked a Friday. Jess had taken that whole "keep my friends close but my enemies closer" saying to a ridiculous level. Their frenemyship, alive and healthy in its fifth year, continued its odd, awkward journey, smoothed out by Mina's genuine friendship with Jess's twin, Sara. Had Jess had the early Friday shift instead of the late, Sara would be here, too. But Friday nights only required a shift sup, the DJ, and one other worker.

Mina's eyes swept the store for signs of Jessica. Seeing none, she plugged in the vacuum. It was too early to vacuum, and she knew it. But the store was empty, and at nine PM, with her folding and floor cleaning done, she was going to dip. Brian was heading to Atlanta with his dad the next day, and every second between getting off work and her curfew, she planned to be with him. Every single second.

"You know you wrong," Vic called from the corner. His teeth shone bright in his handsome, deep dark brown face.

Mina raised her finger in front of her mouth in a shh, and Vic mimed zipping his lips.

She revved up the vacuum, and its growl mixed with Vic's thumping bass.

As the vacuum glided over the already clean floor, Mina did what she did often during Seventh Heaven shifts—think.

She had thought having to work was going to curse her summer, but it hadn't. She wasn't looking forward to August fifteenth, but work kept her too busy, so she wasn't obsessing over it, either. And Brian was traveling so much with his dad for his dad's job, even when Mina wasn't working, he was gone more than he was home.

If their parents were trying to get them used to a long-distance romance, they were doing a good job.

The lemonade was that she and Lizzie were closer than ever. Todd was in Cali and would be until July. So it was almost like back in middle school when even with busy schedules, she and Liz always found time to hang out.

Sometimes, Lizzie dropped Mina off to work on her way to her rehearsal. Or she'd pick Mina up from work after a show. Or, on a rare day off for both of them, they'd hit the beach with the clique, Lizzie sunning, Mina shading under the umbrella, catching up. Mina lamenting, yet not hating, life working with Jessica Johnson; Lizzie sharing some wild tale from Todd's adventure on the left coast.

As Mina vacuumed, lulled by the machine's easy glide across the floor, she had no way of knowing it was the summer they'd never forget. Not for the bonfires, midnight swims, or Ria reunions. Not even for the late-night phone calls of whispered "I miss you's," or hundreds of text messages to stay in touch with one another.

They'd remember this summer because it would set the stage for a junior year of hurtful revelations, broken allegiances, and foolish impulses.

The last summer the clique would remain intact.

A READING GROUP GUIDE

WHO YOU WIT'?
A Del Rio Bay Novel

PAULA CHASE

ABOUT THIS GUIDE

The following questions are intended to
enhance your group's reading of
WHO YOU WIT'?
by Paula Chase

DISCUSSION QUESTIONS

1. Mina and Lizzie's friendship continues to endure despite the various paths they choose. How much should friends' differing opinions on things like sex impact a friendship? A lot? A little? Explain your answer.

2. Each of the girls has a very different type of relationship with her boyfriend. Which relationship do you like the most? Which do you like the least? Which type of relationship do you think you'd most likely end up in?

   Mina and Brian's stable yet constantly evolving relationship?
   Kelly's volatile but never dull relationship with Angel?
   Jacinta's loyal but rocky relationship with Raheem?
   Lizzie's fragile but fresh and new relationship with Todd?

3. Was the abstinence pact something that Lizzie should have discussed with Todd first? Or was it her decision to make free and clear? Is it something that you feel you could comfortably discuss with a guy you're growing closer to?

4. If you wanted to abstain from sex in a relationship and the guy didn't, should you bother to try to make the relationship work?

5. Raheem was surprisingly supportive of the possibility that Jacinta was pregnant. But Jacinta didn't see this as a good thing. Was his support and her reaction to it a surprise to you?

6. Jacinta is constantly torn about her relationship with Raheem. How far should her loyalty go when it compromises her own happiness? How can she get out of the relationship and move on?

7. In a sense, Mina was pressured to have sex with Brian because of her fear that he was seeing someone else. Do you agree with Mina's decision to have sex with Brian? Why or why not?

8. Kelly allowed her ego to make the decision about going to the prom with Angel and it backfired on her. Why do you think she kept Angel's increasingly frantic text messages from her friends? What would you do in that position?

Resources

www.sexetc.org—a site for teens by teens about sex education. Includes resources on relationships, teen sex, teen pregnancy, and sexually transmitted diseases.

www.stayteen.org—facts on dating, relationships, waiting, breaking up, and more.

Stay tuned for the next book in this series:
FLIPPING THE SCRIPT
Available in April 2009 wherever books are sold.
Until then, satisfy your Del Rio Bay craving
with the following excerpt from the next installment.

ENJOY!

The Gang's All Here

"You gon' make us both get into some things
that'll scare grown folks."
—David Banner ft. Chris Brown, "Get Like Me"

I*t's just like old times,* Mina felt like shouting as the clique chilled in JZ's family room. Sitting at the juice bar with Brian, she surveyed the usual chaos, soaking in every ounce of the energy emanating from her friends. Her heart fed off it.

If it weren't for the fir tree in the far corner, a reminder that Christmas was days away, Mina would swear they were reliving a summer night. Todd, Michael, and JZ on the sectional sofa playing Madden, talking smack, insults, and obscenities; Jacinta flitting between plucking with JZ (a happy intrusion to his game that he would have never allowed a year ago) and conversing with Lizzie and Kelly at the arcade-sized Pac-Man game. Greg, standing with the girls, guiding them through each level's danger spots as he waited his turn at the "real" gaming on the sofa.

Greg went with the flow like he'd been friends with all of them forever, fitting in easily since he and Kelly had become an official couple over the summer.

Mina knew if JZ or Michael brought a girl around, it would hardly be as nice a match. And they must have known it, too, because neither of them ever had.

Not that me and the girls wouldn't accept her, Mina thought, checking herself. The fact was, guys seemed to find things to bond over, while girls seemed to focus on the differences.

Brian pulled her stool flush against his, forcing Mina's attention back to him. She draped her legs over his to prevent them from being crushed by the bar stools. His hands cuffed her sides as he leaned in, closing off their part of the room with his intimate stare and seductive grin.

"Did you miss me, toughie?"

"Nah," Mina said, unable to keep a straight face. An explosion of "aw man" went off from the couch, but Mina barely heard. Brian kissed her gently, pulled back and, in a voice that melted her heart, said, "I missed you."

Her heart trotted as Brian kissed her again, this time longer, his hands pressing against her hips as he leaned in closer. Mina's head swam. She and Brian hadn't been this close since August. If you didn't count the few times she'd watched him play basketball on television, it had been four months since they'd seen each other. The time apart had been all text messaging and phone calls. She kept her phone on so much, she'd worn out two batteries already.

Oh my God, I'm swooning, she thought, giddy, and to prove it, lost her balance when Brian eased his hold on her hips.

"Mmm, good hands," she murmured when he rested his hand on the small of her back to steady her.

"Un-huh." A playful smile lit up his face. "What you know about how good my hands are?"

"A little sumpun, sumpun," she said shyly, dumbstruck by his presence.

He was really here, home with her again. She quickly zapped the bothersome side note whispering in her ear that he was only home for a week before heading back to school. Instead, she stared into his face, taking in the way his long eyelashes framed his friendly brown eyes, wanting to make sure the moment was real. Being up close, very close, to her delight, she saw he looked different, somehow older and more mature. A clean thin line of facial hair framed a more square jaw, and his eyes seemed wiser, like he knew things.

How can that happen in four months? she wondered, content to sit there inches from his face, his hands lightly stroking her backside.

His left hand kept up the gentle stroke as his right hand lifted Mina's left hand. His thumb rubbed the silver heart-shaped ring on her finger. He grinned. "Just checking."

Mina's brows furrowed. "You thought I was going to stop wearing it?"

"You know how y'all chicks do." Brian's thumb played with the promise ring he'd given her, twisting it around her finger slowly. He gazed at her, his eyes narrowing as if probing into Mina's mind. "You probably just put it on 'cause you knew I was coming home. I need to do one of those spot inspections on you one day . . . catch you off guard."

Mina chuckled. "And if you do, you're gonna be all burnt 'cause I'll have it on." Her heart did a small happy dance when Brian squeezed her hand lightly and winked. "Shoot, I wish you *would* come home one day on the fly."

He dropped her hand, then gently resumed massaging her lower back. "Yeah, but you know that's not gonna happen. The season gears up for real after break."

"Yeah, I know." Mina frowned. "Am I gonna see you at all?"

"Nope. Not until school ends." He pulled her closer so they were face-to-face, practically sharing his stool. "So you know what that means, right?"

Mina pushed his chest and feigned pulling away. "Don't even say something nasty."

His face fell in exaggerated offense. "I wasn't."

"Yes, you were," Mina said, chuckling. She gave up her weak resistance, resumed their face-to-face stance, and put on her best wary tone. "What? What does that mean, Brian?"

"It means I only have a couple days to tap that ass, so . . ." He threw his hands up as if to say, "What's up?"

He burst out laughing and tugged at Mina as she played mad, pulling away.

"See, I knew you were gonna say something rude," she said, untangling herself.

He grabbed at her, trying to pull her back, but she quickly slipped out of his grip and stood beside his stool.

"Just for that, I'm making you wait," she said, even as her body grew warm thinking about being alone with him.

"Don't be like that, toughie," he said, laughing.

He swiveled in the stool so she was standing between his legs. He wrapped his arms around her and she instinctively put her face up to his for the kiss she knew was coming . . . then pulled back, smiling.

"Still making you wait," she teased before walking off to join the girls and Greg at the Pac-Man game.

"You so wrong for that," Brian yelled after her.

Mina blew him a kiss.

"Brian, you must have lost your touch," Jacinta said. "I thought y'all would have *been* gone."

"Your girl on that tease tip," Brian said. He watched the rowdy game of Madden for a few seconds before standing up and stretching his long legs. He walked over to the more subdued Pac-Man game, bear-hugging Mina from behind. They swayed lightly, side-to-side.

"Shoot, from what she told me, I'm surprised she didn't jump you when you picked her up from work tonight," Jacinta said, her grin sly. She moved away before Mina's smack could connect.

"Don't be telling all my business," Mina scolded.

"Actually, Brian, Mina told *me* that she's ready to take the pact with me," Lizzie said. She winked at Mina and they laughed.

Brian snorted. "What? That abstinence pact?" he hollered over the rising noise. "Todd, you still not handling your business, son?"

A round of bawdy teasing broke out as the guys gave Todd a hard time for complying with Lizzie's yearlong virginity pact. Todd took it in stride. The only evidence that he was embarrassed were his hands, first the right then the left, pushing through his unruly hair.

"She's the boss," Todd said, his blue eyes gleaming playfully.

"Okay, boss," JZ said, never taking his eyes off the plasma screen. "Liz, you my girl and all, but Todd a better dude then me. I would have stepped on you long ago."

"Thanks a lot, Jay," Lizzie said, scowling.

"Hmm . . . Greg not saying nothing," Jacinta said. "Which means either Kelly broke the pact and gave him some or . . ."

"Or, that Greg works out a lot to distract himself," Greg said. His hand went over Kelly's on the game's joystick as he helped her dodge the colorful ghosts hot on her trail.

Kelly smiled, embarrassed, refusing to join the public discussion of her sex life or lack thereof.

Todd ran over from the sofa, his hand up for a high five.

"Dude, that's what I'm saying," Todd said. He and Greg exchanged a hand slap. He yelled over to JZ, "See, Greg knows what it's like to live like a monk. I condition like twice a day so I won't go serial killer."

The clique cracked up at Todd's animated grimace.

"*That's* why you're looking so buff," Mina said.

Brian kneed the back of her leg lightly. "Oh, so you be checking him out?"

"Hells yes," Mina said. She lifted her head for a kiss and Brian leaned over, planting one on her. "Seriously, though. I was like, dang, T is getting huge."

With all the action at the back of the room, JZ and Michael put the game on hold and joined them.

"Ay, I just thought about something," JZ said. He put his arm around Lizzie. "Liz, keep your stuff on lock because I think it's helping T's game."

"I *know* it's helping my game," Todd said, his eyes an exaggerated pool of sadness.

Lizzie put her arms around his waist. "So I improved your game? Cool."

She stood on her tiptoes and laid an affectionate peck on Todd's lips.

"Son, you mad aggressive on the court lately. I never connected it with your dry spell, though," JZ said, marveling at the thought. "Maybe I should try that." He laughed loud and hard. "Sike."

The sound of Lil' Wayne penetrated the clique's laughter. Jacinta pulled her cell phone out of her pocket and the ring tone grew louder, shushing the group.

"Hey," she said into the phone, walking away.

Conversation resumed about Todd's newfound energy and aggression until Jacinta returned and announced, "I'm getting ready to roll, y'all."

JZ's eyebrow rose. "Where you dipping to?"

"That was Raheem," Jacinta said, pushing the cell back into her pocket. "He over at my aunt's house, so I told him to pick me up. Girlfriend duty calls."

Mina caught the hardening of JZ's stare despite how quickly it came and went. Her stomach rolled at the tension she felt in the fleeting glare and she attempted to joke it off. "Jay, looks like you gotta call one of your little jump offs tonight."

"Who said I wasn't gonna do that anyway?" JZ said, smirking. "I was just waiting for all y'all couples to bounce."

"Geez, are you kicking us out?" Lizzie said.

"Well, you know what they say?" A broad grin spread across JZ's face. "You don't have to go home, but you gotta get the hell out of here."

Brain dapped him up. "I know that's right." He squired Mina toward the stairs. "Let's dip."

Kelly, Greg, Lizzie, and Todd followed behind them in the midst of a chorus of good-byes.

"That's messed up about you, Jay," Mina said over her shoulder.

He saluted her. Just as she and Brian hit the stairs, she heard Jacinta say, "You gonna walk me out, big head?"

JZ's voice came back strong. "For what? You don't know your way out all of a sudden?"

Well, that can't be good, Mina thought. Her stomach took another mini-roll at the edge in JZ's voice.

That can't be good at all.